Christmas CHARMS

A small-town Christmas romance
from Hallmark Publishing

TERI WILSON

In loving memory of Bliss...pure
Hallmark magic on four furry legs.

Chapter One

*E*VERYONE TALKS ABOUT CHRISTMAS MAGIC as if it's an actual, literal thing. As real as silver tinsel draped lovingly from the stiff pine needles of a blue spruce tree. As real as snow on Christmas morning. As real as the live toy soldiers who flank the entrance to FAO Schwartz, the famous toy store now situated in Rockefeller Plaza, right at the center of the bustling, beating heart of Manhattan.

But here's the truth—as authentic as those costumed soldiers seem, they're really just actors killing time until they land a role in an off-Broadway play. I know this because a pair of them stood in line behind me last week at Salads Salads Salads during the lunch rush. Dressed in their tall black hats and red uniforms with glossy gold buttons, they piled their bowls high with lettuce, cucumber slices and shredded carrots while discussing their audition monologues for the upcoming revival of *West Side Story*. It was all very surreal and not the least bit magical.

Genuinely magical or not, though, New York is undeniably lovely during the holidays. After four Christmases in Manhattan, I still go a little breathless every year when I catch my first glimpse of the grand Rockefeller Center Christmas tree. Every time I stand on the frosty sidewalk in front of Saks Fifth Avenue for the unveiling of their big holiday light show, I feel my heart grow three sizes, just like a certain green you-know-who.

I love this time of year. I always have, but this particular December is special. This Christmas will be my best yet. I just have to make it through my last day at work before taking off on my first real vacation in eight years—to Paris! My boyfriend, Jeremy, has family there, and this year, he's invited me to spend the holidays with them. Christmas magic, indeed.

Oui, s'il vous plaît.

I pull my coat tighter and more snugly around my frame as I jostle for space on the busy midtown streets. The very second the floats in the Macy's Thanksgiving Day parade pack up and go home, Christmas shoppers and holiday tourists descend on Manhattan in droves. The switch is kind of jarring. One minute, a sixty-two-foot inflated turkey is looming over Central Park West, and the next, his giant, colorful plumage is nowhere to be seen. Swinging shopping bags are the only thing in sight, all the way from one end of 5th Avenue to the other.

The Christmas crowds are predictably terrible, so I always leave extra time during the holiday season for my walk to the upscale jewelry store where I work, just a few blocks from FAO Schwartz and its not-so-magical toy soldiers. A snowstorm blew in last night—

the first of the Christmas season. And even though I'm in serious danger of being swallowed up by the crush of people headed toward the ice-skating rink at Rockefeller Center, I can't help but marvel at the beauty of the season's first snowfall.

Manhattan looks almost old-fashioned covered in a gentle layer of white. Frost clings to the cast iron streetlamps, and icicles drip from the stained-glass windows of St. Patrick's Cathedral. Huge Christmas wreaths have been placed around the necks of Patience and Fortitude, the massive stone lions that flank the main branch of the public library like bookends, and when a winter storm is sprinkled on top, the tips of their front paws and noses are the only visible glimpses of pale gray marble beneath a blanket of sparkling snow. I can almost picture them rising up to shake the snowflakes from their manes and prowling through Midtown, leaving a trail of paw prints in the fresh powder.

I smile to myself as I near the toy store. One of the actor soldiers out front pauses from saluting at passersby to pose for a selfie with a little girl bundled up in a bright red snowsuit. It's an adorable scene, and I let my gaze linger longer than I should. Before I register what's happening, I plow straight into a man exiting the store.

Oof.

We collide right at the edge of the red carpet stretched out beneath FAO Schwartz's fancy marquee. Technically, I'm only partly to blame. The man's arms are piled so high with gift-wrapped packages that I can't even see his face, so I doubt he can tell where he's going or who might be in his way. My gaze snags on the sight of his hands in the seconds just before impact. They're nice hands—strong, capable. The sort of hands that can probably steer a car using only two fingers. Cradle a sleepy puppy in a single palm. Loosen a necktie with one swift tug.

I blink, and then impact occurs and the packages scatter. The rattle of what sounds like airborne Lego bricks and who knows what else snaps me back to attention.

"I'm so sorry. I wasn't watching where I was going," I say. I drop to my knees on the sidewalk to try and collect as many of his gift-wrapped packages as I can before they get stepped on. "Here, let me help you."

We reach for the same box and when our fingertips collide, I realize there's something almost familiar about those nice hands of his. Something that makes my stomach do a little flip, even before I look up to meet his gaze. And when I finally stand and get a glimpse of his face, I'm more confused than ever.

Aidan? My arms go slack, and all the presents I've just scrambled to pick up tumble to the ground again. *Aidan Flynn?*

No. It can't be. Absolutely not.

One of his packages must have conked me on the head or something and made my vision go wonky, because there's no way my high school sweetheart just walked out of FAO Schwartz. The Aidan Flynn I used to know wouldn't be caught dead in New York City. He was a hometown boy, through and through—as much a part of Owl Lake as the snow-swept landscape. Hence, our awkward breakup.

"Ashley," Aidan says, and it's more a statement than a question. After all, he shouldn't be as surprised to see me. I'm the one who belongs here. This is my city, my home—the very same city I left him for all those years ago.

Still, he seems to be almost as stunned as I am, because he makes no immediate move to pick up the remaining gifts scattered at our feet.

"Aidan, what are you..." I clear my throat. Why is it so difficult to form words all of a sudden? "What are you doing here?"

This can't be real. It's definitely some sort of Christmas hallucination. Not magic, definitely not that. Even though I can't exactly deny that there's a pleasant zing coursing through me as we stare at each other through a swirl of snowflakes.

I shake my head. *Get ahold of yourself.* I've moved on since Aidan and I dated, obviously. Eight years have passed, and now I'm practically engaged...sort of.

In any case, I shouldn't be wondering why Aidan looks as if he's just bought out an entire toy store. Is he a father now? Is he *married*? Is he a married to a *New Yorker*? All of these possibilities leave me feeling a little squeamish. I wish I could blame my sudden discomfort on something gone off at Salads Salads Salads, but alas, I can't.

"I'm working," he says, which tells me absolutely nothing. He could be one of Santa's elves for all I know. Or a professional gift wrapper. Or a personal shopper for a wealthy Upper West Sider who has a dozen small children.

Somehow none of those seem like realistic possibilities. Against my better judgment, I sneak a glance at his ring finger.

No wedding ring. My gaze flits back to his face—his

handsome, handsome face. Goodness, has his jaw always been that square?

"Oh," I say. Ordinarily, I'm a much better conversationalist. Truly. But I'm so befuddled at the moment that I can't think of anything else to say.

Plus, I'm pretty sure Aidan noticed my subtle perusal of his most important finger, because the corner of his mouth quirks into a tiny half smile.

My face goes instantly warm. If a snow flurry lands on my cheek, it will probably sizzle. When Aidan bends down to scoop up the packages I dropped, I take advantage of the moment to fan my face with my mittens. Out of the corner of my eye, I notice one of the toy soldiers smirk in my direction. As if I need this surprise encounter with my Christmas past to get any more awkward than it already is.

Aidan straightens, and I jam my mittens back into my coat pocket. I really should get going. My shift starts in less than ten minutes, and Windsor Fine Jewelry is still a good eight-minute walk this time of year.

But something keeps me rooted to the spot, and as much as I want to blame it on simple nostalgia, I'm not sure I can. Aidan is more than my high school sweetheart. He's the personification of another place and time. And every now and then, the memories sneak up on me when I least expect them—now, for instance. Whenever it happens, I feel strangely empty, like one of those chocolate Santas you don't realize are hollow until you bite into them and they break into a million pieces.

That's silly, though. I'm fine, and my life here in Manhattan is great. I'm certainly not on the verge of breaking.

I square my shoulders as if to prove it, but when I meet Aidan's soft blue gaze, my throat grows so thick that I can't speak. Not even to say goodbye.

"It was good to see you, Ashley," he says.

And then he's gone just as quickly as he appeared, and I'm once again standing alone in a crowd.

Chapter Two

"IT'S MAGICAL!"

The little girl stands tippy-toe on the opposite side of the glass display case, beaming at me as she wiggles her hand to and fro. Six whimsical silver charms dangle from the bracelet on her wrist, glittering beneath the twinkle lights of the towering white Christmas trees that Windsor Fine Jewelry is famous for at this time of year.

I grin back at her. "I can't promise it's magical, but it's a beautiful bracelet. Perfect for Christmas in New York."

It's been hours since I ran into Aidan Flynn on the sidewalk, and I've just spent the past thirty minutes helping this sweet child and her father select half a dozen custom charms from Windsor's new holiday collection. I'm back in my element on the fourth floor of Manhattan's finest jewelry store, and I almost feel like myself again. Aidan is part of my past. Period.

After much deliberation, my young customer has

settled on a silver candy cane with stripes in our store's signature blue, a Santa hat, a reindeer with a petite ruby nose, a gingerbread man with three Windsor-blue buttons and a snowflake sparkling with tiny diamonds. Upon my recommendation, they've also added a shiny silver apple charm to represent their holiday shopping trip to the Big Apple.

All in all, quite an extravagant Christmas gift for such a young shopper. But luxury is Windsor's specialty and the primary reason tourists flock to the store's flagship location on the corner of Madison Avenue and 57th Street, especially during the holidays. *Everyone* hopes to find one of Windsor's coveted royal blue boxes under their tree on Christmas morning. Locals and tourists alike.

It's one of the things that makes working at Windsor so exciting. Sometimes I have to pinch myself to make sure I'm not dreaming. Manhattan is only a six-hour train ride away from the small lakeside town where I grew up, but glamour-wise, it may as well be on another planet.

"Thank you, Daddy," the little girl says, turning wide blue eyes toward the man towering beside her. *Adorable.* My heart gives a little clench.

So do my feet, for less sentimental reasons. I've been positioned behind the charms counter for six hours straight with no opportunity to sit. As much as I love my job, the holiday hours are brutal, and with the crush of Christmas shoppers, sometimes it feels like there's no end in sight.

Except there *is* one in sight—the most dazzling, glamorous ending imaginable. And it's headed my way in less than twenty-four hours.

This time tomorrow, I'll be on a plane to the most gorgeous city in the world!

I bite the inside of my cheek to keep myself from squealing out loud.

Across from me, the little girl's father rests an affectionate hand on his daughter's shoulder. "You're welcome, pumpkin."

"Shall I wrap it for you, or would you like to go ahead and wear it?" I shift my weight from one throbbing foot to the other.

"I'd like it wrapped, please. In one of those pretty blue boxes tied with white ribbon?" The sweet child bounces up and down as she offers me her wrist so I can unfasten the bracelet.

"Of course." I wink at her as I release the tiny silver clasp. "I'll be right back. Have some hot cocoa while you wait."

I nod toward the wall of big picture windows overlooking snow-dusted Manhattan, where a gloved coworker dressed in a dark suit and blue silk tie serves hot chocolate from a silver tea service to waiting customers.

We have a dress code here at work—black or the darkest charcoal gray only, with small touches of the store's signature royal blue. The rule applies even during December, which explains both my black turtleneck and the fact that the colorful, hand-knitted Christmas sweater my mom sent me a few days ago is currently tucked away in my bottom dresser drawer. Though in all honesty, the sweater is a better fit for my old life rather than my new one. Novelty Christmas sweaters are all the rage back in Owl Lake, where everyone wears them in a completely non-ironic way. I have an entire photo roll full of texts from my family to prove it. Wearing one in Manhattan, though? That would be a whole different story.

My cute little customer skips toward the hot chocolate stand, and her father follows. I'd be lying if I said watching them together didn't make me feel the tiniest bit wistful about not making the trip home for the holidays. *Again.* But working retail isn't for the faint of heart, and if I ever hope to get promoted to manager, this is where I need to be until I step onto that flight to Paris. I've spent the past three Christmas Eves right here, behind the charms counter. Before that, I was always stuck in Boston working at my college internship. And this year...

Well, this year will be a complete dream come true. My family totally understands. Who could pass up a romantic trip to France during the holidays?

I pick up the charm bracelet and head toward the wrapping station as shoppers mill about, holding steaming blue paper cups while lacy snowflakes dance against the surrounding windows. The air smells like peppermint, warm chocolate and the fine Windsor perfume we sell in engraved silver bottles. Four stories below, pedestrians fill the sidewalks to view the elaborate Christmas windows lining Madison and 5th Avenues while yellow taxicabs crawl slowly past, their bumpers piled high with snow.

One more day. I feel a secret smile tugging at the corners of my mouth while I go over each silver charm with a polishing cloth so the bracelet will look perfect when it's unwrapped. For weeks, Jeremy has been telling me about all the wonderful things we'll see and do once we get to Paris—the Christmas market at the Eiffel Tower, midnight carols at Sainte Chapelle, holiday cocktails at the Ritz. It all sounds like something out of a dream. Mostly, anyway.

I just never quite expected Aidan Flynn to have a surprise walk-on role in my holiday plans.

"Ashley!"

At the sound of my name, I drag myself back to reality and see Maya Sanchez dashing across the sales floor at a speed to rival Rudolph's on Christmas Eve. Maya works on the floor directly below me, selling engagement rings in the lavish Windsor I Do boutique, and she's also been my roommate and closest friend in New York since the day I started working the charms counter.

I stifle a laugh as she skids to a halt beside me. "What are you doing up here? Isn't I Do the busiest section of the entire store right now?"

Every year, the marketing team at Windsor designs a holiday ad campaign for its engagement rings that is so whimsically romantic that it rivals a full-length Christmas rom-com movie. A snowy winter proposal just isn't the same without a diamond from Windsor— that's what our marketing wizards would have you believe, anyway. I have to admit, the ad featuring a tuxedoed man hiding a little blue box behind his back as the unsuspecting love of his life hangs a perfect blue ornament on a Christmas tree hits me right in the feels every single time.

The ad even includes a floppy-eared puppy romping at their feet. It's all picture-perfect—though not exactly realistic. I'm just not sure why the man's fiancée-to-be is wearing a beaded evening gown to decorate the tree.

I'm all for glamour, but that seems like an impractical fashion choice. Just saying.

I guess you can take the girl out of Owl Lake, but you can't quite take the Owl Lake completely out of the girl.

"It's insane down there. You wouldn't believe how many couples are getting engaged this Christmas." Maya's cheeks flush pink, and her gaze shifts to the bracelet in my hands. "Cute. Let me guess—you helped the customer choose the charms?"

"It's my favorite part of my job." I place the bracelet in its box and arrange it just so.

"And you're absurdly good at it." She points to the apple charm. "That's an especially nice touch."

"Thanks. It's a reminder of her trip to New York and at the same time, it sets her bracelet apart from one filled with traditional Christmas charms." I press the box's lid in place and begin unspooling a section of white satin ribbon for the bow. "The best charm bracelets are the ones with little unexpected touches, don't you think?"

"Absolutely," Maya says, and she appears to be biting back a smile.

I narrow my gaze at her. "What?"

She blinks. "What do you mean, 'what?'"

"You're acting weird. Have you been sampling the champagne downstairs? I thought it was only for the customers."

"Very funny." She rolls her eyes as she picks up the scissors to cut the ribbon I'm winding into a bow in just the right spot without my having to utter a word. We've both tied so many white Windsor bows in the past few weeks that we could do it in our sleep. "I just don't see how you can be so calm when you're leaving tomorrow."

My heart skips a beat. I might seem calm on the outside, but on the inside, I'm counting the minutes until our plane takes off. My bags have been packed for days, which is probably a good thing because an hour or so ago, Jeremy popped into the charms department to tell me he wants us to go out after work tonight for a special pre-Paris dinner.

Jeremy works at Windsor, just like Maya and me. Except instead of putting together charm bracelets or selling engagement rings, he helps princesses pick out tiaras and arranges for Hollywood stars to borrow extravagant pieces from the vault to wear to award shows or movie premieres. He works on the first floor in the fine jewels section, where even a single item in the display cases cost significantly more than my parents' modest, Adirondacks-style lakeside home. Jeremy and I met on my first day of work when he'd caught me staring, wide-eyed, at a diamond necklace that had once been worn by Audrey Hepburn. A year later, we started dating.

"Christmas in Paris!" Maya sighs. "It's so insanely romantic, just like those old movies you force me to watch all the time."

"Hey, you loved *Funny Face*. Don't pretend you didn't."

She shrugs one shoulder. "Guilty."

Finished with the bow, I tuck the rectangular box into a matching blue carrier bag. My little customer and her dad are still sipping cocoa by the windows, watching the bright emerald lawn of Central Park slowly disappear beneath a fine layer of snow. I turn to fully face Maya, and sure enough, her lips are starting to quirk back into a secret smile.

"There." I point at her face. I've shared a tiny fifth-floor walkup with her long enough to know when she's trying to keep a secret. "Something weird is definitely going on. You look like someone just told you the exact contents of Santa's naughty and nice lists."

"I don't know what you're talking about," she says in a wholly unconvincing manner. "But let's just say I might know which of those lists *you're* on."

"Maya." I stare hard at her. Hard enough to peer inside her brain, if such a thing were possible. "You're not saying what I think you're saying, are you?"

My heart pounds so hard that I think it might beat right out of my chest.

Here's the thing—when you've been dating a perfectly nice man for three years and he invites you to the most romantic city in the entire world for the holidays, it's not completely out of the realm of possibility that he might be thinking about proposing. I mean, I don't think I'm being over-the-top presumptuous to wonder. Anyone who's read a single romance novel would wonder the same thing.

And when said boyfriend works at the most famous jewelry store in the world, you might also have an inkling where he'd purchase an engagement ring. After all, we *do* get a sizable discount on employee purchases, which would be great if I ever found myself with an invitation to the Met Gala. Sadly, that's not my reality. But my reality does contain a secret weapon in the form of a best friend who works in the very department where Jeremy would purchase an engagement ring, if and when the time is right.

Please let the time be right.

"My lips are sealed." Maya clamps her mouth closed and mimes locking it with an invisible key. Her subsequent silence lasts less than a fraction of a second. "Hypothetically speaking, though, if I *did* know that a certain someone recently made a significant purchase with his employee discount, wouldn't you want to be surprised? A true friend would keep her mouth shut."

"No, she wouldn't." I shake my head. We've been over this before. I don't like surprises, especially ones involving marriage proposals. "A true friend would give me a heads up so I could prepare an appropriate response."

"An appropriate response?" Maya's forehead crinkles in confusion. "You sound like you're talking about replying to a job offer instead of potentially agreeing to marry the love of your life."

A weird lump forms in my throat as her words snag inside my head. *The love of my life.* For a second, the memory of a handsome, chiseled face flits through my thoughts—a chiseled face that doesn't belong to Jeremy at all, but to the man I just saw juggling packages outside FAO Schwartz. I haven't looked into eyes that blue since the *first* time I was surprised by a diamond solitaire.

I blink hard, willing the vision to disappear. I probably shouldn't be thinking about Aidan Flynn at a time like this.

"Jeremy is definitely the love of my life," I blurt out.

"I know. That's what I just said." Maya studies me, frowning. "Are you okay? I thought you'd be over-the-moon excited."

"I am." Of course I'm excited. I'm thrilled to pieces.

Any girl would be. My life is about to seriously resemble one of the Windsor I Do Christmas ads, on multiple levels.

Minus the evening gown, of course.

"Good, because you look a little like you just took a gulp of expired eggnog." Maya's frown deepens. "I'm beginning to think you might be right about that heads up. Clearly you need one."

"I do," I say, and when I realize I sound like a bride, I have the irrational urge to clamp my hand over my mouth.

What is wrong with me all of a sudden? I'm in love with Jeremy. I've been fantasizing about marrying him for months already. Sometimes I even take a slow walk past the beautiful display windows of the Vera Wang boutique down the street and imagine what I might look like in bridal white, heading down the aisle toward him.

"Okay. Well, because I know you and Jeremy are crazy about each other, and it would probably hurt his feelings in a major way if you accidentally got this same reindeer-in-the-headlights expression when he actually proposed, I'm going to go ahead and tell you what I know." She takes a deep breath. "Seriously, I'm only spilling the beans so you can prepare—"

"Oh my gosh, just tell me," I whisper-scream. It's not just that I'm impatient. My customers are probably getting low on hot chocolate by now and wondering why I'm still hanging out at the wrapping station. Plus, the line at the charms counter appears to be multiplying by the second.

"Fine." Maya pauses for dramatic effect. "Jeremy bought an engagement ring last week. Malik helped him pick it out, not me. I guess Jeremy thought I might ruin the surprise."

I can't quite manage to bite back a smile.

"Stop looking at me like that," she says. "I totally could have kept it a secret if you hadn't seemed so freaked out."

An amused silence follows.

"I probably could have, anyway," Maya concedes.

"I believe you," I say, imagining those big shopping bags from the department store down the street that have *Believe* printed across the top in swirling white script.

"The ring was getting sized, so Jeremy picked it up today. That's how I found out. And now he's walking around this very minute with it in his pocket." She starts vibrating with excitement again, like she'd been just moments ago before my minor, pre-proposal panic attack. "You're going to get engaged over the holidays! Maybe even at the Eiffel Tower or on that bridge with all the love locks. It's going to be magical."

A strange prickling sensation crawls up the back of my neck.

Magical.

It's the second time in just a few minutes that someone's used that word. My cute little customer described her charm bracelet the exact same way.

I glance quickly in the direction of the hot cocoa stand and the wall of picture windows overlooking Madison Avenue. The child's father has rid himself of his empty cup and is looking around the sales floor, no doubt pondering what's taking me so long.

"I have to get back to work before I get in trouble," I say.

"Of course you do." Maya waves me off. "I'll straighten up the wrap area and get back downstairs."

"Thank you." I grin. "And thank you so much for running up here to tell me the big news, even though it's supposed to be a secret. I owe you big time."

Maya throws her arms around me before I can take a step. "Ahh! I'm just so happy for you."

She releases me, and I nibble my bottom lip because it's trembling all of a sudden and I think I might cry.

Save it, I tell myself. *Save all your happy tears for Jeremy.*

They *are* happy tears, aren't they?

I give Maya's hand a tight squeeze, take a steadying breath and start walking toward my customers. My mind whirls and the snow outside falls harder than ever, making me feel as if I've been placed inside a snow globe that someone has given a ferocious shake.

The Windsor bag containing the wrapped bracelet shakes in my grasp. Three floors below, Jeremy has an engagement ring tucked into one of his pockets. I try to imagine him slipping it onto my finger at one of the outrageously romantic Parisian sites Maya mentioned. Or maybe someplace different, like the Champs-Élysées, with row upon row of sparkling Christmas lights lining the path to the Arc de Triomphe.

And then it hits me.

Jeremy wants to take me to dinner tonight for a "special pre-Paris celebration." I assumed he wanted to talk logistics for the trip—what we'll do for Christmas Eve and Christmas Day, which sights we'll have time to visit, maybe go over the names of his family members again, so I'll be prepared. But that twinkle in his eye when he mentioned dinner didn't have anything to do with our itinerary, did it?

My boyfriend isn't going to propose on the love locks bridge or anywhere else in France. He's going to ask me to marry him in New York.

Right here.

Tonight.

Chapter Three

MY DINNER DATE WITH JEREMY is scheduled for eight o'clock, two hours after my shift at the charms counter ends.

Once I deliver the Christmas bracelet with the tiny apple charm to the young girl and her father, the rest of the day flies by in a dizzying whirl of engraved heart charms, silver gingerbread men and tiny blue-striped candy canes. The crush of holiday shoppers seems to be growing by the hour, and I barely have time for a bathroom break, much less a chance to figure out how I might be able to squeeze in a manicure before Jeremy slides his ring onto my finger.

Somewhere between my initial panic at the thought of getting engaged and my trek through the crowded city streets to the minuscule apartment I share with Maya, any initial fears about marrying Jeremy melt away like yesterday's snowfall. Thank goodness.

Obviously I want to marry him. I'm madly in love with him—I'm certain of that. We've been dating three of the four years I've lived in New York. Jeremy is kind and thoughtful, and most importantly of all, he understands me. We're like two sides of the same coin.

He gets me, I think as I shrug off my coat, flip on the television and head straight for the card table in the living room that serves as my jewelry-making station.

The apartment seems eerily quiet. Maya is still busy at Windsor, and without her constant stream of chatter to calm my nerves until my big date tonight, I need a happy distraction.

Cue Jimmy Stewart and Donna Reed.

It's a Wonderful Life is playing on the classics channel. Perfect. I still have an hour until Jeremy is supposed to arrive, so I give my make-up a quick once over, adding a classic red lip and a swish of winged eyeliner. Then I change into a new LBD (little black dress) from my favorite retro online shopping site. It's got a nipped-in waist, a full skirt and a faux pearl-encrusted collar. I've been saving the dress for Paris, but there's a timeless quality about it that makes it perfect for an engagement dress, so I remove it from my luggage and put it on.

I do a little twirl in front of the full-length mirror in our tiny bathroom, and then I lose myself in the black-and-white world of Christmas magic on the television screen while I sort through the haul of costume jewelry from my most recent estate-sale splurge.

As much as I love the sparkly new charms in the department where I work, vintage jewelry is my favorite—charms, especially. I adore the way an antique charm bracelet tells the story of the person who wore it. Trinkets and tiny baubles represent favorite vacations, holidays and long-lost loves. When I'm not busy working the charms counter, I love taking my vintage finds and turning them into new, re-crafted pieces. The Santa and reindeer necklace that Maya's been wearing to work since the day after Thanksgiving is a gift I gave her last Christmas, made from a box of charms I found in hole-in-the-wall antique shop on Coney Island.

My current project is a brooch with a Victorian-style heart charm dangling from its center. It looks like a frilly, silver Valentine—perfect for a bride-to-be. If I work fast, I can get it finished before Jeremy gets here. While Clarence the angel takes George Bailey on an eerie and magical journey through Christmas on my television, I secure the heart into place with just enough time to pin the brooch onto the lapel of my best winter coat and give my nails a quick once-over with a coat of holly-red polish. When Jeremy knocks on the door, I'm more than ready for a holiday proposal.

"Hi," he says, smiling down at me from the threshold. His gaze flits briefly to the silver charm dangling from my coat collar, but he doesn't mention it.

A flicker of disappointment passes through me, which is beyond ridiculous. My jewelry designs are just a hobby. Jeremy has always been supportive of my tinkering—he's just not particularly interested in vintage jewelry. Also, the man has a *diamond in his pocket.* "Hi, yourself. You look nice."

He's dressed in one of the sleek suits he always wears to work. Actually, now that I think about it, I rarely catch a glimpse of Jeremy without a tie fashioned into a Hanover knot anchored firmly to the collar of his button-down Oxford.

"Thanks. We have a special night ahead of us, so

it seemed like a good idea to dress the part." He offers me his elbow.

See? Total marriage material. My stomach does a little flip as I loop my arm through his, and we're on our way.

As we walk toward midtown, Jeremy tells me all about the important people he helped at Windsor throughout his shift—the congressman who purchased a string of rare gold pearls for his wife, the Broadway star who needed a pair of flashy earrings for a holiday party at the Rainbow Room. I've been looking forward to telling him about the sweet father-daughter duo I met today and the charm bracelet I designed for the little girl, but I change my mind as he keeps going on about his VIPs.

"I saw Maya just before the end of my shift," he finally says.

My footsteps slow as we approach a street corner where a Salvation Army volunteer in a red apron is ringing a bell beside one of the bright red kettles that pop up all over the city during the holidays. I dig through my red leather crossbody bag for a few dollar bills and drop them into the kettle.

Jeremy doesn't seem to notice I've stopped until he's about to step off of the curb and realizes I'm no longer beside him. "Ashley?"

"Sorry." I dash back to his side. "What were you saying?"

He sighs and waits for me to catch up. "Nothing, really. Just that Maya seemed awfully happy about something. She was even more animated than usual."

I bite the inside of my cheek to keep from laughing. If there's an award for world's worst poker face, Maya's the winner, hands down. "Her holiday spirit must have kicked in."

"She's not the only one." Jeremy reaches for my hand and gives it a squeeze. "Do you mind if we make a quick stop before dinner? I've got a special Christmas surprise for you."

This is it.

I grin up at him. I'm practically sparkling. "I'd never turn down a Christmas surprise."

"Wonderful," he says, releasing my hand to pull on a pair of sleek leather gloves. "You're going to love this."

I dig through the pockets of my coat for the mittens my grandmother crocheted for me back when I was in college. I can't quite give them up even though they're woefully out of place in an environment like Windsor. But this is date night—we're not going to Windsor Fine Jewelry.

Except the closer we get to my mysterious surprise, the more familiar the direction we're heading begins to feel. We pass FAO Schwartz, where the doormen are dressed as toy soldiers and a seven-foot teddy bear looms in the front window, and I can't help but think about Aidan. I glance at the entrance to the famous toy store, half-expecting to see him still there, arms laden with packages and shopping bags. He's not, of course, and the keen sense of disappointment that courses through me catches me by surprise.

I take a deep breath and force my gaze elsewhere. Horse-drawn carriages decorated with clusters of jingle bells clip-clop toward Central Park, and the Plaza Hotel stands in the distance with its grand thirty-foot

Christmas tree shining bright behind the hotel's fancy iron gates.

Are we going back to Windsor?

The store is a stone's throw away, right across the street. Maybe Jeremy's forgotten something and needs to fetch it before we get on with the important part of the evening. Or maybe he's taking me someplace nearby. That has to be it. Windsor isn't even open this time of night.

But as we near the crosswalk, he takes hold of my mittened hand and leads me straight toward the stately jewelry store. Swaths of evergreen decorate the windows, and a wreath crafted exclusively from bright blue boxes tied with white ribbons hangs above the revolving door at the entrance to our workplace. It's undeniably beautiful, even for a building I see on pretty much a daily basis.

"Here we are," Jeremy says, gazing up at the shop windows, glowing gold for six towering stories. "Are you ready for your surprise?"

My breath hitches, and I have a sudden vision of being led to the I Do section and presented with case after case of engagement rings to choose from, like Reese Witherspoon's over-the-top proposal from Patrick Dempsey in *Sweet Home Alabama*. But wait—didn't that particular engagement end in disaster?

"I am," I say, and my breath hangs in the air in a cloud of frost and anticipation.

We bypass the front entrance for the side door the employees use to enter the store, and the same security guard who waved goodbye to me two hours earlier smiles and holds the door open for us.

"Hi, Ashley." He winks. "Merry Christmas."

An amused look passes between the security officer and Jeremy, and my face grows hot. Am I supposed to be the last person in the building to hear about my own engagement?

"Merry Christmas," I say.

The guard nods at Jeremy and glances at his watch. "Everything's ready. You've got twenty minutes."

"Perfect," Jeremy's grin widens and his hand slides onto the small of my back.

I'm getting more confused by the second, especially when he guides me in the opposite direction of the elevators that lead to the coveted I Do section and instead escorts me toward the sparkling glass cases on the first floor sales boutique. Another security guard—Sam, a retired police officer who typically works the overnight shift—is situated by the stationary display case that holds a place of honor at the very center of the room. On my first day at Windsor, I stood in front of the same exact display case, mesmerized by its contents. It's where Jeremy and I first met.

The case contains a diamond necklace that Audrey Hepburn wore in one of her most iconic movie roles. A still from the movie is featured on the bottom corner of the display, with the necklace's large center stone—a rare pink diamond—shining brightly from the dip between her collarbones. During store hours, the exquisite piece is always surrounded by a crowd of tourists. It's strange to see it shining all alone in the dimly lit sales area now.

Even stranger—the door to the case is standing open. My eyes grow wide.

"What's going on?" I ask, unable to tear my gaze from the glittering pink jewel.

"Your favorite necklace is being moved to the fancy Christmas party upstairs, along with some of our other more extravagant pieces. I know how much you love Audrey Hepburn and all those old movies, so I thought you might like to try it on while it's out of its case."

"Seriously?" I blink, and my hands fly to my throat. "Try it on? Me?"

I'm so stunned that I can't seem to form a full sentence. Somewhere beyond my complete and utter shock, I'm vaguely aware that Jeremy's surprise hasn't turned out to be an engagement ring. But that's okay. I'm going to get to try on Audrey's necklace—the same outrageously glamorous diamond piece of jewelry that drives scores of visitors to Windsor every day. It's not as exciting as a proposal, but it's close.

"Yes, you." Jeremy shrugged one shoulder. "I checked with the senior manager and he said it's fine, as long as we're quick. No pictures, though. We can't let tourists think they can drop in and ask to try it on. And Sam here needs to keep an eye on us the whole time."

Sam grins. He knows I loved Audrey. Pretty much everyone at Windsor does.

I nod. "I can deal with those rules."

Jeremy's eyebrows lift. "Are you surprised?"

"Yes." I let out a laugh. "Stunned, actually."

"Good. I wasn't sure what to get you for Christmas, and this seemed as good as anything I could have bought and wrapped up in paper." Jeremy waves toward Sam with a flourish and the guard begins removing the necklace from its black velvet cushion with gloved hands.

My smile stiffens into place.

But what about the ring in your pocket?

I don't say it. Of course I don't, because what Jeremy has just arranged means the world to me. Truly, it does.

But his comment about not knowing what to get me for Christmas confuses me, considering Maya's insistence that he's just purchased a diamond solitaire. If the ring isn't for me, then who could it possibly be for?

Never mind. I force myself to concentrate on the iconic necklace glittering like crazy in Sam's gentle grasp. The engagement ring will probably make its appearance during our holiday in Paris. Jeremy is simply trying to keep it a secret. In the meantime, getting to wear Audrey's pink diamond, even for a moment, is a precious, precious gift.

I turn to smile at him, but he's drifted back to the entrance where we entered the building and is busy chatting with the doorman. I'm pretty sure they're discussing Jeremy's fantasy hockey league, one of my boyfriend's favorite topics.

Sam clears his throat, and my attention darts back to the necklace, draped carefully over his fingertips.

I take a deep breath, and for the first time since Jeremy arrived at my doorstep that evening, my holiday cheer takes a serious hit. It would be nice if Jeremy could don a pair of white jeweler's gloves and put the necklace on me himself, but I realize that's probably impossible. Looking after the expensive piece is Sam's job.

Still. Doesn't Jeremy at least want to watch me try it on?

Sam casts a disapproving glance in my boyfriend's

direction, so fleeting that I almost think I imagined it. Then he refocuses his attention on me and gives me a grandfatherly smile. The kindness in his gaze makes me inexplicably wistful. "Go on, then. Turn around and I'll help you get it on. I'm sure it will look beautiful on you, Ashley."

"Thanks." I give him a wobbly smile, spin around and gather my hair in one hand so he can fasten the valuable string of diamonds around my neck.

The large center stone rests heavily against my skin, and before I examine my reflection in one of the nearby mirrors, I take a moment to close my eyes and remember the first time I saw it on film.

It was at the historic movie theater, back in Owl Lake. Aidan, my high school sweetheart, had taken me to my very first classic movie marathon, and I'd fallen instantly in love with the sweeping scores, the musical numbers and all the old-school Hollywood glamour. Classic movies became our thing after that. Aidan and I never missed the Palace Theatre's monthly marathon. If he could see me now, wearing this necklace, he wouldn't believe his eyes.

My eyelashes flutter open. At the first glimpse of my reflection, I hardly believe it myself. Nor can I fathom why memories of Aidan keep invading my thoughts today. Bumping into him shouldn't be affecting me like this. It's most unsettling...

Especially on a night when I thought I might be getting engaged to someone else.

I turn hopeful eyes in Jeremy's direction, but his back is still turned toward me.

"Lovely," Sam says, meeting my gaze in the mirror. "Just lovely."

"It is, isn't it?" My face goes warm. The diamonds around my neck sparkle brighter than the Rockefeller Center Christmas tree, and tomorrow I'm leaving for Paris with the man I love. I tell myself that Maya is right—this is going to be the Christmas of my dreams.

But somewhere deep down, I'm not sure I believe.

After we leave Windsor, Jeremy and I go to a little hole-in-the-wall pizza place off Central Park with red-checkered tablecloths and clusters of plastic grapes dripping from the ceiling. It's not Jeremy's favorite, but I've always liked it because it reminds me of the quaint, cozy restaurants back home upstate.

Nestled at a table by the corner where we can watch the horse-drawn carriage wind their way through the park, we sip red wine and eat huge slices of pepperoni pizza, folded into a v-shape at the crust, New York-style. It's the perfect dinner before our trip to Paris, a festive farewell to the city we both love so much.

Throughout the meal, my phone vibrates like crazy in my handbag. A tiny peek earlier showed me that Maya is on a major texting spree, begging for a play-by-play of the proposal that hasn't quite happened yet, and my mom is still sending me photos of Owl Lake, all decked out in its holiday finest. She does this every year during December—her way of making sure I feel included in Christmas back home when I'm stuck working overtime at Windsor.

When Jeremy steps outside to take a work call, I sneak another glance at my text messages. The most recent photo from my mom is a shot of the Owl Lake firehouse. A huge wreath hangs over the station's massive red doors, and swags of evergreen garland decorate the building on all sides. My throat goes thick as an unexpected wave of homesickness washes over me. I can't remember the last time I set foot inside the firehouse. My dad retired as chief shortly after I moved to Manhattan, but our family celebrated many a holiday with his fellow firefighters during my childhood—Thanksgivings around the station's long, rough-hewn farmhouse table and Christmas mornings filled with stockings, gingerbread and a fir tree in the corner, topped with a firefighter's helmet instead of a star.

"Sorry about that," Jeremy says, sliding back into his chair. "One of the managers had a question about the party guest list."

Another text from Maya pops up on my screen.

Please let me be your Maid of Honor. A string of prayer hands emojis follows, and I shove my phone back into my bag as fast as I can.

"Duty calls, no problem," I say with a smile. The pizza I just consumed suddenly feels like a boulder in the pit of my stomach.

Jeremy studies me from across the table. "Is everything okay? You seem a little…"

"I'm fine," I say brightly. Too brightly, if I'm really being honest. "I was just thinking about Christmas traditions and family. That sort of thing."

"Ah." Jeremy nods as he repositions his napkin over his lap.

"How does your family celebrate? Will we go caroling? I'm not sure I know any French Christmas songs." I've spent the past month trying to learn as much

French as I can from a foreign language app on my phone, but it's sadly lacking in holiday content.

Granted, Jeremy's family isn't actually French. His father is the vice president of a global bank, so they're basically expats. Still, when in Rome and all that. For my very first Christmas in the City of Lights, I want to at least be able to say *Joyeux Noël* with a proper French accent.

Jeremy practically snorts. "You're safe. There definitely won't be any caroling."

"Oh. That's good, I suppose." I pick up my wineglass.

"The holidays are going to be a little different than usual this year, anyway. My mom has already booked the ballroom at the Ritz the day after Christmas for the engagement party."

I nearly choke on my Chianti. "Engagement party?"

Did I miss the part where Jeremy proposed?

Surely not. That definitely seems like something I'd remember.

"Didn't I tell you? My brother is proposing to his girlfriend on Christmas Eve." Jeremy lets out another snort, followed by a dramatic roll of his eyes.

I stare blankly at him, unsure which gives me more pause—his brother's potential engagement or the massive eye roll. "Um, no. You haven't mentioned it."

"Well, he is. They've only been dating a few months. Can you believe it?"

It does seem lightning-fast compared to the three years Jeremy and I have been seeing each other. I try to convince myself the brevity of their coupledom is the reason for my boyfriend's apparent cynicism, and then I try even harder to imagine how fun Christmas in Paris will be with a double engagement.

It *will* be fun. Maybe the party at the Ritz is for all of us and Jeremy just can't say so without ruining the surprise of his own proposal. But if that's the case, why mention the party at all?

"That is so exciting!" But even as I say the words and bounce a little dance in my seat, I realize that somewhere along the way, Maya and I might've both jumped to conclusions...and those conclusions could be wrong.

So.

Very.

Wrong.

"We'll see. Let's hope she says yes." Jeremy shrugs. He couldn't appear more disinterested in the topic at hand. "Josh asked me to buy the engagement ring for him with my employee discount. It's already been sized, so it's nonreturnable."

I go still as he takes a giant bite of pizza. Part of me was expecting this from the moment he mentioned his brother. I didn't want to believe it, but there isn't any use in lying to myself anymore. The ring he's been carrying around in his pocket all day isn't for me. It never was.

Perhaps a small part of me should be relieved. I did, after all, experience a slight moment of panic when I'd first heard my boyfriend had been shopping in the I Do boutique.

But the sudden tightness in my chest doesn't feel at all like relief. Nor do the unshed tears clouding my vision or the way my pulse has begun to pound so hard that I can't fully catch my breath. This sensation isn't relief at all. It feels more like heartbreak.

My phone buzzes again from the depths of my handbag. Maya, most likely. She's probably sending me options for bridesmaid dresses. I want to crawl under the table and hide.

"It was nice of you to buy the ring for your brother," I say, because I can't keep sitting here in silence. That would definitely make Jeremy realize something is wrong.

But there's an unmistakable tremor to my voice. I hear it. Jeremy hears it. Even the couple sitting at the table beside us hears it, if their sidelong glances are any indication. Hashtag awkward.

Jeremy frowns at me over his slice of pepperoni. He has a rogue string of mozzarella cheese stuck to his chin, which ordinarily would be something we'd both laugh about. Looking at it now makes me inexplicably weepy.

Get yourself together. An hour ago you were wearing Audrey Hepburn's necklace, and tomorrow you'll be on a plane to Paris. Everything is fine.

"What's wrong?" Jeremy asks.

"Why did you roll your eyes just now?" The question slips right out of my mouth before I can stop it.

Jeremy's brow furrows. The mozzarella on his chin doesn't budge. "When?"

"Just a second ago, when you said Josh will be proposing to his girlfriend on Christmas Eve." My voice has gone eerily calm with no trace of a tremor whatsoever. "You rolled your eyes so hard that I thought they might roll right out of your head."

Jeremy stares at me for a beat before lowering the

piece of pizza in his hand back down to the plate in front of him. "It didn't mean anything. I just think it's a little cliché, that's all. I'm sure you agree."

"With what, exactly? Is it a holiday engagement that's cliché or the idea of marriage in general?" For the record, I don't agree on either count. In fact, both options sound perfectly lovely to me.

Jeremy shakes his head, clearly baffled. "I don't understand why you're getting upset."

Don't say it. Now is the time to swallow my disappointment, save what's left of the evening and go home to get a good night's sleep before our flight in the morning. If I admit that I heard about the ring and assumed it was meant for me, there will be no going back.

I don't have to say it, though. The truth is apparently written all over my face.

"Oh no. No, no, no, no." Jeremy's eyes go as wide as saucers. "Maya told you about the ring, didn't she? And you thought…"

My face burns with embarrassment.

"You said you had a special Christmas surprise for me tonight," I say in my defense.

"And I did! The necklace, remember?" He nods enthusiastically, as if he's accepting an award for Boyfriend of the Year. I'm feeling less and less inclined to tell him about the cheese stuck to his face. "Why in the world would we want to get *married?*"

Ouch.

I feel like crumpling right here in full view of the other pizza shop patrons. A woman at a nearby table groans out loud.

"Wait, I didn't mean it like that." Jeremy holds up a

hand, backpedaling before I can articulate a response. "You know how much I care about you."

Do I, though?

He loves you. Of course he does.

A rebellious tear slides down my cheek as I remember how alone I felt in Windsor an hour ago when I couldn't even get him to look at me—and earlier at my apartment when he noticed and then immediately dismissed the new vintage charm brooch I'd been working on for days. Tiny things I've tried my best to overlook suddenly seem like monumental red flags.

This night is a disaster.

"I only meant that marriage isn't for people like us," he says, as if that's supposed to make me feel better.

"People like us?" I echo.

"You know what I mean."

Why does he keep saying that? I'm beginning to think Jeremy doesn't actually get me at all.

"I honestly don't." I wrap my arms around my myself tightly in an effort to hold myself together.

"Babe." He reaches for me from across the table, and I somehow manage to let him hold my ring-less hand. "Marriage? *Really?* Why would we want to go down that road? We're living the dream."

I nod mutely, trying my best to hold onto the feeling of Audrey's pink diamond resting against my skin. Audrey Hepburn would handle this sort of disappointment with grace and poise. She'd never weep into a slice of pepperoni pizza.

"Look around." Jeremy waves his free hand toward the view outside the window. Central Park dazzles with twinkling lights, and the gentle snowfall is so beautiful, it nearly makes me cry. I push back the urge since no matter how desperately I want to believe the gorgeous holiday scenery is the reason for the tears just on the verge of brimming, I know better. "Tonight, it's Manhattan. Tomorrow, it'll be Paris. We've got the sort of glamorous lives that most people only dream of."

Paris.

During the past few devastating minutes, I'd somehow forgotten all about our romantic holiday vacation.

I take a deep breath. Back at my apartment, my passport is probably diving back inside a drawer, never to be seen again. As much as I've always wanted to go to Paris, it's the absolute last place I want to be with Jeremy at the moment. "So you're saying that after three years together, you're not ready to get engaged."

He gives me a tentative smile. "I guess so, yeah. But babe, that doesn't mean..."

I stand without letting him finish. I've heard enough.

"Please stop explaining—it's okay," I say.

Really, it is. Because the more I think about it, the more I realize I'm not ready for marriage, either. Not to Jeremy, anyway. Not after tonight.

I slide into my coat, and the charm on my vintage pin gives a little jingle. Such a Christmassy sound. So joyful, when I'm feeling the exact opposite.

"I hope you and your family have a very merry Christmas," I say, and then I give Jeremy one last wobbly smile before heading out into the cold.

Alone.

Chapter Four

"PLEASE TELL ME YOU AT least left him sitting there with cheese stuck to his chin." Maya passes me the small carton of gingerbread ice cream she dug out of the freezer the minute I turned up back in our tiny living room wearing my broken heart on my sleeve.

I blink back tears and dig in with my spoon. If there's a genuine cure for heartbreak at Christmas, it's got to involve gingerbread. "I couldn't. It seemed mean."

Before leaving Jeremy at the pizza place, I'd caved, handed him a napkin and told him about the cheese. I figured I owed him that much after three wonderful years together.

Although, truth be told, I'm not sure they'd been altogether wonderful. I'm not sure of *anything* at this point.

"He deserved it," Maya says, jabbing at the air with her spoon for emphasis. "He deserved worse.

You should have dumped your pizza on his head and smeared the tomato sauce in his hair. You dated for *three years*, and he's still rolling his eyes at the thought of marriage. He deserves way more than public humiliation by way of cheese."

I try to laugh, but I can't. All that comes out is a pathetic strangled noise. Somewhere between Central Park and my living room sofa, I've gone numb. I'm not going to Paris for Christmas. There will be no candlelight service at Sainte Chapelle, no Christmas Eve stroll along the Seine, no fancy party at the Ritz. Jeremy and I are finished, all because I'd suddenly believed that we lived in a Windsor holiday ad when in fact, we do not.

What was I thinking? I'm almost twenty-seven—far too old to believe in Christmas magic.

Maya sighs. "Come to think of it, *I* might be the one who deserves punishment. I feel like this is all my fault. I should never have mentioned the ring."

"Stop." I shake my head. "Don't be silly. You were just looking out for me."

"I'm sorry. Seriously, Ash. So, so sorry." Her face crumples, and just when I think it's impossible to feel any worse about this evening's dire turn of events, I do.

"Please don't apologize. None of this is your fault." I nibble on my bottom lip and pause before continuing, "I've actually been wondering..."

"What?" Maya's spoon comes to a halt midway to the pint of ice cream. We've nearly plowed through the entire thing already. "I don't like the guilty look on your face. Surely you're not blaming yourself for your boyfriend's general cluelessness."

"*Ex*-boyfriend." Maybe if I say it enough times it will begin to feel real. "And I'm not blaming myself."

But perhaps I sort of am—not because of anything that transpired between Jeremy and me, but due to the nagging sense that my current predicament smacks of terrible irony.

Is this how Aidan felt all those years ago?

I try not to think about the answer to that question, because if I'm really being honest with myself, he was probably even more heartbroken than I am right now. Isn't that the way it always is with young love—first love?

On the rare moments when I allow myself to remember how Aidan and I said goodbye, I crumble inside. No one gets *engaged* at the tender age of eighteen, though. Saying no to him was the hardest thing I've ever done. But it had been the right answer, the *only* answer.

Hadn't it?

I take a ragged inhale. "Do you think what happened with Jeremy could be some kind of cosmic payback for breaking someone else's heart? I mean, maybe I deserve this."

Maya tilts her head, not catching my meaning at first. After a moment, she says, "Wait, are you talking about your old high school boyfriend—the one who proposed back when you were still teenagers?"

"Aidan," I say, and his name tastes too familiar on my tongue. Too sweet. I put down my spoon. Clearly, I've overdosed on frozen gingerbread. "Aidan Flynn."

I still haven't told her about running into Aidan outside of FAO Schwartz earlier. I'm not sure why, exactly. I usually tell Maya everything.

I think I was just intent on believing that seeing Aidan again after all this time was a non-event. Certainly not anything meaningful or fated. But the longer I go without mentioning it, the more important the encounter begins to feel.

Maya studies me, and when she speaks again, her voice has gone soft. Serious. "What exactly happened back then? You never talk about it beyond the bare minimum."

"The night before I left for college, he surprised me with an engagement ring. We'd already planned on dating long distance since I'd gotten a scholarship at MassArt in Boston and he was staying to study at the local college in Owl Lake, but we'd never discussed marriage before." I glance down at the bare ring finger of my freshly manicured hand.

I can still picture that ring with perfect clarity—antique, rose gold with a small emerald-cut center stone, surrounded by a decorative halo of tiny diamond chips. It looked like it could have been right out of one of the classic movies we loved so much—absolutely breathtaking. Even after four years of working at Windsor, and even after having Audrey's infamous pink diamonds placed around my neck, that modest vintage ring is still the most beautiful piece of jewelry I've ever set eyes on.

"I just sort of...panicked." I shook my head. "We were so young. In love, yes, but going in completely different directions. I'd lived in Owl Lake my entire life. I was excited about moving away and seeing the world. He knew my plans. All I could talk about was getting my degree and moving to New York or London or Paris, like Audrey Hepburn's character in *Sabrina*. I wanted to start my own jewelry line someday. I loved him with my whole heart, but promising to marry him would have changed everything. Does that make sense?"

"Of course it does. You were practically kids," Maya says.

"I asked him if he could just hold onto the ring and ask me again later, when we were older. When we were *ready*. He agreed, but after I left Owl Lake, things just...ended. I think he was crushed that I'd said no, and I felt too guilty to face him again. I've hardly been back to Owl Lake at all since I left. My college internship kept me insanely busy, even during the holidays, and you know how crazy it gets at Windsor."

"Wow, that's such a sad story." Maya reached for my hand and gave it a squeeze. "But it's ancient history and it certainly doesn't have anything to do with Jeremy. I don't want to hear another word about you being punished for it. You're one of the kindest people I know. No one deserves to have their heart broken, least of all you. You deserve to be happy, Ash. You still deserve the Christmas of your dreams, with or without Jeremy."

"Ha." I stand to throw away our now-empty ice cream carton and put our spoons in the sink. "That ship has most definitely sailed. Or, more accurately, that plane will be taking off for Paris in about eight hours. Without me."

"So does this mean you're staying in New York for the holidays? I know you've already asked for the time off, but you know how chaotic Windsor gets this time of year. They might give you some hours if you ask. You could come with me to my mom's on Christmas Day, like you always do." Maya grins hopefully at me, and then my phone chimes with yet another incoming text.

I freeze right where I'm standing.

"Do you think that could be Jeremy?" Maya asks, wide-eyed.

Both of our heads swivel toward my phone, sitting innocently on the kitchen table in its protective silver glitter snowman case.

"You look," I say. "I can't bear it."

What if he's had a change of heart? Although, at this point, what could he possibly say that would convince me to climb aboard a flight to France?

Just kidding! I do want to marry you.

Not likely. Such an about-face would probably take a Christmas miracle. I'm not sure I even want him to change his mind, anyway.

"It's a picture of your parents." Maya holds up my phone for inspection. My mom and dad, all bundled up in winter gear at a Christmas tree farm, grin at me from the tiny screen.

My stomach tumbles. "My mom's been texting me all day. She's afraid my phone won't work overseas, and she doesn't want me to miss Christmas at Owl Lake."

But I'm not going to be in France for the holidays anymore, which means I don't have a single legitimate reason not to go home. My vacation days from work are already booked, and my packed suitcase is still sitting by the door. I could beg to get back on Windsor's Christmas schedule, but if my family found out that I had the time free and deliberately chose not to come home, they would definitely be hurt, and that's the last thing I want.

Besides, it's not like I've been actively trying to

avoid Christmas in my hometown in recent years. Other things have simply gotten in the way. I need to show the management team at Windsor that I'm a devoted employee if I ever hope to get promoted, and devoted employees work on Christmas Eve. A trip to France was about the only thing that could drag me away from the charms counter on the busiest shopping day of the year.

You're not going to Paris anymore, remember?

The truth is finally beginning to sink in.

Maya's eyebrows lift. "I'm guessing you haven't told your folks about you and Jeremy yet."

I shake my head. "No, not yet."

We've been broken up for less than two hours. I don't feel like reliving the humiliating pizza dinner again—not yet. There will be time to explain later. Maybe it will seem less mortifying if I tell my mom and dad what happened in person, over a warm cup of hot chocolate topped with marshmallows and a dash of cinnamon, the way my grandma used to make it. Maybe the perfect way to get over heartbreak is to spend Christmas Eve taking dinner to the old firehouse with my parents and then to wake up in my childhood bedroom on Christmas morning. Maybe a trip back home for the holidays is just what I need.

It's not Paris, but it might be the next best thing.

Owl Lake, here I come.

With only ten days to go until Christmas, Grand Central Station is a complete madhouse the following day. The annual holiday fair is in full swing, with booths stretching from one end of the station's historic Vanderbilt Hall to the other, selling everything from original artwork to toys and craft items. Shoppers, commuters and tourists alike weave through the crowd carrying colorfully wrapped packages and parcels decorated with ribbons and bows. In between announcements for departing trains, Christmas music plays over the loudspeakers, and even though everyone has places to go and people to see, the mood in the station is festive. It almost feels like a party, albeit a party to which I am a surprise guest with no plus-one.

I arrive at Grand Central bright and early and manage to snag the very last ticket on the evening train with a stop at Owl Lake. I should be home by bedtime. Since my hometown is such a small village nestled far upstate in the shadow of the Adirondack Mountains, only a few trains per day run from Manhattan to Owl Lake's tiny railway station. There are about half a dozen stops at various points in between, so when I drag my suitcase—still stuffed with everything I so lovingly packed for Paris—onto the train, most of the seats are already taken. I make my way down the aisle until I finally spot an empty window seat next to an older woman wrapped in a pretty red cape with her snow-white hair swept up into a magnificent bun.

"Is that seat taken?" I ask.

She looks up from the bundle of knitting in her lap, and I see that her reading glasses are red-rimmed with clusters of holly leaves and berries decorating the corners of the frames. "It's all yours, dear," she says, gathering her things so she can stand and let me by.

I feel myself smile ear-to-ear. She's giving off a major Mrs. Claus vibe that I find particularly endearing. "Thanks so much."

After the passenger across the aisle helps me heave my bag onto the overhead rack, I settle in beside my seatmate and check my phone. Still no conciliatory text from Jeremy, which I pretty much expected. He's probably halfway to France by now.

Last night, I decided to keep my trip to Owl Lake a secret, just in case. I haven't told my parents I'm coming, lest Jeremy make some sort of last-minute grand gesture that will undo the misery of the night before. Which is ridiculous, because after tossing and turning all night, I'm not even sure I *want* a grand gesture from him. Somewhere deep down in the pit of my stomach, I'm not sure there's anything he could say or do to convince me that I actually want to marry him. Everything has gotten so confusing. It's not until the train begins pulling out of the station that I fully absorb the fact that Jeremy won't arrive, running through the station at the last moment while the music swells, to tell me he can't live without me. There will be no trip to Paris with a ring on my finger. I'm actually going to sleep in my childhood bed tonight, far away from the glittering lights of New York and an entire world away from the Musée du Louvre.

I take a deep breath and focus on the scenery on the other side of the train window. The farther we crawl away from the city, the thicker the snowfall becomes, until the ground is covered by a deep layer of sparkling white. Icicles cling to the tree branches, and the train casts a cool blue shadow over the horizon. I almost feel like we're headed toward the North Pole.

"Are you on your way home for the holidays?" the older woman beside me asks.

I glance at her hands and the careful, rhythmic motion of her knitting needles and catch sight of a flash of silver dangling from one of her wrists. "Yes, you?"

She nods. "Oh, definitely. It's that time of year, isn't it?"

My heart gives a little tug. Before I left Owl Lake for college, if anyone would have told me I'd miss eight Christmases in a row at home, I never would have believed them. Then again, I'd never have believed I'd turn down a proposal from Aidan Flynn either.

I press my hand against the ache in my chest.

"I'm Ashley," I say. "Ashley James."

"Nice to meet you, dear. My name is Betty." She pauses from her knitting to offer me her hand.

As I shake it, I get a better look at the bracelet I spied earlier on her wrist and gasp. "Oh my, look at your charm bracelet. Is it vintage?"

It shimmers under the fluorescent lights of the train. Sterling silver, possibly even white gold. The charms are like none I've seen before—as if they're from another era, like perfect, tiny images from Christmas cards that have been lovingly saved and pressed into the pages of a scrapbook. I spy a silver dog with a red enamel bow around its neck and a Christmas tree topped with a glittering gold star. There are more, and all of them seem to be either winter or Christmas-themed. It's a lovely piece of jewelry, and when she withdraws her hand from mine, the movement of the charms sounds like jingle bells.

"This old thing?" She laughs. "Indeed. It's even older than I am."

Timeless, I think. "It's quite beautiful. I've never seen one like it, and charms are kind of my thing."

"Is that so?" She tilts her head and regards me with an intensity that makes my cheeks go warm. "Tell me more, dear."

So I do. I tell her all about my job at Windsor and every collection of charms that has graced the display case in my department since I started working there four years ago. I tell her about the necklace I made for Maya with the Santa charm and eight tiny reindeer. I tell her about all my favorite booths at Brooklyn Flea and which ones have the best selection of antique silver pieces.

"Charms really are your thing, aren't they?" she says.

I nod. "I studied jewelry making in college. Re-crafting vintage pieces is my specialty."

Betty frowns down at her knitting and the click-clack of her needles stops. "Then why aren't you selling your own designs?"

"You mean I should open an Etsy store or something?" I've considered it, but with all my hours at Windsor, I've never found the time to make enough pieces to keep a side business up and running.

"Not exactly." Betty gives me another of those soul-piercing looks that makes my cheeks warm. "If you don't mind my saying so, you just might need to learn to dream bigger."

Seriously? Windsor Fine Jewelry is one of the most glamorous and recognizable jewelry stores in the world. It's legendary. What could be bigger than working there? But as Betty's charm bracelet rattles, drawing my eyes to its silver shimmer, I get the distinct feeling that Betty isn't talking about Windsor at all.

"Dream bigger." I let out a laugh. "You sound like my roommate. She keeps telling me I'm going to have the Christmas of my dreams, even though it's been pretty much of a disaster so far."

"I sensed something might be amiss. You seem sad, dear, and no one should be sad at Christmas. It's the most magical time of the year."

There's that word again. *Magical.*

Something inside my chest loosens, like a shiny satin ribbon unspooling. I have the sudden urge to tell Betty everything, even though she's a total stranger. "I suppose I am sad. I thought my boyfriend was going to propose last night, but it was just a crazy misunderstanding. And now he's no longer my boyfriend."

"I'm sorry," she says.

"Me too." I sigh. "I'm supposed to be in Paris with him right now, actually. But I couldn't bring myself to go after the non-proposal."

Betty's lips curve into a sympathetic smile, and her glasses slip to the very tip of her nose. I desperately want to tell her that she looks exactly how I've always pictured Mrs. Claus, but I don't want her to take it the wrong way.

Plus, I'm not quite sure how to explain the impression she's made on me. It goes beyond appearance. Talking to her is astonishingly comforting, even though she's a stranger. Against all odds, I'm starting to feel like everything will be all right. Even better than all right, maybe. A warm glow starts to wrap itself around me, and I feel like I'm brimming with possibility.

With hope.

"Do you think I did the right thing?" I ask, and I'm not altogether sure why. Betty has never even met Jeremy, and I've only known her for the better part of an hour. Her opinion shouldn't carry much weight, but for some strange reason, it does.

"Only you can answer that question, my dear." Her eyes shine as she speaks.

And then the strangest thing happens. I start telling her more and more about my life in New York. I tell her about Audrey's pink necklace and the gingerbread ice cream I shared with Maya last night. I tell her about our shoebox of an apartment and how the television is always set to the classic movies channel. I tell her about the thick, plush carpet at Windsor, the view from the big picture window and how on a crisp clear day, I can stand at the charms counter and see the tower of Belvedere Castle looming over Central Park.

I don't stop there. I talk and talk, pouring my heart and soul out to this kind woman who, like Maya, seems to have more faith in me than I have in myself. I tell her how much I used to love Owl Lake, and I even admit that I'm a little bit nervous to be going back there again. I know it can't be the exact same town that I left all those years ago, but I admit that part of me hopes that it is. It would be nice to think that the most precious things in life can be preserved somehow, immune to the passage of time—kind of like the vintage jewelry I love so much.

Betty knits as she listens, and my gaze goes back to her bracelet again and again, drawn by the movement of the charms as the stitches on her needles pile up, row upon row. When at last I run out of things to say, a perfect red Christmas stocking hangs from her knitting needles. The overhead lights of the train have gone dim, and the only thing visible on the horizon is the glint of snow beneath a sliver of December moon.

My eyelids grow heavy. I am exhausted all of a sudden—tired to the bone. Tired of my fast-paced life in Manhattan, tired of wondering why I'm not enough for Jeremy, tired of thinking about the past. I can't wait to get home.

"I thought this was going to be a new beginning," I murmur as my eyes drift shut. "I believed. I really did. I thought this would be the Christmas of my dreams."

"Perhaps it still will be," Betty says quietly.

And then the last thing I hear as the rocking motion of the train finally lulls me to sleep is the gentle music of her charm bracelet, as tender and soothing as a Christmas lullaby.

"Attention, passengers. This is your conductor speaking. We're nearing the Owl Lake Station, our final stop. All train passengers must disembark. Thank you for traveling by rail, and have a happy holiday season."

I jolt awake, disoriented as the train comes to a stop. The overhead lights have been turned up brighter, and I seem to be the only person left in my car. My heart sinks as I realize that the seat Betty occupied is now empty.

I've missed the chance to tell her goodbye.

I sit up, rubbing the sleep from my eyes, and something in my lap shifts. When I look down, I spot a familiar red bundle—it's the stocking Betty had been knitting while I shared my story. There's a small lump near its toe, and when I gather the stocking in my hands, it makes a jingling sound.

No. My heart hammers in my chest. *It can't be.*

I reach inside, and as soon as my fingertips brush against cool silver, I know it's true. Betty has left me her vintage charm bracelet.

My astonished gaze travels over it, moving from charm to charm, and I run the pad of my thumb over the bracelet's interlocking links. The charms swivel in place, almost as if they're winking at me. I can hardly believe it. This bracelet can't possibly be mine. There's no way I can accept it. It's far too precious for Betty to give it away to a perfect stranger.

I glance up and down the aisle, but she's nowhere to be seen. She must have gotten off at an earlier stop, and I slept right through it. How can this be happening?

I peer inside the knit stocking, hoping she's left me her contact information. If so, I'll return the bracelet the first chance I get. Sure enough, there's a small piece of paper folded into a square deep inside the stocking's round toe. But when I unfold the note and scan Betty's swirling cursive script, there isn't a hint of an address or phone number. Not even her full name. She's only written a single, mysterious sentence.

Please wear this and have the Christmas of your dreams.

I'm not sure what it means, exactly. I guess she noticed how much I loved the bracelet and probably felt sorry for me. I had, after all, just spent the past several hours opening my heart to her, even though we'd never so much as met before.

Somewhere in the periphery, I'm aware of a throat clearing. When I look up, the coach attendant is standing in the center aisle, scowling down at me. "Excuse me, miss. Perhaps you missed the announcement? It's time to disembark."

I stand and immediately bump my head on the overhead luggage rack. *Ouch.* The attendant lets out a weary sigh.

Bah humbug to you, too.

"Yes, I know. I'm so sorry, but the lady who was sitting beside me left something behind. It's valuable." My fist tightens around the bracelet. Part of me thinks I should turn it over to the train personnel, but I wholeheartedly doubt that Betty would want me to leave it behind with this cranky person. I need to find her. "Did you happen to notice where she exited the train? She had pale silver hair and wore reading glasses decorated with holly sprigs. Her hair was in a bun, and she wore a red cape with white trim."

The attendant snorts. "Sure, a man with eight reindeer friends and a belly that shook like a bowl full of jelly picked her up a while ago."

So helpful. "I'm being serious. Didn't you see her?"

"No, and I really need you to get off of the train. There's an ice storm headed this way, and we need to clear the track. You've got three minutes." He turns on his heel and leaves, muttering something about visions of sugarplums dancing in my head as he goes.

Okay, then. I'm stuck with the charm bracelet—at least for the time being. I look down at Betty's note again.

Please wear this...

I take a deep breath, unfasten the bracelet's catch

and secure it around my wrist. I tell myself it's only temporary, so I won't lose it before I manage to track Betty down. I'm afraid I might accidentally misplace the lovely piece of jewelry if I jam it back inside the stocking while I gather my things and get off the train. It will be safer if I wear it. I already have a handbag and a giant wheeled suitcase to keep track of, and the Grinch himself is rushing me out the door.

The charms tinkle as I gather my things together, and a strange shiver runs up and down my spine.

Welcome home.

Chapter Five

I GRAB THE LONE CAB AT the small taxi stand outside the station instead of calling my dad to come get me, because, true to the Grinch's word, it's already started sleeting outside. Granted, my dad spent a large part of his career maneuvering the OLFD's 42-foot-long ladder truck over steep mountain passes in all sorts of weather, but it's bad enough I'm showing up unannounced. I really don't want to make him climb out of his favorite recliner and drive to the train station when it's on the verge of raining ice cubes outside. And anyway, the sooner I can get indoors for the night, the better.

Sleet pings against the taxi's windows, and the driver makes animated chitchat as the cab winds its way from the railway station toward Main Street. The town's namesake lake shimmers in the center of our small village, surrounded by a three-mile walking trail that runs the length of downtown. On the opposite side of the lake, homes sit perched above the frozen water. In the summertime, the surface of Owl Lake is like a smooth mirror, reflecting everything in sight. Now, with the lake frozen over and piled with snow, it's a breathtakingly pristine blanket of white.

I lean closer to the window for a better view, my breath fogging the glass. I clear it away with a mittened hand, and the charms around my wrist jingle again. The sound is somehow comforting. My heart starts hammering hard in my chest as soon as the lights of downtown come into view. I haven't seen my hometown all decked out for Christmas in years, and even though my mom has been peppering me with photos, the images on my phone can't compare with the real thing. Sights I've known for as long as I can remember make me feel as if I've stepped back in time—the old stone church at the corner with its original Tiffany stained glass windows and exposed rafters of polished maple; the Christmas lights and fir garlands trimming the gabled roof of the chalet-style inn with its sweeping view of the lake; the letters that spelled out *White Christmas* and *Holiday Inn* on the Palace Theatre's glittering gold marquee.

A sign announces that the monthly classic movie marathon is showing on the twentieth of the month, just as it always has. My throat grows thick with emotion. With memories.

Not everything has remained unchanged, though. The boughs of the evergreen trees lining the walking trail are covered in snow and twinkle lights as always, but they're much taller than they were the last time I saw them. I remember my dad and the other firefighters volunteering to plant them as saplings when I was in sixth grade, and now they tower over the roofs of the quaint shops and restaurants on Main Street.

Everything is just like I remember it, but also different, all at the same time. It makes me nostalgic for years gone by, and a very small part of me wonders if coming here is a mistake. I'm confused enough about the state of my life as it is. Do I need the emotions of an overdue homecoming piled on top? I take a deep breath and toy absently with the charms on Betty's bracelet as we pass the firehouse, standing sentry over Owl Lake at the top of the hill. A sign advertising the annual Firefighters' Toy Parade stretches from one end of the apparatus bay to the other.

"Almost there," the cab driver says. "You got here just in time. This storm is supposed to be a doozy."

Just in time, I repeat to myself. Of course coming back to Owl Lake isn't a mistake. This is where I belong. I'm home, even if home doesn't quite feel the same as it used to.

The taxi crests the small hill that leads to my parents' lake house, where a ribbon of smoke rises from the chimney. One of the fir trees growing in the front yard has red velvet bows tied to its branches and shimmers with white lights. An antique sleigh sits in the middle of the lawn looking like something out of a Christmas card. My parents have always been big on decorating for the holidays, but they've really gone all out this year. I press my hand against the window and squint in the direction of the front porch. The interior lights are still on, and I breathe a sigh of relief that I won't have to sneak inside while my mom and dad are sleeping.

But then I blink—hard—convinced I'm seeing things.

There's a dog sitting on the welcome mat on the shelter of the wide, wraparound porch. With its luxurious honey-colored coat and gentle expression, the dog looks like it might be a golden retriever mix. A huge red bow is tied around its neck and, despite the icy conditions, the pup looks as if it just arrived straight from a grooming appointment at the pet salon.

When on earth did my parents get a dog? I begged and begged for one when I was a little girl, but the answer was always a firm no. And why hasn't my mom mentioned it to me?

All those text messages, and zero mention of a new, furry family member. It doesn't make sense.

"Let me help you with your luggage," the driver says as I hand him a ten-dollar bill.

"That's okay, I can get it. I'm sure you want to head home before the roads get any worse." I climb out of the backseat. "Thanks so much for the ride."

"Sure thing. You have a merry Christmas, now." He grins at me as I shut the car door. While I haul my suitcase to the walkway, he turns the cab slowly back toward the main road.

I eye the strange dog warily as I approach the front porch. It stays seated, greeting me with a wide doggy smile and happy swish of its tail. There's something so familiar about the animal, from its sweet expression and the tilt of its head to the massive bow around its neck. I'm certain I've never seen it before, though—definitely not at my parents' house.

"Good boy," I murmur once I get a closer peek at the animal.

The tail wagging intensifies as the golden gives me a melting look that makes my heart feel like it's being squeezed in a vise. I reach out a tentative hand, and I'm immediately rewarded with a swipe of a warm, pink tongue.

"What's your name?" I bend to check the dog's collar, but he's not wearing one. The bow's red satin ribbon is the only thing wrapped around his thick, furry neck.

What are my parents thinking? It's not safe for a dog to be outside on his own, especially without any sort of identification tag. And right now, there's an ice storm on the way. This sweet pup should be lying by the hearth, gnawing on a soup bone or something.

"Don't you worry. We'll get you right inside." I knock on the front door, and the dog rises to stand beside me, tail beating against my leg with glee.

The door swings open almost instantaneously, and my mom goes wide-eyed at the sight of me.

"Ashley?" She clasps her hands to her mouth, then lets out a full-on squeal. "You're home!"

She throws her arms around me and squeezes me tight, and I feel my eyes fill with tears. I clamp them shut in an effort not to cry. There's nothing like a hug from Martha James.

"What are you doing here?" She releases me from her embrace, but keeps her hands planted on my shoulders, as if trying to anchor me in place. "You're supposed to be in Paris."

"Right...that..." An anguished sniffle escapes me, despite every effort to maintain a brave face.

"Never mind. It doesn't matter. We can talk about that later. The important thing is that you're home for the holidays." My mom's gaze shifts from me to the dog. Her forehead crinkles in apparent confusion. "And you brought a dog with you?"

"What? No? That's your dog." I glance down at the sweet pup who's begun to lean against my leg, all softness and comforting warmth.

"Don't be silly," my mom says, waving a dismissive hand. "You know we don't have a dog."

"Then what's he doing here, sitting on your doorstep, all dressed up for Christmas?"

Before my mom can respond, my dad ambles toward the door from the direction of the den. He's wearing his favorite flannel buffalo plaid shirt—always a staple during the holidays—and the slippers I sent him for Christmas a few years ago. "What's all the commotion out here?"

He stops in his tracks when he spots me, and his face splits into a wide grin. "Well, what's this? It must be a Christmas miracle. Ashley's home!"

"Hi, Dad." Feeling bashful all of a sudden for turning up out of the blue, I give him a little wave.

He wraps his arms around me in a big bear hug, no questions asked.

Well, technically there's one question...

"When did you get a dog?" He rests one of his big hands on the golden retriever's broad head, and the dog responds with a full-body wag.

"He's not my dog," I repeat. Something seriously strange is going on. "Are you two playing some kind of joke on me? The dog was sitting right here by the door when the cab dropped me off. His fur isn't even wet. He couldn't have been out here long. I thought maybe you'd just let him out to do his business a second ago, and he was ready to come back inside."

"Speaking of getting inside." My mom peers out at the icy drizzle and shivers. "It's freezing out here. Ed, grab Ashley's bag. Let's get her out of the cold."

"But what about the dog?" I say as my dad reaches for my suitcase.

"Honestly, you don't need to make up a cute story, sweetheart. We don't mind that you brought your dog. We're just pleased as punch to see you." My dad winks at me as he carries my luggage over the threshold. "He can come inside."

I gape at the back of my father's head as he walks into the house. The dog glances up at me, eyes dancing, before trotting after my father as if he owns the place.

What. Is. Happening?

Hesitantly, I step over the threshold. My dad can't possibly think I invented the golden's mysterious appearance on their porch just to sneak a dog into the house, can he? But if he doesn't belong to my parents, then where did the furry little guy come from? He's too calm and well cared for to be a stray, but there's no sign that he belongs to anyone, either. Animals don't just appear out of thin air with red satin bows tied around their necks.

The dog pauses halfway to the den and cocks his head as if to ask what's taking me so long.

"I'm coming," I say, smiling despite the completely bizarre circumstances. The pup seems really sweet, regardless of where he came from or who he belongs to.

"Are you hungry, sweetheart?" My mom heads straight for the kitchen while my dad carries my things to my old bedroom. "I'm assuming you took the train, and I'll bet you haven't eaten. How does leftover pot roast sound?"

My stomach grumbles. "I'm famished, actually— and pot roast sounds great."

"Perfect. I'll heat some up for you." She reaches into the refrigerator while I scan the area for any signs of pet ownership, coming up empty.

No food or water bowls. No leash hanging on the row of hooks by the back door. No fluffy dog bed tucked by my dad's recliner in the den. (And that's definitely where it would be, if it existed).

Once we're both indoors, the dog won't leave my side. He's velcroed himself to my leg and keeps gently tucking his head beneath my hand, politely demanding to be petted. I acquiesce, because why not? He's the most devoted male I've crossed paths with in a long, long time.

"So what's his name?" my mom asks as my plate of leftovers spins round and round in the microwave.

She's talking about the dog. I can tell.

My mom's face is open and honest. It always has been, so I can also tell she's not faking anything or putting me on. She genuinely thinks the friendly pup belongs to me.

"Fruitcake," I deadpan.

Because something truly nutty is going on.

An hour or so later, I'm back in my childhood bedroom, rummaging through my suitcase for my pajamas. My parents have been incredibly kind and patient about my unexpected visit, even though I sort of skimmed over the details of my breakup with Jeremy.

Full disclosure: my parents aren't exactly his biggest fans—and that's not anything new. Jeremy has never set foot in Owl Lake, but my mom and dad met him on a few occasions when they visited me in the city. I always thought they'd eventually get along like gangbusters once they had a chance to really get to know one another, but it seemed like every time we all got together, Jeremy either got called away to deal with some big work emergency at Windsor in person, or his cell phone blew up like crazy and he gave it all his attention instead of interacting with us. Either way, my mom's smile would always grow increasingly strained around the edges, and one time, I overheard my dad mutter something terrible under his breath.

That Jeremy is no Aidan Flynn.

We'd been out to brunch at The Mark—Jeremy's treat—and I'd walked Jeremy to the lobby after he'd been summoned back to Windsor to assist a celebrity client who was having some sort of diamond crisis. Once I'd seen him off, I returned to the table just in time to accidentally hear my dad's rather blunt assessment of my new boyfriend.

"It's not a contest," my mom had said, in true mom form.

And despite the fact that my father's words hadn't actually had anything to do with me personally, my face burned with shame. I managed to slink to the bathroom and hide for a few minutes until I could force a smile and return to the table.

I frown as I tug my candy cane–striped pajamas

from my luggage. It's funny, I haven't thought about the brunch incident in a long time. Years, probably. It happened about six months into my relationship with Jeremy. Maybe I shouldn't have been so quick to ignore my father's opinion.

But he'd compared Jeremy to Aidan. *Really, Dad?* Aidan hasn't been part of my life since the summer after high school. By the time they met Jeremy, Aidan and I were ancient history. And now our relationship is even *more* ancient. The concept of Aidan and me is basically prehistoric.

Then why do you keep thinking about him?

I roll my eyes at myself. It's kind of hard not to think about Aidan Flynn, given my current surroundings. Our prom picture is still hanging on my bedroom wall, while faded, dried flowers from the wrist corsage he gave me at our senior homecoming dance are still pinned to the bulletin board. And somewhere at the bottom of my jewelry box, Aidan's class ring is probably buried beneath my earliest attempts at jewelry design.

All the mementos are messing with my head, that's all. So I turn my back on them and find Fruitcake stretched out on the foot of my bed like he's lived here all his life. His tail beats wildly against the duvet when I meet his gaze. Thump-thump-thump.

"Where did you come from, and what are you doing here?" I ask. Then, more pointedly, "Why me?"

I'm talking to a dog.

No, it's worse than that—I'm talking to a dog as if he knows the answers to all of my life's questions. I've got to stop doing this. First Betty, now Fruitcake.

I pull on my pjs and climb into bed. Fruitcake is

basically a giant, furry foot warmer, and I have to admit—it's not terrible. He's really rather cozy, and I have to remind myself that he doesn't actually belong to me, despite whatever my parents may think. I need to try and find his owner, just like I still need to locate Betty so I can return her bracelet.

While I'm thinking about Betty, I reach to unclasp her charm bracelet from around my wrist. I can't exactly sleep with it on. Most of the bracelets we sell at Windsor feature a toggle clasp, but this piece is older and it connects with a simple silver spring ring. Spring rings date back to around 1900, which matches my best estimate for the time period of the charms.

I press on the clasp's tiny lever with the pad of my thumb, but it refuses to budge. Weird. It must be jammed or something.

I try again…and again. Still nothing. The lever is completely unmovable, which seems extra strange, considering I had no trouble at all with it when I put the bracelet on earlier. And I'd even been in a rush at that point.

Fruitcake shimmies further toward the head of the bed until he's close enough to rest his head in my lap. He watches, eyes shining, as I continue struggling with the bracelet.

It's no use. My thumb is tender and throbbing, and I've made no progress whatsoever with the clasp. I *am* going to have to sleep with it on—and just hope that I don't accidentally stab myself in the eye with the sharp edge of a tiny charm in the middle of the night.

I do a quick inventory of the charms, checking for anything particularly pointy. There's a snowman with nice, rounded edges—perfect. But as I keep flipping through the tiny silver pieces, I spot a house charm that makes my eyes widen. It's an old-fashioned cottage that looks like it came straight out of Owl Lake. A fir tree with minuscule little bows on its branches sits in front of the cottage, along with—prepare for goosebumps—a replica of Santa's sleigh.

No way.

The tableau is an exact replica of the house I'm sitting in, decorations and all. Adirondack-style Christmas cottage, check. Fir tree tipped with bows, check. Antique sleigh, check. What are the odds?

While I'm staring at the charm, the bracelet makes a sudden tinkling noise, like the ring of a bell. I'm not going to lie. I'm a little freaked out. More strange things have happened to me today than the rest of my life put together.

Fruitcake lets out a snuffling sound and nudges the bracelet with the tip of his nose. He cocks his head, and at first, I'm grateful for the interruption. Betty, the bracelet, the house charm, Fruitcake himself—they're all just funny coincidences. There's really no other explanation.

But then I catch a glimpse of the charm dangling right beside the little silver house—it's the one that originally caught my eye when I first spotted the bracelet on Betty's wrist. It's a tiny silver dog with a red enamel bow on its neck. I hear the same distinct tinkling noise again, and my eyes go wide.

Jingle, jingle.

The charm looks exactly like Fruitcake.

Chapter Six

The following morning, I'm awakened by the persistent ringing of my cell phone. At first, I try to ignore it. I didn't get to sleep until the wee hours of the morning, thanks to my pathetic attempts to remove the strange bracelet.

I'd tried liquid soap and Vaseline, but neither would make the lever on the spring ring slide free. Then I'd done my best to fold my hand into a tiny enough contortion to slide the bracelet off my wrist, but after an hour or so of bodily origami, all I was left with was a cramp in my wrist and a vague sense of panic.

"Are you even real?" I'd asked Fruitcake as I stroked his warm head and tried my best to fall asleep.

It was a ridiculous question. Our house was just as real as it had been for decades, even though a small silver version of it dangled from the bracelet. Following that logic, Fruitcake should also be real.

He certainly seemed real at the moment—writhing around on his back on the bedroom floor and woofing with glee. He's a morning person, because of course he is. It only makes sense that a magical dog would be an early riser.

He's not *magical,* I tell myself as I fumble around for my phone. My eyes open wider and I sit straight up when I see Maya's name on the screen.

I tap the green button to accept the call. "Maya, thank goodness it's you."

"Good morning to you too," she says. "What's wrong? You sound odd."

"Things here are just a little—" I pause, searching for the right word. There's no way the charms on the bracelet are coming to life. That's just not possible. "—*weird.* Actually, they're a lot weird. It's good to hear your voice."

Fruitcake pops to his feet and lets out a bark. I'm guessing he needs to go outside.

"Did I just hear a bark? I didn't know your parents had a dog," Maya says. In the background, I hear honking horns and the wail of sirens and I wish I was back in New York.

"They don't." *He's imaginary!* "Never mind. It's a long story. What's up? I thought you were scheduled to work this morning."

"I am. I'm on my break, and I desperately need a gingerbread latte. I also needed to step outside so I could call you, because I have huge news."

She's talking a mile a minute, in true Maya form. I throw off the covers and shove my feet into slippers so I can sneak into the den and take Fruitcake outside while she gives me her news. I refrain from asking if it involves an engagement ring this time.

The house is quiet. Nobody stirs, not even a mouse.

My parents are either still sleeping, or they're out front shoveling snow.

"There's a management position opening up," Maya says, pausing for dramatic effect as I open the sliding glass door and step outside onto the backyard deck. "And it's in *your* department."

Fruitcake romps into the yard, clearly a fan of the brisk winter weather. As for me, I'm thinking I should have put on a coat because it's *freezing* out here. But I don't mind because Maya was right. This news is indeed huge. "Are you serious? There hasn't been an open management position in the charms department the entire time I've worked there."

"Well, there is now. And rumor has it, they want to fill it by New Year's Day."

My elation takes a serious hit.

No! No, no, no, no, no. This can't be happening while I'm miles away in Owl Lake. It's the very first Christmas since I started at Windsor that I've been here instead of dutifully standing behind the charms counter. Out of sight, out of mind and all that.

"I need to get back to Manhattan," I blurt.

Simultaneously, Maya says, "You need to get back to Manhattan."

Finished with his business, Fruitcake spins joyful circles around me. Is this dog ever in a bad mood?

"I'm not sure I can go, though." There's no way I can tell my mom and dad that I'm already leaving from my first visit in years. I've been here less than twelve hours.

"Maybe you can just come up for the day, throw your hat into the ring *in person*, and then catch the train back to Owl Lake. Think about how much initiative that would show."

She has a point. The upper-tier management at Windsor is all about initiative. And it would show a definite lack of initiative if I didn't come in to apply since everyone in the building probably knows by now that I'm not in France. Note to self: don't date people I work with anymore.

"Good idea." I nod, and Fruitcake nods back at me, as if I'm talking to him and him alone. "That's what I'll do."

Once we hang up, I feel infinitely better about the immediate future. I know I just got here, but getting out of Owl Lake for the day sounds wonderful, given all the odd things that have happened since I left the city. I try the bracelet's clasp again and give it a little tug. No dice. Since two of the charms have already mysteriously come to life, I'm afraid to examine the others too closely.

Not that there's anything to be afraid of. Because it's all just a coincidence, anyway. Right?

Of course it is. Bracelets do not have magical powers, and Christmas is Christmas. There will always be some real world overlap between Christmas-themed charms and actual, real-life Christmas.

Still, I'm looking forward to a day in the city. Maybe I'll even manage to get some sort of hint to Betty's whereabouts while I'm on the train.

When Fruitcake and I go back inside, my parents are both bustling around the kitchen in their bathrobes. My mom pours coffee into three mugs. It's clearly some sort of holiday flavor, because the air smells

like cinnamon rolls and coffee beans. My dad sneaks
Fruitcake a slice of bacon while she's not looking.

"Good morning," my mom says brightly.

"Morning." I smile.

My mom and dad both smile back, and a pang of
guilt hits me right behind the breastbone. They're going to be disappointed that I'm leaving already, even if
I turn around and come right back.

It's just for the day. Worst case scenario: overnight.

I plaster on the widest grin I can manage. "You'll
never believe what Maya just called to tell me. It's the
best news."

Mom lowers her coffee cup. "What is it, dear?"

"There's a management position opening up in the
charms department. I've been there a few years now,
so I think I've got a shot."

"That's great," my dad says with genuine enthusiasm.

"But they want to fill it before New Year's," I add,
grin freezing in place. "I need to have a meeting with
my boss as soon as possible so I can explain to her in
person why I'm the best choice for the job."

My mom's brow furrows. "But you just got here."

"I know. It will only be a quick day trip. I'm coming
right back, I promise." I shrug like it's no big deal, but
I'm already glancing at the time on my phone, growing
more antsy by the second. I'm not quite familiar with
the train schedule, but I'm pretty sure I need to hurry
and get to the train station if I'm going to make it to the
city and back by tonight. "I should probably get ready."

"Wait." Dad holds up a hand. "Honey, there was an
ice storm last night, remember?"

I nod, thinking about the layer of frost covering the

majority of the backyard. Only the area beneath the pergola my dad built ages ago had been spared. The grass had made little crunching sounds beneath Fruitcake's paws when we'd been out there just now.

"But the sky seems clear," I say.

"The temperature is still below freezing. The train station will be closed until the tracks can get de-iced." My father shakes his head. "I'm afraid you're stuck here."

"Are you *sure?* A little ice never shuts down the trains in Manhattan for more than a few hours once the storm has stopped."

"You're not in Manhattan anymore." Dad's tone is careful. Gentle. But the look on his face is all too familiar. I've seen that look before.

That Jeremy is no Aidan Flynn.

He's disappointed in me, which seems really unfair. Does he want me working the charms counter for all eternity when going into Manhattan for just one day could be the key to my career?

Besides, I can't be trapped in Owl Lake. I've got a bracelet stuck to my wrist and two of the charms on it have somehow come to life. I need a break from whatever holiday craziness is going on. Maybe if I leave and come back again, everything will go back to normal.

I try to call the station to check and see if the trains are running, but the phones are down due to the storm.

"I'm going to Owl Lake station, just in case. There's got to be a train out of here today. I *promise* I'll be back in time for dinner." Hopefully, with a shiny, new promotion. It's time to turn this unlucky Christmas around.

Fruitcake trots at my heels as I dash back to my bedroom to change. For a split second, I wonder if he'll still be here when I get back. If he's really a charm come to life, he can't be an actual, permanent dog, can he?

Then I remind myself that jewelry doesn't come to life. Fruitcake's resemblance to the charm is a complete and total coincidence.

Which is a good thing because, weirdly enough, I think I might miss him if he suddenly disappeared.

An hour later, the same cab driver who took me home last night drops me off at the train station. Back home, the front yard is a frozen tundra, the angle of the grade making it far more treacherous than the back yard. I couldn't possibly ask my dad to brave the sheet of ice covering our driveway to get me here. But that's okay, because here I am, even though the taxi driver drove at a turtle's pace the entire way due to the icy roads and the whirl of snow that's starting up again.

The parking lot of the station looks practically empty, but I can see plenty of people milling about inside. I exhale a sigh of relief. Surely the trains are up and running, and my dad was just being overly cautious. It happens…a lot. It's a firefighter thing—safety first! I've always been rather fond of Dad's protective streak.

Speaking of firefighters, when I reach the platform, Owl Lake's bravest are all over the place. At first glance, it appears that every single person in my line of vision is dressed in bulky cargo pants and a dark quilted jacket boasting the OLFD crest. A few are even wearing full turnout gear, helmets and all.

"Excuse me, miss. You can't be here," someone behind me says.

"But I'm here to catch the...um..." I start to say, but any attempt at speech becomes impossible as I turn around and get a glimpse of the firefighter who seems to be in charge of whatever is going on.

It's Aidan.

Again.

But why is he here, and why, oh why, is he wearing an Owl Lake FD helmet with his last name emblazoned on it?

I blink as hard as I possibly can. Is there an ex-boyfriend firefighter charm on Betty's bracelet that I somehow failed to notice? This can't possibly be real.

Then he scowls at me, and I know that I'm really standing face-to-face with Aidan in full hero mode. Because there's nothing at all imaginary about his cranky expression.

Nice to see you too, Firefighter Grumpy Pants.

Ugh, why does he have to be a firefighter? He looks like he's on his way to pose for one of those fireman bachelor calendars. So strong. So *heroic.*

"Ashley." He clears his throat.

There's a slight tremor of surprise to his voice, and the fact that he seems as shocked as I am makes me feel a tiny bit better—the smallest possible amount. He's clearly more rattled to see me here in Owl Lake than he was back in Rockefeller Plaza.

"Aidan," I manage to say, and wow, why on earth do I sound so...so....*breathless?*

He arches a brow, and I wish I could melt away and vanish like Frosty the Snowman. "You've come home."

Finally. The word floats between us, unspoken but very much there.

He's judging me—for all the Christmases I've missed in Owl Lake, for leaving the way I did all those years ago, for so many things. Or maybe he's not. Maybe I'm judging myself.

I lift my chin to fully meet his gaze. When did he get so tall? He seems even bigger than he had just a few days ago. "Yes, but what are you doing here? You told me you worked in the city."

"No, I didn't," he counters.

Didn't he?

His frown deepens. "I said I was working. I was there to collect a donation for the Firefighters' Toy Parade."

So he really, truly *is* a fireman—right here in Owl Lake at the station where my dad used to be the chief. I can't believe Dad failed to mention this significant fact. We're definitely having a chat about that when I get back from the city.

Right...the city...where I'm supposed to be heading right now instead of shivering on the platform in Owl Lake, thinking about how handsome my high school sweetheart looks in his OLFD uniform, glowering expression and all.

"Okay, well." I swallow hard. There's an annoying lump in my throat all of a sudden, for reasons I don't even want to begin to contemplate. "It was nice seeing you again. I have a train to catch."

The moment the words leave my mouth, I realize there's not another traveler in sight. While I was right about there being plenty of people in the station, I'm the only person in the vicinity who's not wearing either fire-retardant clothing or some sort of railway uniform, and the train itself is nowhere to be seen.

"No, you don't." Aidan shakes his head. "The storm shut down the station. The tracks are iced over, and we're out here supervising the de-icing efforts. Everything should be back up and running in forty-eight hours."

"Forty-eight hours?" My jaw drops.

"I'm afraid I'm going to have to ask you to leave." A muscle in Aidan's jaw flexes. Still, his expression is a blank slate. He's as stiff and unyielding as a robot.

He didn't used to be this way. I don't like it. I'd almost prefer more glowering.

"But I can't wait that long," I say. "I need to get back to Manhattan right away."

He narrows his gaze at me. His eyes are the same striking shade of blue they've always been. *Forget-me-not blue*. The lump in my throat grows threefold. I could never, ever forget Aidan Flynn, not if I tried.

Nor would I want to. I just wish he would smile at me again, for old times' sake. Aidan always had the best smile. It never failed to make me weak in the knees.

"I just saw you two days ago in the city. You have to have just gotten here," he says stonily.

"I got in late last night." Not that it's any of his business.

"So you've been home all of twelve hours, and you're already itching to go back." He shakes his head and looks about as thrilled as a kid who just found a lump of coal in his stocking on Christmas morning. "Sounds about right."

I've changed my mind about the glowering. I definitely prefer the robot treatment. But at least with this last comment, his standoffishness suddenly seems more understandable. To him, I'm just the girl who broke his heart and turned her back on her small town for a new life in the big city.

But that's not who I am.

Is it?

My chest grows tight as I realize all available evidence supports his theory. Here I am—back for my first Christmas in Owl Lake in years—and all I can think about is finding a way to get back to Manhattan.

"It's not what you think," I say, blinking against a sudden whirlwind of snow flurries. "This is just a day trip. I'm coming right back."

He goes silent for a beat. After a long, painfully awkward pause, his blue eyes soften—ever so slightly. He clears his throat. "Not today, you're not. All trains have been cancelled."

Oh yeah. He already mentioned that, didn't he?

"That's unfortunate." I try my best not to sound like a snobbish big city princess, and to be honest, I'm not sure I'm successful. What would Aidan think if he knew I was supposed to be in Paris right now? And why does his opinion still matter after all this time? "I guess I'll call the cab to come back."

Aidan gives me a slow nod, then squints against the snowfall and glances around at his fellow firemen.

"No need. I can take you home," he finally says. He zips his jacket the remaining two inches until it's snug against the base of his throat. His neck is thicker than it used to be—corded with muscle.

The Aidan I used to know was a boy; the person standing in front of me right now is very much a man.

"You don't have to do that," I say softly. For some reason, his kindness is more difficult for me to accept than his earlier crankiness.

He shrugs one shoulder. "I know."

And then he strides toward a shiny red fire truck parked parallel to the railway tracks, leaving me no choice but to follow.

My high school sweetheart is giving me a ride home. In a fire truck.

Minutes later, I'm seated up front in the ladder truck, right beside Aidan as he navigates the rig over the ice-covered streets of Owl Lake toward my parents' lake house. Everything about the experience is nostalgic, which does little to alleviate the ache in my chest. When I was a little girl and my dad was chief, he would prop me up in the front seat of the various fire trucks all the time. I felt like a princess, and my dad's heavy chief's helmet was my crown. Now, here I am again, in a fire truck in my hometown, only the man sitting beside me is Aidan. Never in a million years would I have predicted this turn of events, but it feels right somehow. Fated, if I'm really being honest.

Aidan's own father died in a car accident when he was just a little boy. He and my dad have always been close. The fact that he's followed in my father's footsteps must mean the world to Dad.

Still, this trip down memory lane would be a lot nicer if it were a bit more quiet. Thanks to the siren, every head turns our way as we pass, from the good people of Owl Lake who are outside shoveling snow to the white-tailed deer prancing among the fir trees. Super. Just what I need for this awkward reunion—an audience.

"Is the siren really necessary?" I ask over the ear-splitting wail of the fire engine.

"Sorry." Aidan silences the siren, and I catch the telltale hint of a smirk on his lips. He's enjoying this little rescue mission, probably because he can tell I find it wholly embarrassing.

I face forward and do my best to ignore his presence, but of course doing so is impossible. The air in the cab of the fire engine is thick with memories and the warm, masculine scent of woodsmoke and evergreen. Adult Aidan is as appealing as s'mores cooked over an open campfire on a cold winter night, all melty warmth and starlight. The miles between here and Paris seem longer than ever.

"Why are you in such a hurry to get back to the city?" Aidan asks without tearing his eyes off the road.

I tell myself he's only being safety-conscious, not trying to avoid meeting my gaze, but his white-knuckle grip on the steering wheel says otherwise.

"I found out this morning that a promotion has opened up at the jewelry store where I work, and I really want it—but they're looking to fill it right away. If I wait until after the holidays to talk to my boss about it, it will be too late."

Aidan nods.

"I truly was planning on coming right back," I say.

He sneaks a sideways glance at me, and my heart gives a little squeeze. My stupid, stupid heart. "I believe you."

I cannot be attracted to Aidan Flynn. I have far more important things to worry about at the moment, not least of which is the fact that I just broke up with the man who I foolishly believed was about to ask me to marry him. The butterflies zipping around my insides are just nerves, nothing more.

The ride to my parents' lake house is quick, especially since we're pretty much the only vehicle on the road. Dad wasn't kidding when he insisted that the storm had shut down the entire town. Several of the local businesses seem to be open, but people are out walking from place to place instead of driving. The sledding hill behind the fire station appears to be the hottest spot in town.

"How's your mom?" I ask. "And Susan?"

Aidan's sister used to be one of my closest friends, and I suddenly miss her so much that her absence in my life feels like a physical ache, deep in my chest. Why is coming home always so hard?

"They're both great," he says without elaborating.

Okay, then. I was hoping he'd tell me about the twin nieces I've already seen in dozens of pictures (thank you, Facebook), but I guess we're past the point of sharing personal details about our lives. The ache in my chest is beginning to feel more like a chasm.

We arrive home in a matter of minutes, and I quickly realize that Aidan may have turned off the siren, but he left the engine lights on. They sweep across the snowy front lawn in dancing rays of red and gold. The effect is oddly beautiful.

"When did your parents get a dog?" Aidan says as his mouth curves into a smile at long last.

Fruitcake is sitting by the front door in the same

spot where I first found him last night. He cocks his head when he sees me, as if he's been waiting there for me his entire life, tail wagging like a pendulum.

I shake my head. "They didn't. He just sort of keeps...appearing."

Aidan turns toward me and regards me with sudden interest, like he might not have me quite as figured out as he'd thought.

You have no idea, I almost say. *There might be a magic bracelet stuck on my wrist.*

I can't tell him that, obviously. It sounds completely nuts. But despite the years stretching between us, he's still the person I most want to confide in. I don't know why. It doesn't make sense, but then again, since the moment I woke up on the train in Owl Lake, *nothing* has.

"I found the dog right there on the porch last night, or maybe he found me. I'm not exactly sure which. I should probably try and figure out who he belongs to." I really should get right on that, especially since I'm apparently stuck here for the time being. There's got to be a logical explanation for his presence. Golden retrievers don't just materialize out of thin air. "He doesn't have a collar or ID tags, so I've been calling him Fruitcake."

Aidan arches a brow. "Fruitcake?"

"Christmas and all," I say by way of explanation, leaving out the part about my recently nutty life.

"Cute name." Aidan smiles again until he seems to realize that he's no longer scowling at me and his lips straighten into a flat line. "I should probably be getting back to the train station."

"Right, of course. Thanks so much for the ride."

I start to climb down from my seat, but Aidan hops down and opens my door for me before I manage to do it myself.

The gesture is so reminiscent of the many times he brought me home after a date back in high school that my cheeks grow warm. I wonder if he's thinking the same thing, but when I climb down to the snowy ground and look up to meet his gaze, his expression is still a complete blank.

"Thanks again," I say, doing my best to ignore the disappointment I have no business feeling. Then I turn to go, anxious to get inside and put an end to this uncomfortable encounter.

"Hey," Aidan says, stopping me in my tracks.

I turn around to face him, and his gaze shifts to Fruitcake for a second and then back to me.

"I can ask around about the dog, if that helps. One of the guys at the station is bound to have heard about a missing dog." Aidan shrugs. "You know how small towns are."

"Thank you. I'd appreciate that," I say.

It's been years since I've been home, but yes, I do know how small towns are. Much like those eyes of his, bluer than the bluest of Christmases, there are certain things a girl never forgets.

No matter how long she's been away.

Chapter Seven

THE HOUSE IS THICK WITH the smell of warm sugar and vanilla when I stomp the snow from my boots and let myself in. By my side, Fruitcake's nose twitches. My stomach rumbles, and I pause in the entryway to take a deep inhale.

"Mom must be baking Christmas cookies," I say, because I'm apparently becoming the sort of person who talks to strange dogs as if they're human.

I can't help it. He's so sweet. So...*devoted*. A flicker of panic passes through me at the thought of Aidan actually tracking down Fruitcake's real owner, which is absurd. This dog is *not* mine. He didn't just magically appear on the porch with a big red bow on his neck just for me. He's probably supposed to be a Christmas gift for someone else and somehow got lost, but he's gazing up at me as if I'm the long-lost inventor of dog biscuits.

"Stop looking at me like that," I say, and his ears

prick forward. "Aidan is going to help me figure things out, so you can go home."

"Ashley, is that you?" my mom calls from the kitchen. She sounds utterly delighted that I've only been gone an hour instead of a full day.

When I round the corner, she's wearing a full bib-style apron covered with little cartoon gingerbread men and pulling a tray of sugar cookies from the oven. There are at least two dozen of these, already decorated with colored icing and sprinkles, piled onto platters on the kitchen island next to a fresh batch of chocolate walnut cookies. The big electric mixer is poised, ready for another round of batter, and I know instantly what's going on.

"Do you still make cookies every year for the firemen?" I take a closer look at a vanilla-iced snowman cookie and, sure enough, my mom has piped a cute little firefighter's helmet onto his round head.

"Of course I do." She peels the oven mitts from her hands and arches a brow at me. "It doesn't look you made it very far."

"I didn't." I shake my head. "Dad was right. The train station was closed."

"I'd ask how you got home, but I saw the ladder truck's flashing lights out front just now," Dad says, strolling into the kitchen from the direction of his man cave down the hall, where he's apparently been spying on me from the window overlooking the house's snowy street.

I don't need to ask if he knows who was behind the wheel of the ladder truck, because his amused expression says it all.

"About that." I jam my hands on my hips. "How am I just finding out that Aidan is a firefighter?"

"You were in a terrible hurry to leave this morning, honey," Mom says.

My dad shrugs. "If you'd stuck around longer, we might have had a chance to get you caught up on things around here."

Touché. "Point taken, but seriously? We talk all the time and Mom texts me every day. How has this never come up in conversation?"

"Well. A while back you said you didn't want to talk about Aidan, remember?" My mom flips through her recipe book—the same one she's used since I was a little girl. The pages are soft and worn, with faded ink and dots from spilled vanilla.

"That was seven years ago. I was trying to get over our breakup."

"And are you?" Dad says. "Over it?"

Of course I am. I can't believe he's even asking me that question. But when I try to form an answer, the words stick in my throat. I blink back at him until Mom changes the subject.

"Now that you're back, why don't you join me?" Mom offers me an apron covered with layer upon layer of peppermint-striped ruffles. It's the very antithesis of basic Manhattan black.

"You know I can't bake." The stove in the apartment I share with Maya has a grand total of one useable burner, and the tiny oven is filled with takeout menus. I'm not even sure it actually works. "These cookies are gorgeous. I'd only end up ruining the rest of the batch."

My mom shakes her head and forces the apron into my hands. "You're forgetting something very important—holiday baking isn't about a perfect end result. It's about the process. Besides, Aidan just rescued you and brought you home in a fire engine. The cookies will be a nice thank-you gesture."

The kitchen window doesn't look out to the drive-way, but Mom's not guessing—she's absolutely certain that Aidan's the fireman who drove me home. I knew it. My ride with Aidan has already made the Owl Lake gossip rounds. There was probably a phone tree or something, and now everyone in town is talking about it.

"It was hardly a rescue." I tie my apron strings into a bow with a tad too much force. "He offered me a ride, that's all. And he didn't exactly seem thrilled about it."

But he'd also offered to help solve the Fruitcake mystery, so maybe I should overlook his comment about me being in such a hurry to get back to the city. Besides, I had been in a hurry to get back to Manhattan. I still am.

"You two have fun." Dad winks at me before swiping one of the chocolate walnut cookies for himself. "I'll go check the smoke alarms, just in case."

"Very funny," I say, but already I'm forgetting the difference between baking soda and baking powder. Which is the one with the arm swinging the little gavel? Or is it a hammer? And what do either of those have to do with baking?

"Here you go, honey." My mom slides the recipe book across the counter toward where I'm standing beside the mixer. "Why don't you get all the ingredients together and get the batter started while I frost the batch that just came out of the oven? Put twice the amount listed for everything so we can make a double batch."

I can do this. It's just measuring things and stirring them together, right? It's got to be easier than wielding a pastry bag and drawing cute little details with icing, like my mom's doing. Already, she's drawing a tiny, intricate fire hose in the hands of a gingerbread firefighter.

Automatically, I move to unfasten the charm bracelet from my wrist so it won't get dirty in what's sure to be a messy attempt at holiday baking. But of course the clasp still refuses to budge. Why didn't I bring my jewelry-making tools with me on this trip? If I could get my hands on the right pair of pliers, I could probably get this silly thing off in no time.

For now, I tuck the charms into the sleeve of my black turtleneck sweater as best as I can.

"You're so good at this, Mom." I attempt to measure out two and half cups of flour and am immediately covered in a cloud of fine white powder. Fruitcake is sitting at my feet and sneezes four times in rapid succession.

"I've been doing it for more than thirty years," she says. "It just takes practice."

"Thirty years. Has it really been that long?" Is that sugar that I just added to the flour, or was it salt? I definitely shouldn't be trying to carry on a conversation while I'm doing this. I add a little extra sugar, just in case.

"I started the first Christmas your dad was a rookie firefighter. We were engaged, but not yet married. I turned up at the firehouse a week before Christmas with the most pathetic looking gingerbread firemen and iced sugar cookies anyone had ever seen."

I look up from the bowl in front of me, now overflowing with ingredients. Somehow, I've never heard this story. Probably because I haven't helped my mom with her firefighter cookies in years. I used to love dressing up in one of her holiday aprons and licking the batter from the beaters of the mixer when I was a little girl. But as I grew older, I became far too intimidated by the perfection of her end results to try my hand at helping, convinced I'd just mess everything up. And lately, I haven't been home during the holidays at all, as Aidan was so keen to point out earlier.

"I don't believe that for a minute," I say.

"It's true. They looked like a mess, but your dad and the other men at the fire house loved them—or at least, they loved that I'd made an effort—and somehow it became a Christmas tradition." She's moved on from the gingerbread men and is now dusting the snowflake sugar cookies with shimmery edible glitter.

"And you're still baking them, even though Dad retired." I feel myself smile at the idea.

"Of course. The firehouse is a very important part of the community, and really, I can't imagine giving up the tradition just because your dad isn't the chief anymore. To him, the men at that station are still family. They always will be."

And now that family includes Aidan. My heart gives a little twist, and I add an unspecified amount of ground ginger to my batter. It's hard to measure when my hands are trembling.

I don't want to be this rattled by my latest encounter with Aidan. I really don't. I just want to think about ordinary things, like getting my promotion and making my way to Paris for Christmas someday all on my own. But instead, I'm back in Owl Lake with a strange bracelet stuck on my arm and all sorts of strange and confusing feelings clouding my head over a man who hasn't been a part of my life in almost a decade. Although truthfully, those feelings have been fluttering through me since I first ran into him outside of FAO Schwartz.

It doesn't help that my mom's story about baking for the firemen when she and my dad were newly engaged is giving me major *It's a Wonderful Life* vibes. I could have had that life. I could have been the one baking terrible cookies for my firefighting husband-to-be all those years ago, but I chose another path.

Rightly so, I remind myself. As Jeremy said the other night, I'm living the dream.

I flip the electric mixer to the on position. Fruitcake leans heavily against my leg, all warmth and comfort. He's got a dusting of flour on his head, and it makes him look like he's been outside playing in the snow. I smile, and as the cookie dough spins round and round, I realize just now was the first time Jeremy has crossed my mind all day.

Maybe my heart isn't quite as broken as I thought it was.

"I can't believe you're making me do this." I take one last look at the platter of cookies in my hand and wince.

They're every bit as bad as I expected them to be—worse, because I had such a good time with my mom in the kitchen that I let her talk me into trying to decorate the last batch of gingerbread firefighters and snowflake sugar cookies myself. Let me tell you, drawing things with frosting is a lot harder than it looks. My poor gingerbread firemen look like they're wrestling yellow snakes instead of wielding fire hoses. Happy holidaysssssssssssss.

"You helped make the cookies, so of course you should help deliver them too," my mom says as we walk up the sidewalk toward the firehouse. Fruitcake trots alongside us on a candy cane-striped dog leash my dad picked up on one of his errands this afternoon. Any day now, the dog will probably have his own Christmas stocking hanging from the mantle. "Besides, it will be fun."

"Are you just saying that because you don't want anyone to think you're the one responsible for the snake cookies?"

"Absolutely not. They'll be thrilled to see us—and thrilled with the cookies. Just wait." My mom laughs and gives me a little nudge, because the closer I get to the station, the more I'm dragging my feet.

What am I doing here? More to the point, why does one of our biggest family traditions have to involve delivering homemade baked goods to Aidan's workplace?

With any luck at all, he'll be out on a call. Not that I want anything in the nearby vicinity to catch on fire, but isn't there a kitten in a tree somewhere that needs saving?

But the ladder truck, the pumper truck and the small engine are all present and accounted for, lined up side by side in the apparatus bay, as shiny and red as Rudolph's famed nose. A wreath hangs on the grill of the ladder truck, and I can't help wondering if Aidan hung it there himself. I'm guessing his job is more than a basic fireman. Since he drove me home in the rig, he must be the fire engineer responsible for the ladder truck.

I remind myself I'm not here to see Aidan. I'm here for my mom and her favorite Christmas tradition. But somehow my heart doesn't seem to get the memo. It beats wildly out of control as Mom knocks politely on the door to the fire house.

"Martha!" The current fire chief's face splits into a wide grin when he opens the door and sees my mom. His gaze sweeps over the trays of cookies in her hands, and then he does a double take when he spots me standing beside her. "Ashley? Well, aren't you a sight for sore eyes."

"Merry Christmas, Uncle Hugh." Hugh took over the chief's position after Dad retired. He's been with the department since my dad's early days with the OLFD, and while we're not technically related, he's always been like an uncle to me. Somewhere along the way, I started calling him Uncle Hugh and the nickname stuck.

He winks at me. "I heard you were in town for the holidays."

I'm sure you did. I paste on a smile and try not to think about my absolute certainty that everyone in Owl Lake is talking about my ride through town earlier in Aidan's truck. It was *not* a rescue, despite how it looked.

Hugh's grin widens, and he tries to hug me, but

it's difficult with my platter of mortifying gingerbread firemen stuck between us. I pray for fate to be kind and intervene just enough for my cookies to slide to the floor and immediately get trampled underfoot so no one will ever see them, but alas, no such luck.

"Who's this?" Hugh asks, ruffling the fur on Fruitcake's head.

The dog's entire back end wiggles with delight.

"Oh, that's Fruitcake. Ashley's dog," my mom says.

Uncle Hugh straightens and rests his hands on his hips. "That makes perfect sense."

"It does?" I say, before I can stop myself. I can't help it because so far, nothing about Fruitcake has made sense.

"Sure. When you were just five or six, you said you wanted a big yellow dog for Christmas. You asked Santa for that very thing at the Firefighters' Toy Parade. All this furry guy needs is a shiny red bow around his neck." Uncle Hugh laughs. "As I recall, that was an important detail in your Christmas wish."

"Oh, that's right!" My mom nods. "I'd forgotten that you specifically wanted a yellow dog with a fancy red bow. You were so earnest and so certain about what you wanted—but you were also so little at the time. We weren't sure you were ready to take care of a pet."

I nod as if in a daze.

A big yellow dog with shiny red bow.

I'd forgotten the specifics of that particular Christmas wish, but now they feel strangely significant because the wish seems to have inexplicably come true.

Or not. There's got to be a rational explanation. I glance down at Fruitcake. If only he could talk, then I could demand one.

"Come on in." Uncle Hugh opens the door wider and waves us inside. "The guys are going to be thrilled to see you two. Your cookies are always one of the highlights of Christmas around here, Martha."

He leads us through the dispatch area, toward the large common room where two rows of plush leather recliners embroidered with the OLFD crest face a big flat-screen television. A long, rustic table sits just past the TV area, and I know from experience that this is where the on-duty firemen share their meals and where the big communal dinners are held on holidays like Thanksgiving and Christmas, when the firehouse is full of the OLFD's family members. It's the same table where I sat, year after year, before I moved away from Owl Lake. Somewhere on its worn chestnut surface, it probably still has marks from my old crayons.

Firefighters are milling about the station—most I recognize, but a few I don't. Word spreads quickly that there are cookies on the premises, and soon we're surrounded by a group of men and women in dark blue OLFD sweatshirts. I'm immediately swept up in a wave of hugs and introductions. Fruitcake is showered with pats and adoration, while I nod and make polite conversation. But all the while, I'm hopelessly distracted, waiting for Aidan to make an appearance.

His absence should be a relief. After all, it's exactly what I'd hoped for. Instead, I'm hit with a nonsensical tug of disappointment.

I inhale a steadying breath, but then Aidan strolls toward our group from the direction of the locker room and sleeping quarters. Fruitcake bounds toward him, wagging a greeting, and I'm suddenly overly aware of the sound of my own heartbeat.

He's here.

Of course he is. He *works* here, what did I expect? Still, I have an urge to pitch my sad little cookies into the nearest trash can before he can see them. This is like our high school home economics class all over again.

Aidan greets my mom with a friendly hug but gives me a wide berth after waving and saying hello. The space between us seems infinite.

"Hi," I say back.

The rest of the group clusters around the platters of cookies my mom made, gushing over her artistry and her commitment to the annual cookie tradition. I'm hoping no one notices my lone tray of gingerbread firemen. Maybe they'll get overlooked in the mix.

But of course Aidan notices them straightaway, and his lips quirk into a grin.

"Sure, *those* you smile at," I mutter. I understand why he doesn't seem happy to see me, I really do, but I'd be lying if I said it didn't make me sad. I never wanted to hurt Aidan.

He looks up, blue eyes dancing with amusement. "You made these yourself, didn't you?"

I feel impossibly warm all of a sudden, despite the snowflakes swirling outside. "How could you tell?"

He picks up one of the cookies and squints at it. "They look great, but I'm trying to figure out why the gingerbread man is holding a giant spaghetti noodle."

"That's a firehose," I say flatly.

Matt, one of the firefighters I met a few minutes ago, reaches for a gingerbread man, and Aidan shakes his head. "You might not want to do that if these are anything like the cookies Ashley made back in high school. As I recall, she started a fire in the home economics lab."

"It wasn't a fire," I protest. "Just a minor smoke incident."

Matt laughs. "Thanks for the warning, but I'm sure they're delicious."

He bites into the gingerbread man's leg and his eyes widen with something that really doesn't look like delight. He chews for a ridiculously long time before slipping the rest of the cookie to Fruitcake when he thinks I'm not looking. Fruitcake wolfs it down, and then promptly spits it out.

Aidan notices, of course, and I long for the floor of the fire house to open up and swallow me whole.

But then Aidan reaches for one of my cookies, pops it into his mouth and swallows it after a few quick chews. Then he eats another and another, holding my gaze the entire time.

My heartbeat seems even louder. Surely everyone can hear it.

I reach to cover the platter of gingerbread men with plastic wrap to prevent him from eating a fourth cookie. He's already moved his way straight to the top of my nice list. There's no need to make himself sick. I don't think eating too many of my cookies could poison anyone...but I wouldn't want to stake someone's life on that.

He's mid-reach though, ready to choke down another one, and his hand collides with mine. A spark of electricity passes between us, and I freeze.

What was *that?*

I search Aidan's gaze, wondering if he felt it too. But his gaze isn't fixed on mine anymore. Something else has captured his attention, and that something is the mysterious bracelet as it jingles on my wrist.

"This is pretty," he says, running his fingertips over the dangling silver charms. "Is it from the jewelry store where you work?"

"No. It's…um…an antique." *And possibly magical.*

No, no, no. It's not magical. I'm sure loads of little girls wish for big yellow dogs with red shiny bows for Christmas and then years later one prances right into their lives after meeting a stranger on a train. Totally normal. Nothing to see here.

Really, though. I'm being paranoid. Being away from the city is getting to me. The dog and bracelet can't possibly have anything to do with each other.

Aidan's expression softens, and it seems as if his eyes glitter with a thousand yesterdays. "You always did love vintage things."

Warmth fills my chest, until Aidan stops to take a closer look at one of the charms. His eyebrows shoot up. "Wow, look at this one. It's just like your Christmas cookies."

Jingle, jingle.

Oh no, not again. "Did you just hear that?"

Aidan's gaze collides with mine. His nearness makes it hard for me to breathe. "Hear what?"

"Nothing. Never mind." I gnaw on my bottom lip, afraid to look at the charm. But Aidan is right there, going over it with the pad of his thumb, waiting for me to comment on the tiny silver trinket.

I have no choice. I can't tuck the bracelet back beneath my sleeve and ignore it like I've been trying to do all day, so I look.

And there it is, right beside the dog charm—a tiny

silver platter of gingerbread men and cookies shaped like snowflakes, carefully arranged on a rectangular tray with handles shaped like holly leaves. Aidan is right.

It looks like an exact replica of the platter of cookies sitting on the table beside us.

Chapter Eight

I'D LIKE TO SAY THAT I handled things with Hepburn-like grace when Aidan pointed out the Christmas cookie charm, but alas, I didn't. I snatched my hand away and basically fled, telling my mom I wasn't feeling well and needed to go home.

It's not a lie.

I *do* feel sick. There's a knot of panic in my chest and I'm shaking all over by the time I get home and shut myself in my bedroom. I've got to get rid of the bracelet. It's seriously starting to freak me out. Two charms that flawlessly match what's going on in my life could possibly be chalked up to coincidence, but three, right in a row? Doubtful. The cookies on the charm are too tiny to tell if their decoration is as sloppy as my real-life efforts, but the shapes are plain as day. Even so, I *might* have been able to convince myself nothing strange is going on, if not for the charm's little silver cookie tray. It's a perfect replica of the platter with my gingerbread men and snowflake cookies on it, all the way down to the decorative holly leaf handles. The tray has been in our family for generations, and now its tiny identical twin is dangling from my wrist.

What is going on?

Deep breaths. Stay calm. There's no such thing as magic.

Right...except I'm wearing a vintage piece of jewelry that says otherwise. I mean, what next? Is there a charm representing of my current panic attack? Because there probably should be.

I can't bring myself to look too closely at the other charms. Not yet. First things first—there's got to be something I can use to unjam the bracelet's catch. After a quick scan of the room, I finally find a stray bobby pin in one of my dresser drawers. With a pang, I realize that I probably last used it to sweep my hair up into a fancy twist for prom with Aidan. But I refuse to think about that now as I bend the bobby pin and ram the tip of it against the tiny knob on the spring ring.

Spoiler alert: it doesn't budge. Beads of sweat break out on my forehead, but no amount of poking and prodding will force open the catch. Fruitcake flops into a down position on the floor and gazes up at me wistfully. I feel like whining myself.

I toss the useless bobby pin aside and take another deep breath. It's time. I can't get the thing off, I have no idea how to track Betty down, and now three of the charms have seemingly come to life. I'm going to have to seriously examine the remaining silver trinkets and get a good look at what might be coming next.

"Okay, charms of Christmas future, show me what you've got," I mutter. Fruitcake cocks his head.

Oh, goody. I'm talking to the bracelet now—because I wasn't delusional enough already.

My hand trembles like crazy, and the charms tinkle against one another, making a deceptively lovely and simple sound. I swallow hard and take an inventory of the remaining charms. There's a silver Christmas tree with a gold star on top, a wrapped Christmas gift, a teddy bear, an ice skate, a snowman with an orange enamel carrot for a nose, a delicate filigree tiara topped with a snowflake and finally...

A ring.

At the sight of that last one, my breath catches in my throat. It looks like a miniature engagement ring and appears to have a tiny diamond chip in the delicate setting. Funny, I don't remember seeing that one when I first noticed the bracelet on Betty's arm during our train ride.

I go over the charms again, one at a time. Honestly, with the exception of the ring, they don't seem especially significant. At first glance, it's simply an innocent collection of winter and Christmas charms. Maybe I really am jumping to conclusions.

There's still no rational explanation for Fruitcake's appearance, though. Or the eerily perfect match of the cookie tray. Or why the house charm is decorated exactly like my childhood home.

But why is the ring there? The mysterious force behind whatever Christmas magic is going on must have missed the memo about my non-proposal.

It's just a bracelet, I remind myself, but I must not be very persuasive because I'm not entirely convinced.

I'm not altogether sure how I feel about the ring charm. It doesn't seem possible that it could be some kind of premonition. I still haven't heard a word from Jeremy. He's probably sipping champagne in a gilded room at the Palais Garnier opera house or something equally posh right now, while here I am...

Trying to make sense of my vague feeling of disappointment over the fact that none of the charms on my wrist appear to have anything to do with Aidan Flynn.

I wake up the following morning on a mission.

Maya called while I was at the firehouse last night, and by the time I finally listened to her voicemail, it was too late to call her back. Totally my fault for getting distracted by the bracelet, which is, of course, still stuck on my wrist. A collection of mangled bobby pins sits on my nightstand in an ineffectual pile. At one point last night, I tiptoed down to the basement in search of my dad's bolt clippers but they were far too bulky for the task at hand.

According to Maya's message, while I was busy yesterday riding around in a fire truck, doting on my mystery dog and baking Christmas cookies, a handful of candidates interviewed for the management position. How can this be happening? Other than a few afternoons off when my parents came up to Manhattan for a visit, this is the *one* time I've actually taken vacation days, and I'm going to get passed over. I just know it.

I ring my boss, but of course Windsor isn't open yet and there's no answer. I leave another message indicating I'm interested in the position, but it's clearly not enough or I'd have heard back, letting me know that I'm at least in the running. I *have* to get back to Manhattan.

Staying in Owl Lake and waiting for the train station to re-open isn't an option, but that's fine. There are plenty of other ways to get from here to Manhattan. Okay, there's actually just one other way—by car. Granted, I don't own a vehicle, because renting a parking space in the city is basically the equivalent of renting an apartment for your Ford Fusion. But I can certainly rent a car overnight. Easy peasy.

I let Fruitcake out, then get dressed in another classic black cashmere turtleneck and simple black slacks as fast as I can while Betty's charm bracelet rattles on my wrist.

Not much longer.

Once I'm back at Windsor, I will definitely be able to get it removed. It will probably take all of two seconds for one of the jewelry repair specialists to open the clasp. So, there—I've officially got two perfectly valid reasons to beat a hasty trail to the city.

Just like the day before, my parents are dressed in their matching plaid bathrobes, sipping cinnamon roll–flavored coffees at the kitchen table when I make my way downstairs. It's starting to feel sort of like the movie *Groundhog Day* around here, but in a good way. From the ongoing Christmas traditions to my mom and dad's quiet morning rituals, there's a rhythm to Owl Lake that sets it apart from the hustle and bustle of my usual life. I've forgotten how comforting the routine of small-town life can be—probably because I've always been so anxious to spread my wings and experience something bigger and better.

"Sweetheart, are you sure you want to try to drive?

The roads are still pretty icy," Mom says when I announce my plans to rent a car and drive into the city for the day.

"The forecast calls for more snow," Dad adds.

I glance out the big picture window facing the lake. There's not a snowflake in sight. A pale lavender mist covers the icy surface of the water, and as I'm taking in the breathless serenity of an Adirondack sunrise, a snowy white owl swoops from the branches of a blue spruce tree and glides through the air in a smooth, graceful arc.

It's my first real owl sighting since being back in town, so I watch until the big white bird disappears into the mist. Snowy owls like to fly close to the ground—just a little nugget of owl lore my grandmother taught me when I was little. She also told me that snowy owls were supposed to symbolize big dreams and new beginnings. They've always been my favorite.

"The weather seems fine," I say. Seeing the owl feels like a sign—that promotion is mine. I just have to grab hold of it. "I'll be back as soon as I can. I promise."

My dad smirks. "The last time you said that, Aidan ended up driving you home in the ladder truck."

Like I need the reminder.

I roll my eyes. "That won't be happening again, I assure you."

"If you say so," he says, smirking far too much for my liking.

Have my parents forgotten that I lead a perfectly independent life in the biggest city in the country? I don't need Aidan—or anyone else, for that matter—to rescue me. Certainly not on a daily basis.

Fruitcake shuffles toward the kitchen table, turns

three circles and plops down with his chin on my dad's foot. Honestly, whose side is he on?

The rental car place is right on Main Street, close enough to walk. When I get there, it seems as if I'm the only person in Owl Lake interested in renting a car. I decide this is a good thing. Surely that means that there are plenty of cars available and my magic bracelet hasn't somehow orchestrated events to keep me stuck here in Owl Lake.

I shake my head. It's a *bracelet*, not a magic wand.

"Here you go," the clerk says, handing me a set of keys. "We don't have any utility vehicles left, but the car has all-wheel drive, so you should be good to go. Just be careful out there. We're expecting a lot snow today."

I peel off my mitten and take the keys. "Thanks so much."

Snowflakes swirl lightly against the windshield as I crank the engine. By the time I travel the length of Main Street and turn onto the highway, the snow is beating against the windows in thick white clumps.

Admittedly, the roads are a little treacherous in this kind of weather. Conditions are always more severe upstate in the mountains, though. Once I get to Albany, the halfway point, I'll be home free.

I lean closer to the windshield, squint hard at the horizon and try to lift my spirits by visualizing myself as a manager at Windsor Fine Jewelry. The windshield wipers are working overtime as I approach the town line. *Swish swish swish.* Still, it's starting to feel like I'm heading straight into a wall of white. The car is crawling forward at barely ten miles per hour. At this rate, I can forget about arriving in time to plead for the promotion—I'll get back to Windsor when it's time for me to retire.

I can do this...I *need* to do this.

The *Now Leaving Owl Lake, Owl Capital of the Adirondacks* sign is just ahead, barely visible through the swirl of snow. Somehow, I feel if I can only get past it, everything will be fine. My foot presses just a little bit harder on the gas, and the next thing I know, the car is drifting sideways, sliding off the road.

No!

Following my dad's rulebook for what to do when you hit an icy patch on the road, I take my foot off the accelerator and allow the car to slow. Again, I tell myself that everything is *fine*, and it totally is...

Until the car drifts slowly into a snowbank with a muffled thud.

Snow is piled up on the side of the road in a mound nearly as tall as my rented vehicle, and within an instant, I'm a part of it. The windshield is packed with snow, and I can't see a thing. But somehow, I've yet to actually make it past the Owl Lake's town limits.

Don't panic. At the moment, getting back to Windsor seems less important than getting out of this car, so I push the door open to make sure I'm not about to be buried alive.

It opens just fine. Only the front part of the car is stuck. But when I get back inside and crank the engine again, the wheels spin and spin against the snowy ground without actually going anywhere.

I'm officially stranded.

I reach for my cell phone, but there's not even a hint of bars in the upper left-hand corner. No service whatsoever. Maybe it's the weather, but somehow I doubt it. Was I really just waxing poetic about small-town life earlier? This would never happen in Manhattan.

My eyes drift shut and I rest my forehead against the steering wheel. What am I going to do? The wind outside sounds like an entire chorus of owls, eerily beautiful. I'm too far from Main Street to try to walk home, especially in the snow. And I can't exactly stay here until the salt trucks come out to clear the roads.

But just as the first flutter of panic begins to stir deep in my belly, I hear a familiar noise in the distance, coming closer and closer.

And closer.

I groan, torn between dread and relief, because it's the unmistakable wail of a fire engine.

I squeeze my eyes closed tight.

Not him, please.

Anybody but him.

Okay, yes—I've been feeling a bit fluttery lately in Aidan's presence. There, I've admitted it. But butterflies aside, I really don't want him to be behind the wheel of the red truck making its way toward me, lights flashing through a dizzying twirl of snowflakes.

For starters, there's the whole damsel in distress thing. I don't want to look like the big city girl who doesn't know how to take care of herself once she's away from concrete and Starbucks. And I *really* don't want to seem like I need a Prince Charming on a shining red firetruck to come save me.

Mostly, I don't want to see the disapproving look on Aidan's face when he sees that I'm trying to escape Owl Lake again when I'm supposed to be enjoying the holidays with my family. Last time, his scowl spoke a thousand words, and I'm really not in the mood to hear any of them again.

Never mind that any and all of the accusations he could choose to throw at me are technically true—I am out of practice at driving in the snow, I very much need saving at the moment and I'm indeed mid-flight back to Manhattan. It would just be really great if Aidan didn't have a front-row seat to my most recent humiliation, especially after he'd already gallantly saved me from public embarrassment the previous day by force-feeding himself my sad attempt at homemade gingerbread men.

Making those cookies had been fun, though. My mom was right. The end result didn't matter as much as spending time with her in the kitchen and seeing how happy we made the firefighters. Life is messy, so it only makes sense that baking gets messy too. And who am I kidding? Aidan choking down those terrible cookies meant far more to me than if they'd been perfect and delicious. Jeremy would have never done such a thing. Not many men would, I suppose.

Three sharp knocks on my driver's side window force my eyes open, and sure enough, the chiseled face I see peering down at me belongs to Aidan Flynn. Snow tips his eyelashes, and even his bulky firefighter helmet can't hide the square set of his jaw and his perfectly defined cheekbones. Still, I'm both mortified and disappointed to see him. The sudden pounding of my heart is just a result of my recent near-death experience. Obviously.

I feel a little breathless, but I know I must be taking in oxygen because the window goes foggy as I sit there, staring at him. When I wipe it clean with my mitten, I have a very clear view of Aidan's judgmental frown. Honestly, is he the *only* firefighter in the OLFD? Where's Uncle Hugh when I really need him?

I sigh, and since I've made no move to open the car door, Aidan does it for me.

"Going somewhere?" He arches a brow.

"Apparently not." I scramble out of the car so I can stand eye-to-eye with him, but it's no use. He towers over me. Plus all his firefighter gear makes him seem huge—quite literally larger than life.

"Are you okay?" He looks me up and down, and despite the fact that I have to blink against the snow, my face goes hot. "You're not hurt, are you?"

Nope. Just my pride.

I lift my chin. "I'm fine."

"Good," he says flatly. Why do I get the feeling he'd be far happier if I'd twisted an ankle or something, preventing me from limping out of town until after Christmas? "Because getting back to the city isn't worth risking your life in a snowstorm."

"For your information, I wasn't 'risking my life.'" I attempt to make sarcastic little air quotes, but since I'm wearing mittens, the gesture is impossible to pull off with any sort of flair. I look like I'm giving him a cutesy, double-fisted wave.

He accidentally smiles before rearranging his features back into frown. "You slid right off of the road."

"Just a little bit," I counter.

His ice-blue gaze flits to the front end of my rental car, currently buried beneath a pile of white, and then back at me. "Would it kill you to stay put for a few days? Couldn't you see how happy your mom was last night at the station? Your Uncle Hugh, too. Everyone in town is ecstatic that you're back."

Everyone?

I don't dare ask, mainly because I'm afraid of what his answer might be.

"I wasn't going back to Manhattan for good." I wish I didn't have to keep saying this, but even more so, I wished everyone believed me when I did. I'm not quite sure they do, probably because I haven't been home for Christmas in years. I haven't spent much time in Owl Lake at all since I moved away.

My gaze drops to the snowy ground. Suddenly, I can't seem to look Aidan in the eye anymore. I blink against the wind and my teeth start to chatter.

Aidan clears his throat. "Once the snow lets up, I can come back and tow your car out of there. Meanwhile, will you let me take you home?"

He's asking my permission, like a gentleman. He could have simply ordered me to get in the firetruck since this is technically a rescue mission, and as a bona fide hero, he's probably honor-bound not to leave me stranded here in the snow. But he didn't, because Aidan isn't like that.

"Yes, please," I say. Maybe it's not such a bad thing that he's the one who turned up to help me. "But I suppose this means I owe you more cookies."

His laughter warms the chill out of my bones. "Not necessary. We're good, Ash."

I hope we are, I think. I truly do.

The inside of the firetruck is toasty warm, and I sink into the leather passenger seat while Aidan closes me in and stomps through the snow toward the driver's side. We're in the OLFD small rescue vehicle this time, not the ladder truck. It's more like a glorified SUV than an actual fire engine, which explains why Aidan is operating it without a crew.

"How did you know I'd gotten stuck out here?" I ask once he's sliding in place behind the steering wheel.

He removes his helmet and sets it on the console between us. "A trucker saw you drift into the snow-bank and called 911."

"I'm surprised you're still on duty. Isn't it usually twenty-four hours on, forty-eight hours off?" A fire chief's daughter knows these things.

Aidan shrugs. "One of the guys is down with the flu, so I volunteered for some overtime."

"Ah." I nod as he steers the truck off of the snowy shoulder and onto the road, deftly avoiding the dark icy patch that caused me to go into a slide.

On the way back, the ride is brief. Within minutes, we're turning onto Main Street. The Palace Theatre's marquee glitters gold in the midst of the storm. Classic movie night is only four days away, and a very real part of me is tempted to ask Aidan if he might want to go. Just for old times' sake, of course.

But the other part of me—the rational, sensible part—knows this would be a mistake. I still have every intention of getting back to Manhattan after this holiday visit is over. I'm scheduled to be back at work two days after Christmas. Since that means I only have a limited amount of time to spend with my parents, I definitely don't need to be filling up my schedule with social outings, no matter how badly I find that I want to. Besides, he could have a girlfriend for all I know. Classic movie night could be *their* thing now. The thought makes my heart clench, even though I know I have no right whatsoever to be jealous.

Still, when we drive past the theater, I sneak a glance at Aidan. His gaze fixes with mine, and his lips curve into a tiny smile of remembrance. Memories flash through my mind like a montage from a rom-com—the two of us sharing a bucket of popcorn in the dark, Aidan draping his high school letter jacket over my shoulders as shadows move across the screen, the look in his soulful blue eyes when I'd said I thought Audrey Hepburn was the most beautiful woman in the world.

It's you, Ash, he'd whispered. *It will always be you.*

I swallow hard as Aidan's smile fades and he turns his attention back to the road.

"You left the station awfully suddenly last night," he says. Once again, a telltale knot of tension is visible in his jaw.

"Oh." A weight settles in the pit of my stomach as I realize what he's thinking.

We'd had a moment when our hands collided. The briefest, most innocent of touches had sparked something to life inside of me, like a thousand shimmering Christmas lights. Aidan had felt it too.

And within seconds, I'd fled.

It was the bracelet's fault, I start to say, but how absurd would that sound?

I glance down at the collection of silver charms lying against my black cashmere sleeve and vow once again to somehow get the clasp open—today, if at all possible. The sooner, the better.

"I wasn't feeling well," I say, because I can't exactly change my story now.

But he knows it's nothing but an excuse—I can see the sadness in his expression, and it makes me want to rip the bracelet off my arm and hurl it out the window.

A few awkward seconds pass until the firetruck slows to a stop in front of my house.

"Here you go," Aidan says, smiling in a way that doesn't quite reach his eyes. "Home sweet home."

There are so many things I want to say, but before I can even utter a heartfelt thank you, his radio crackles and dispatch comes through, sending Aidan out on another call.

"Be safe," I say as I step out into the cold, but he's already driving away.

I watch the firetruck until it's nothing but a hint of red on the horizon. When I finally turn to walk up the pathway to the lake house, I notice Fruitcake waiting for me by the door, and this time, it doesn't surprise me in the slightest. His fur is warm and dry, despite the swirling snow, which doesn't make any sense whatsoever, but I know better than to question it.

Christmas is a time of magic, and little by little, I'm starting to believe.

Chapter Nine

"How's Aidan?" my dad asks when I walk inside with Fruitcake trotting at my heels.

My parents are sitting at the kitchen table, putting together a 1,000-piece jigsaw puzzle of a cozy Christmas scene. Mugs of hot cocoa sit in front of them, topped with whipped cream and curls of dark chocolate ribbon. Their little tableau is all kinds of adorable, so I decide to overlook the I-told-you-so lurking beneath Dad's question.

"He's fine," I say. "I drove into a snowbank and he gave me a ride home, but why do I get the feeling you two already know all about it?"

My mom pops a puzzle piece into place and shrugs one slender shoulder. "Hugh called to let us know."

Of course he did.

"Quick question—did you guys put Fruitcake outside before I got back?" I'm sure they didn't, and Fruitcake somehow appeared on the porch all on his own out of thin air, sort of like Clarence in *It's a Wonderful*

Life. But I should probably make sure, even though the fact that all of this is beginning to seem normal is probably cause for concern.

"Of course not. He likes to stay snug and warm in your room when you're gone," my dad says. "Good dog you've got there, honey."

I bend to wrap my arms around Fruitcake's furry neck and breathe in the scent of winter and candy canes.

"Sweet boy," I whisper, and his tail thumps against the hardwood floor.

I spend the rest of the morning helping Mom and Dad with their puzzle until the snow finally stops coming down and the world beyond the picture window is a glittering winter wonderland. The afternoon sky is robin's egg blue—the peaceful, perfect calm after a storm.

"I think I'll take Fruitcake for a walk." I reach for my red coat. The charm pendant I pinned onto the lapel a few nights ago is still there, even though that evening is starting to feel like it took place a lifetime ago.

"Don't forget about the Christmas tree lighting tonight," my mom says.

"That's tonight?" I had indeed forgotten all about the annual Owl Lake tree lighting ceremony, plus I'd had no idea it was this evening.

"It sure is. We should probably leave around six so we can get a good spot."

"We'll be back in plenty of time. I promise." Maybe getting stuck in that snowbank wasn't so terrible. I wouldn't want to miss my first Owl Lake Christmas tree lighting in years. "Come on, Fruitcake."

The dog scrambles to his feet and romps toward me, while my dad shoots me an amused glance.

I narrow my eyes at him. "Don't say it, Dad."

I swear, if he tells me to say hi to Aidan again, he's going straight on the naughty list. Surely I can manage to walk my dog without managing to be escorted home in a fire truck again.

He mimes zipping his lips closed and locking them with a key, just like Maya always does. It never works.

"Cute." I roll my eyes.

Fruitcake trots politely at the end of his leash as we head toward Main Street. Snow crunches beneath our feet and Fruitcake's breath comes out in tiny puffs of vapor, pink tongue lolling out of the side of his mouth. Clearly, he's enjoying himself, and I'm glad, even though the purpose of this walk is actually twofold.

Yes, my mystery dog probably needs some exercise. But this morning, I'm pretty sure I spied a new—or at least, new to me—jewelry store tucked into one of the quaint shopping centers along the lake. If they're open, they might be my best shot at getting the bracelet off my arm. Surely they can help.

"Hi, Ashley!" Our neighbor, Jerry, is out front, shoveling snow when we walk past. He stops to lean against his shovel and grin at Fruitcake. "My, that's a handsome dog."

"Thanks." Fruitcake wiggles his entire back end with excitement, so we pause and let Jerry scratch him behind the ears. "He doesn't, um, look familiar or anything, does he?"

"No, the first I saw of him was when you came back from the big city," Jerry says. Why am I not surprised? "Are you back to stay?"

"I'm not." I shake my head. "Just visiting for the holidays."

"It's good to see you, all the same. I'm sure your parents are happy you've come home. We're having our annual New Year's Eve Scrabble tournament. Your parents are already invited, of course, and we'd love to have you join them if you're still in town."

"Oh. Wow." The invitation catches me by surprise. I'm oddly touched to be invited to Jerry and Arminda's big Scrabble party. "I'll probably be back in Manhattan by then, but thank you."

"You're always welcome if you change your mind." Jerry bends down to give Fruitcake a parting pat. "You can bring this guy, too."

"Look at you," I say to Fruitcake as we resume our walk. "Mr. Popularity."

As if to prove my point, we're stopped almost every block by old hometown friends and acquaintances who want to pet the pretty dog. Usually they don't even realize I'm the one on the other end of the leash until Fruitcake has already flopped down on the sidewalk for belly rubs. We run into my third-grade teacher, who wants to hear all about my life in Manhattan while Fruitcake offers his snow-covered paw for a shake. When we pass the shop on the corner that sells hand-carved rustic furniture and other Adirondack-inspired designs, the owner, Mr. Garcia, comes outside to offer Fruitcake a biscuit. While he chomps it down, Mr. Garcia reminds me of the time a black bear wandered out of the nearby forest and took a stroll down Main Street when I was just a little girl. He still has a picture of the bear pausing in front of his shop on the wall by the entryway.

The greetings repeat themselves three or four more times, and before I realize it, I've reconnected with people who'd been part of my daily life when I was growing up—people I haven't thought about in a long, long time. It's nice. Fruitcake is a total friend-magnet, and I'm starting to actually feel like I belong in Owl Lake again, even though I've spent half of my time here trying to get back to the city.

"Merry Christmas, Ashley," the mailman calls from across the street.

"Merry Christmas!" I wave a mittened hand and Fruitcake lets out a friendly woof.

The jewelry store stands just a few feet away, next to Mountain Candy. As usual, the candy store somehow envelopes the entire block in its rich cocoa aroma. I pause on the cobblestone walkway to take a deep, chocolate-scented breath and study the jewelry shop's exterior.

A swinging sign hangs from the rafters with a swirl of hand-painted letters that spell out the name *Enchanting Jewels*. I've never seen the store before, so it must have opened sometime in the past eight years or so. The windows are filled a mixture of new and vintage pieces—modern classic solitaires surrounded by halos of pavé diamonds and other Art Deco settings that look like something out of *The Great Gatsby*. I feel myself smile. There's no doubt that I'm going to love this place. I can already tell.

A bell chimes as I push the door open, and just as I'm about to ask if it's okay to bring Fruitcake inside, my gaze fixes on the woman standing behind the display case.

I gasp. "Susan?"

She looks up, and her eyes go wide. "Ashley! Aidan told me you were back, and I almost didn't believe it."

Susan Flynn is Aidan's sister and one of my best friends from high school. Relief floods through me at the sight of her, because even though my time in Owl Lake thus far has been nice—kind of great, actually—I miss Maya like crazy. Strange things have been happening left and right, and...well, I could really use a girlfriend right about now.

Susan runs around the display case to hug me, and she wraps her arms around me so tightly that before I know it, I'm blinking back tears.

"It's *so* good to see you," she whispers, and there's an unmistakable catch in her voice.

"You too." I hug her back with all my might.

Fruitcake lets out a little whine, presumably picking up on my messy emotional state. As much as it pains me to admit it, Susan and I haven't exactly kept in touch. There have been countless times I've wanted to pick up the phone and call her, but after breaking her brother's heart, I couldn't bring myself to do it. She must have felt the same way, since I haven't heard from her, either. Admittedly, I've been Facebook stalking her for a while, so I know she's married now and has two adorable daughters—twins. But she's probably the last person I'd have expected to find at the jewelry shop which is starting to feel like my only hope for solving the charm bracelet mystery.

"Look at you." She pulls back, hands still on my shoulders as she sweeps me up and down with her gaze. "Classic black turtleneck, winged eyeliner and red lipstick..."

I cringe, waiting for the inevitable "big city princess"

comment that's sure to follow, but instead what she says renders me speechless.

"...Aidan was right. You look just like Audrey Hepburn." She reaches to tuck a stray lock of hair behind my ear, and it feels like we're back in tenth grade again.

I blink at her, struggling to absorb what she's just told me. "He did *not* say that."

Impossible. It's the single best thing Aidan could say about the way I look after all this time, and he knows it. Granted, he didn't say it to my face, but even the idea that he said it at all makes me go all aflutter. Butterflies the size of flying reindeer are swarming around my insides.

"He absolutely *did* say that." Susan lifts a knowing brow. "He was right, by the way. You look beautiful. City life certainly agrees with you."

I have the sudden urge to change the subject. For once, I don't want to talk about Manhattan. "You look great, too. I can't believe you're a mom!"

We spend the next half hour getting caught up. Susan assures me Fruitcake is more than welcome, and he curls up in a contented ball behind the sales counter as if he belongs there while we sip hot chocolate and talk so much that my throat gets hoarse. Customers come and go, and while Susan waits on them, she lets me scroll through the camera roll on her phone so I can see all the latest pictures of her girls. The most recent ones are from their visit to Santa, and they look precious in matching red dresses with huge tartan plaid bows in their hair. I've never seen such an adorable pair of five-year-olds in my life.

Aidan is in a good number of the pictures too,

which makes sense, obviously. Still, I'm not quite pre-pared for the way I go breathless when his face looks back at me from the screen. Susan's husband, Josh, is a fireman too, so there are several photos of the two of them together—standing in front of the church steps holding firemen's boots overflowing with dollar bills during the Muscular Dystrophy Association's Fill the Boot Drive, side-by-side at the grill for the fire depart-ment's summer barbecue, washing the ladder truck with big, soapy sponges. Josh must have been off-duty last night when my mom and I visited the firehouse. He shows up in dozens of casual family photos with Susan and the twins, but I can't help noticing there's not a single shot of Aidan out of uniform.

That, plus the fact that Aidan was working an over-time shift when he rescued me from the snowbank this morning, leads me to believe he must work a lot. All the time, from the look of things.

"Does your brother own any clothes without the OLFD logo on them?" I ask when I hand the phone back to Susan.

She shakes her head. "You noticed, huh?"

"It's kind of hard not to."

"He loves his job." Susan smiles, but there's a quiet tension to the set of her mouth that makes me wonder if there's more to the story.

I know I shouldn't press, but I can't help it. "That must not leave much time for a personal life."

Susan gives me an amused once over. "Are you asking if Aidan is seeing anyone?"

"Gosh, no." I wave a dismissive hand, and the charms on my bracelet clink together. "Well, maybe."

She stares at me until a flush of heat crawls up my

neck and settles in my cheeks. Super, my face is probably as red as a potted poinsettia.

"Fine." I sigh. "Yes, that's exactly what I'm asking."

"I knew it. You went all starry-eyed as soon as I mentioned his name." She laughs. And for the record, I did *not* go all starry-eyed. Much. "To answer your question—no, there's no one."

"No one at all?" Rudolph and company take flight in my tummy again, and I take a giant gulp of hot chocolate to try and quiet them down.

It doesn't work.

"Nope." Susan shrugs. "He dated other girls for a year or two after you first moved away, but never anyone long-term. For the past five years or so, he hasn't dated anyone at all. Since he joined the fire department, it's become his whole life. Sometimes I think he'd rather run into a burning building than risk his heart again."

I lower my gaze to the marshmallows melting in my cup. As much as I'd sort of hoped Aidan was still single, this news makes my heart wrench.

"What about you?" Susan asks, voice going soft. "Anyone special?"

"No, not anymore." I wait for the pang that hits me whenever I think about Jeremy—and Paris and the proposal that never happened—but weirdly enough, it doesn't come. I feel...fine, really. Interesting. "I mean, there was, but not anymore."

Susan nods, then takes a sip of hot chocolate, and before I can stop myself, I'm telling her everything that's happened in the past week—from trying on Audrey's necklace and the subsequent breakup with Jeremy to meeting Betty on the train, the strange appearance of Fruitcake and all the charms that seem to be coming to life. It all just comes spilling out of me. It feels so good to finally tell someone what's been going on and to get all the craziness out in the open that I could weep with relief.

Susan's face has gone as white as Owl Lake's snow-covered landscape by the time I finish. Her eyes—the same beautiful blue as Aidan's—flit toward the charms splayed out innocently on the wrist of my sweater. "Is that it? That's the magical bracelet?"

"Yes. I can't get it off. The catch won't open, no matter how hard I try." The charms sparkle beneath the ultra-bright lights of the jewelry shop.

The store is, for lack of a better word, charming. I've had a chance to poke around, and I practically swooned over the case containing vintage rings, brace-lets and old-fashioned brooches. There are even a few charm bracelets that look like they're from the 1950s, but I'm not going there. I never thought I'd say this, but I have enough charms in my life as it is.

"Actually, that's why I came in here in the first place. I was hoping someone could help me get this thing off, once and for all. I just didn't expect it to be you." Happiness, mixed with a dash of hope, fills me from within. "But I'm really glad it is."

Susan beams. "So am I." But then her gaze drops once again to the bracelet. "Are you sure removing the bracelet is really what you want, though?"

Seriously? Of course it's what I want.

I nod. "I have an entire collection of ruined bobby pins to prove it."

She holds up a hand. "Hear me out for a minute. *If* the bracelet is somehow magical and *if* the charms are coming to life, maybe it's all happening for a reason. What did Betty's note say, again?"

I know exactly what the note says. I've read it so many times that the words are probably permanently engraved in my brain. "It said, 'Please wear this and have the Christmas of your dreams.'"

Susan picks up her mug to take another sip of hot chocolate and then frowns when she realizes it's empty. By now, we've been talking for over an hour.

More than anything, I'm simply glad she seems to believe me. After years of silence in our once-strong friendship, I've just shown up out of the blue and told her that a strange woman on a train gave me a magical bracelet. It's a wonder she's even taking me seriously. Not many people would. I'm hyperaware of the fact that I couldn't even manage to convince my own parents that Fruitcake isn't my dog. Although, let's face it, he's definitely starting to feel like mine.

"I have to say, that doesn't sound so bad. Who wouldn't want to have the Christmas of their dreams? Maybe you should stop fighting it and see what happens," Susan says.

"But..." *But this isn't the way my Christmas was supposed to go. It's* definitely *not the Christmas of my dreams.* I stop short of saying it, because I'm not altogether sure what the Christmas of my dreams looks like anymore. "...this is just crazy. I can't keep living in a fantasy world."

"Think about it, though. All those movies where characters switch places or live a different version of their lives all have some kind of lesson the main character needs to learn. Maybe that's what's happening to you." She bounces a little on her toes, and I can't help but remember that while I was watching *Roman*

Holiday on constant repeat back in high school, Susan had developed an obsession with *Big* starring Tom Hanks.

I breathe a silent sigh of relief that my current problems are limited to magic charms. It seems like a far easier conundrum than what poor Tom went through in that movie. "But what sort of lesson am I supposed to be learning?"

"I don't know. Is there anything the charms have taught you so far?"

I bite my lip and consider the charms that have come to life. If there's a lesson to be learned from the house charm, it's that I've waited far too long to come home for Christmas. I won't be making that mistake again.

I glance down at Fruitcake as I contemplate the dog charm. He's sleeping soundly, paws twitching as if he's dreaming about romping through the forest, chasing snowshoe hares. I've wanted a dog my whole life, but I never realized what actually having one would be like. Everywhere we go, people respond to him—my parents, Uncle Hugh, all the people we chatted with on our walk. Aidan. Fruitcake is helping me reconnect with all the people I've lost touch with since I moved away. I'm not sure I realized that until this very moment.

As for the Christmas cookies, my mom's story about baking for the firefighters back when she and my dad were engaged sums things up perfectly. Sometimes the act of doing something is more precious than the final result. And now that I'm really thinking about it, those cookies seemed to have reconnected Aidan and me in the tiniest way.

Or they had until I'd fled.

I shake my head. It's too much. Can't I just have a

normal holiday? I don't want to spend the rest of my Christmas vacation terrified of what might happen next. I can't even think about what the engagement ring charm might mean. The bare idea of it thrills and terrifies me at the same time.

I thrust my wrist towards Susan. "Please take it off. *Please.*"

"Okay, fine. If you insist." She reaches into a drawer beside the cash register and pulls out a jewelers' kit wound in a black velvet roll.

The kit contains all the basic tools—pliers in assorted sizes, needle-nose tweezers, ring clamps, a bench knife, a mallet—the whole shebang. Susan starts with the smallest pair of pliers, and I hold my breath as they clamp down over the bracelet's catch. My heart pounds in my chest as Susan's words come back to me.

Are you sure removing the bracelet is really what you want?

I swallow hard. A tiny flicker of doubt passes through me, but I push it down and squeeze my eyes shut tight, waiting for the snapping sound as the weight of the charms fall away and I'm finally free. And then...

Nothing.

The pliers are useless against the silver links, as is the next tool Susan tries and the next one after that. One by one, she tries them all and nothing makes a dent in the bracelet. All that effort, and not even a scratch.

It's then that I finally accept my fate—nothing short of magic is getting this bracelet off of my wrist.

Chapter Ten

MOM GREETS ME WITH A shiny gift bag over-flowing with glittery tissue paper when Fruitcake and I make it home from En-chanting Jewels. My head is still spinning from my conversation with Susan. For the entire walk back to the lake house, I've been trying to figure out the reason I'm stuck with the Christmas charms bracelet.

I mean, I do love charms and vintage jewelry. But why me? *Why?* I'm pretty sure George Bailey felt the same way at some point.

I do my best to forget about the charms for the time being, though, because my mom is clearly excited about whatever is in the bag.

"Go ahead," she says. "Open it."

"Now?" I eye her dubiously. Our family never opens Christmas gifts before Christmas Eve.

She nods. "Yes, now."

I wade through what seems like a thousand layers of tissue until I finally reach something soft at the bottom of the bag. It's a sweater, and when I unfold it, I see that it's a slightly smaller version of the one my mom is wearing—an "ugly" Christmas sweater, complete with every form of rhinestone and holiday bauble imaginable. There are even swags of sparkly green garland adorning the front of it.

It's...a lot. The entire garment shines as bright as a disco ball.

"I noticed you forgot to bring the other Christmas sweater I sent you," my mother says.

I didn't forget. My bags were packed for Paris, and it just didn't seem like the sort of thing to wear on the Champs-Élysées.

"I thought it would be fun to wear tonight for the Christmas tree lighting," Mom adds, and there's so much joy in her expression that there's no way I can refuse.

To top it off, my dad strolls in at that exact moment, and guess what he's wearing. (Other than an expression that's a mixture of amusement and mortification.) Yep, you guessed it.

"So this is really happening?" he says.

"It looks that way, Dad," I say, unbuttoning my coat so I can go change out of my basic black cashmere and into the heavily adorned sweater. When I pick it up, it jingles even louder than my charm bracelet.

This is no magical sweater, though, because everyone seems to hear it. Fruitcake's ears swivel back and forth, prompting my mom to dart over to the Christmas tree and pluck another gift from beneath it.

"You should probably go ahead and open this one, too," she says, grinning from ear to ear.

"Oh, no." Dad laughs, and his sweater goes into jingle overdrive. "Not the dog, too."

My dad has always been a good sport about this sort of thing, pretty much wearing whatever my mom brings home and hangs in his closet. And crazy holiday sweaters are beloved in Owl Lake probably more than anyplace else on earth. But again, this is one *decorative* piece of clothing.

"I didn't want him to feel left out," my mother says as I pull a dog sweater out of the gift bag.

Yep, we're the dorky family that's about to attend one of the biggest holiday events our town has to offer dressed in matching hideous sweaters. Strangely enough, I wouldn't have it any other way.

"Thanks, Mom." I hug her as fiercely as I possibly can, and the affection sparkling in her eyes tells me I'm forgiven for leaving the other sweater back in my drawer.

A half hour or so later, we're all dressed in our matching sweaters—Fruitcake included, obviously—as we head toward Main Street. The sidewalks are bustling with other Owl Lake residents, all moving in the same direction.

For as long as I can remember, the town Christmas tree has been set up directly in front of the Owl Lake Inn, a sweeping chalet-style boutique hotel situated at the end of Main Street, at the top of a gently sloping hill overlooking the entire village. This year is no exception, and with the recent snowfall, the inn looks Christmas-card perfect with icicles dripping from the forest-green shutters and gabled roof. Swags of evergreen intertwined with twinkle lights stretch from one end of the alpine-white building to the other. A gazebo sits lakeside, and for this major Owl Lake occasion, it's housing an old-fashioned cart selling traditional roasted chestnuts and mulled cranberry-apple cider.

The tree is a noble fir with blue-green branches that look almost silver in the twilight sky. It stretches so tall that it towers over the inn. As I inhale its deep, Christmassy scent and tip my head back to take it all in, its beauty takes my breath away.

It's hard not to compare the tree and the surrounding scene to the Rockefeller Center Christmas tree lighting back in Manhattan, which Maya and I have attended every year that I've lived in the city. But the crowds are always so thick that we barely manage to catch a glimpse of the tree at all, much less the moment when the lights flicker on for the first time. Being able to be so close to such a majestic tree is nice, and when I look around, I realize I'm surrounded almost entirely by people I've known my entire life instead of a mob of strangers. I've almost forgotten what it feels like not to be just another anonymous face in the crowd.

Of course I can't take a step without having someone compliment Fruitcake's silly sweater. The dog clearly loves the attention, strutting at the end of his candy cane–striped dog leash with his head held high. Two identical little girls in winter-white parkas with fur trim run to greet him. They're so bundled up that it's not until their parents almost catch up to them that I realize these cute children are Susan's daughters.

Aidan's nieces, I think as I search the space around Susan and her husband. He's not with them, though. Strange. I really thought he'd be here.

Although who am I kidding? The sudden clench in

my stomach feels more like disappointment than surprise.

"We meet again!" Susan says, throwing her arms around me. "I was hoping we'd run into you here."

"I wouldn't miss it," I say.

Susan says hello to my parents and then introduces me to Josh and her girls, Olivia and Sophie.

"So this is the famous Ashley James," Josh says, eyes twinkling. "I've heard a lot about you lately."

"Is that so?" I ask, and my gaze flits to Susan.

She gives me a tiny, nearly imperceptible shake of her head to assure me that she's kept my possibly-magical charm bracelet a secret. Thank goodness. My return to Owl Lake has been eventful enough so far without the entire town knowing I believe that I might have had a run-in with the actual Mrs. Santa Claus.

Is that what I believe?

My breath goes shallow. I'm not sure what to think about the bracelet anymore. I just know I'm stuck with it for the time being.

"Your dog is pretty," Olivia says, rubbing one of Fruitcake's silky ears between two delicate fingertips.

Sophie nods. "I like his sweater."

"I'll let you in on a little secret," I tell the girls in a mock whisper, and then I flash open my red coat to reveal my matching ugly sweater.

My parents do the same, and the girls collapse into a pile of giggles. They're precious—identical from the tiny furrow in their foreheads when they laugh all the way to the perfect turnout of their feet. I remember the pictures on Susan's phone of Olivia and Sophia dressed in fluffy pink tutus and soft ballet slippers at their recent ballet recital. And suddenly, I'm not thinking about Aidan anymore. Instead, I'm thinking about Jeremy and the things he'd said about marriage and family.

Marriage isn't for people like us.

Had he really thought I'd never want what Susan, Josh, Sophie and Olivia have? Sure, I have goals and aspirations for my career, but marriage and a family are also a part of my dreams. A big part, I realize, as Fruitcake happily leans into the little girls' pats and my throat goes thick.

When I look up, I find Dad watching me with a sad smile. He clears his throat, pulls a few dollar bills out of his pocket and presses them into Sophie and Olivia's mittened hands.

"It looks like you two could use some spiced cider," he says with a wink.

"Thank you!" they cry in unison, gazing up at Susan for permission to skip over to the gazebo.

My parents exchange a meaningful glance, and my mom volunteers to accompany Susan, Josh and the girls on their quest for warm treats.

"We'll be right back." She gives me a wink.

And then it's just Dad and me, standing beneath the shelter of the noble fir's stately branches. I take a deep inhale. The air smells like evergreen, roasted chestnuts and fresh sparkling snow—like Christmas in the Adirondacks. It's the scent of my childhood, and I suddenly wish I could bottle it and take it back to the city with me, so I never lose my home again.

"You've made your mother's Christmas," my dad says quietly. I had a feeling he orchestrated the group exit so we could have a moment alone together, and it seems as if I was correct. "Mine too, obviously. But thank you for going along with it all—the cookies, the sweater. It means the world to her."

"It means the world to me, too," I say. He has no reason to believe me since I've been so bad about visiting, especially during the holidays, but I hope he knows how much they mean to me. I hope with my whole heart.

"I'm sorry about what happened with Jeremy, honey. I want you to know that." My father zips his puffer coat up to his chin and tucks his hands into his pockets. It's starting to snow again, and his broad shoulders are covered in a fine layer of frost. "We're happy to have you home, but we know it's not what you'd planned. Owl Lake can't exactly compete with Paris."

I shake my head. "It doesn't have to compete. Christmas in Owl Lake is special, all on its own."

All around us, people warm their hands on hot cups of cider and cheer as a fire engine pulls slowly up to the inn. I recognize it at once as Aidan's ladder truck, and it's rimmed in flashing multi-colored Christmas lights. Illuminated snowflakes decorate the front bumper, and a pair of firefighters are leaning out of the truck's back windows, tossing candy canes into the crowd.

I glance at my dad and grin. He's behind the Owl Lake Fire Department's participation in the Christmas tree lighting. About a decade ago, the town tree was so tall that no one had a ladder high enough to reach its upper branches and place the star on top. As fire chief, my dad's solution was to extend the ladder on the department's biggest engine and have one of the firefighters climb to the end and secure the star in place. As we were walking over, Mom told me that it's now a town tradition.

Suddenly, the fact that Aidan didn't accompany his family to the tree lighting ceremony makes more sense. I suppose I should have known he'd be the one doing the honors this year.

"I know you weren't fond of Jeremy," I say. If Dad and I are having a heart-to-heart, we may as well put all of the cards on the table. Even the messy ones. "I'm sorry I didn't pay more attention to your opinion. As it turns out, you were right about him."

"Oh, sweetheart, don't be sorry. All I want is for you to be happy. That's the most important thing of all to me and your mom."

He wraps a warm arm around my shoulders as Mom, Susan, Josh and the girls return from the gazebo just in the nick of time. The ladder on the fire truck is fully extended, and a fireman in a Santa hat is climbing up its rungs.

"Uncle Aidan!" Olivia shouts, jumping up and down.

Sophie gives my hand a tug. "That's our uncle up there."

"Wow, you must be really proud of him," I say, and out of the corner of my eye, I see Susan watching me with an expression so wistful, it makes my chest ache.

Once Aidan reaches the top, the mayor of Owl Lake leads the final countdown to the moment when the lights will flash on. The shouts around me are earsplitting, echoing in the frosty night air.

10, 9, 8...

A shiver runs up and down my spine, and I'm not sure if it's a shiver of anticipation or just the sentimental pride of knowing how much my Dad has contributed to this moment and to all the Christmases in Owl Lake's future. All I know for certain is that I'm glad Aidan is the one putting the star on top of the tree tonight. It seems fitting somehow.

7, 6, 5...

Even Fruitcake gets in on the action, letting out a woof with each number.

4, 3, 2...

And in the final moment before the mayor flips the switch and I'm bathed in shimmering light, Aidan looks down. Sophie and Oliva squeal, Josh lets out a loud whoop, and Susan and my parents wave like crazy. Aidan's gaze sweeps the crowd until his attention finally comes to rest on our little group, and I'm the one he's looking at. Our eyes lock, and I can't seem to breathe. I can *feel* his stare, every bit as real as if he were standing beside me and holding my hand.

1!

He's so high up, balancing a star in his grasp, but by the way my pulse roars, it could be my heart resting solidly in his hands once again.

It's not. I know it's not, but as the lights come to life and Aidan places the star on the tiptop of the beautiful tree, he smiles at me. It's a smile that lights up his entire face, and it feels like everything.

It feels like...

Magic.

Mission accomplished, Dad. I smile back at Aidan. Snowflakes catch in my eyelashes, but the thousands of glittering Christmas lights shining from the tree's graceful branches warm my face. *I'm happy.*

And then, somewhere above the noise of the crowd, I hear the tinkling sound I've come to know all too well.

Jingle, jingle.

After the tree lighting, Susan invites me out for gingerbread lattes with her family. I'm consciously aware that Susan's family includes Aidan, so I do my best to bow out. I'm still feeling distinctly floaty from the look that passed between us as he placed the star at the top of the tree, but I have no idea what it actually meant, if anything.

Maybe I simply imagined it. Or maybe it was quite literally the product of wishful thinking, brought to life by the magic bracelet. The jingle of the charms as the lights came on was unmistakable, and to be honest, the sound made my heart sink. I want Aidan to smile at me because he wants to, not because a vintage piece of jewelry somehow ordained it.

"I should probably get home," I say, glancing at my parents and silently pleading with them to agree.

Clearly, they're oblivious to my reluctance to join the Susan and her family on their quest for hot holiday beverages, because they urge me to go out with my friends and have a good time.

"Please come with us," Olivia pleads. "Pleeeeeease."

Even Fruitcake turns his melting brown eyes toward me. It's hopeless. There's no way I'm getting out of this.

"Okay, sure," I relent. "So long as I'm not intruding."

Susan rolls her eyes. "Don't be ridiculous. Of course you're not."

My parents hug me goodbye and within minutes, I'm seated in a comfortably worn leather booth at a cozy bistro called The Owl's Nest. It sits directly opposite the Owl Lake Inn, overlooking the grand town Christmas tree on one side and the frost-covered frozen lake on the other. The lights from the majestic tree reflect off its icy surface, making the lake look like liquid gold.

"Sorry I'm late," Aidan says as he joins us about fifteen minutes after our gingerbread lattes arrive. "I had to get the ladder truck back to the station."

He presses gentle kisses to the tops of his nieces' heads before taking a seat beside Josh, across from me. If he's surprised by my presence, he hides it well.

"Hi, Ash." He reaches for a drink menu.

"Hi." I gesture toward the mug sitting in front of me, towering with whipped cream and a little gingerbread man cookie balanced on the rim at a jaunty angle. "Do you really need to look at the menu when you can order this sugar-laden work of art?"

"Point taken." The corner of his mouth quirks into a half grin.

"Another gingerbread latte, coming right up," the server says.

"It looks like someone has found her Christmas spirit," Aidan says after the waiter is gone. He takes in all the shiny bits and bobbles of my glaringly green Christmas sweater and arches a brow.

"Isn't it the fanciest sweater you've ever seen?" Olivia bounces in her seat.

"Fruitcake has one just like it," Sophie adds.

"Does he, now?" Aidan's brow creeps even higher.

I nod. "So do my mom and dad. It's a whole thing."

Fruitcake chooses that moment to rouse himself from the floor, where he's been sleeping beneath the table, and plant his head in Aidan's lap. His tails wags so hard against my shins that I'm convinced everyone in The Owl's Nest can hear it.

I love that Owl Lake is the sort of place where dogs can sleep under the tables in public diners and no one gets upset. I'd forgotten that little detail about my hometown. It seems I've forgotten quite a few things.

Like the way Aidan's smile can light up a room. And the way he always seems to roll up his sleeves just enough to afford a glance of the rugged muscles moving beneath the skin of forearms. And the way my heart beats fast when I see the tiny flecks of gold in his blue eyes, as shimmery and luminous as starlight.

I knew tagging along on this family outing was a bad idea. I'm ogling a man's forearms. This can't be normal.

I lift my latte my lips and take a gulp.

Olivia is seated next to me, and as I reach for my drink, her gaze follows the musical sound my charm bracelet makes every time I move my arm.

Her eyes go wide, and she points to my wrist. "Look! It's the Owl Lake Christmas tree!"

I follow the aim of her delicate little finger. The silver Christmas tree charm dances and swivels on its chain, and the diamond at the center of its gold star seems to wink at me beneath the moody lighting of the bistro.

"Wow, it does look like the town tree, doesn't it?" I shove my hand back beneath the table, out of view.

"But on some level, don't all Christmas trees look the same?"

Olivia blinks up at me innocently, unconvinced. Probably because she's right. Just like the other charms that have somehow come to life, the silver tree charm is indeed a perfect replica of its full-size counterpart. It looks exactly like the enormous tree we just watched light up the sky atop the snowy hill overlooking our town. I checked as soon as the bracelet jingled.

But how am I supposed to explain the striking similarity to an entire table full of my hometown friends?

"All Christmas trees look the same?" Aidan frowns. Here we go again. "That's a little on the cynical side, don't you think?"

"Or just a simple observation," I retort.

"If you say so," he says.

"Aidan." Susan pins her brother with a glance of warning. "Leave Ashley alone. She's only saying that *all* Christmas trees are beautiful. Right, Ash?"

"That's exactly what I meant. I love Christmas trees." I flash my sauciest smirk at Aidan. How dare he insinuate I'm a Scrooge. "Have you forgotten that I'm practically wearing one?"

I gesture, Vanna White–style, toward my flashy sweater.

"Touché." Aidan rolls his eyes, but he's smiling again—wide enough for me to catch a glimpse of the dimples beneath the scruff lining his jaw.

My stomach flips and, caught up in the moment, I blurt the first thought that pops into my head. "Do you still think I look like Audrey, even without the black turtleneck?"

Susan practically chokes on her latte. She's going to kill me. I've just majorly broken BFF code by repeating something she shared with me that her brother had likely told her in confidence.

Oddly enough, Aidan himself doesn't seem fazed.

"Better," he says quietly, "I think you look like Ashley."

Someone might need to scoop me up and put me back together, because I'm on the verge of melting into a puddle.

"Who's Audrey?" Josh asks, glancing back and forth between Aidan and me.

"Audrey Hepburn. Ashley's always been a big fan. She loves old movies," Susan says. "Just like Aidan does."

I busy myself with another gulp of my drink, because I can't look Aidan in the eye. Gingerbread is one of the only things getting me through the holidays at this point.

"Really? Huh." Josh shrugs, and then a light bulb seems to go off in his head. "Hey, the Palace Theatre is having a classic movie night the day after tomorrow. You two should go."

I open my mouth to protest and let Aidan off the hook, but no words come out. Not a single one. Zero. My lips seem to freeze into a perfect, soundless O, like one of those porcelain Victorian carolers in a Dickensian Christmas village display.

Because the truth of the matter is that I want nothing more than to sit in a darkened theater and watch black-and-white Christmas movies with Aidan. I want to share popcorn from a giant bucket and feel a tingle when our fingertips collide. I want to watch shadows move across his handsome face and lose myself in the swell of theatrical music. I want to sink into one of the Palace Theatre's red velvet seats and feel as if I'm falling back into the past—not simply a grainy, reel-to-reel motion picture past, but *my* past, when things were so much simpler between Aidan and me.

I want those things more than I've wanted anything in a long, long time.

The bistro is bustling with a steady stream of customers, but an uncomfortable silence falls over our little table. The only discernible sounds are the twins slurping their mugs of hot chocolate and a muffled thud somewhere beneath the table, which is either Fruitcake shifting his position or Susan kicking her husband in the shin for prompting such a painfully awkward moment. My money's on the latter.

I squirm in my seat. "Um...I don't think...I mean..."

Aidan graciously interrupts my nonsensical stammering. "We could."

My gaze flies to his, and all at once, the veil of our shared history seems to slip away and he's looking at me with such an aching vulnerability in his moody blue eyes that my heart feels like it might break clean in two. Or maybe I'm mistaken, and this is what it feels like when a heart starts to mend itself and come back together, beautifully unbreakable.

My mouth is suddenly bone-dry.

I lick my lips.

"We could?" I say, and my voice is scarcely more than a whisper. I clear my throat and nod furiously. "I mean, yes. *Yes*. We could."

"Okay, then." Aidan nods. I suspect everyone at the table is staring at the both of us, but I can't say for certain because wild reindeer couldn't drag my gaze from his. "It's a date."

I beam, drunk on gingerbread and happiness. "It's a date."

Chapter Eleven

"IT'S NOT A DATE," I say to Maya the following morning when we've finally managed to put an end to the incessant game of phone tag we've been playing the past few days. "Not a real one, anyway."

Ever the optimist, Maya disagrees. "Of course it is. Didn't you just tell me those were Aidan's exact words?"

"I did, but I doubt that's truly what he meant. It's only an expression."

Fruitcake plops his head into my lap, and I run my free hand over his silky ears. I'm sitting up in bed in my candy-cane pajamas, not quite ready to step out of my room and face the day. I've been sleeping like a rock the past couple of nights. It's amazing how soothing a snowy silence and the soft hoots of owls outside my window can be, almost like a lullaby.

"Right, but given your history, I highly doubt Aidan

would toss that word out unless he really meant it," Maya says.

She's right, I know she is, but for some reason I can't let myself think about our movie night as an actual date.

"You know, Ash. It's okay to wish for things. I know it's scary, and I know you're still tender after the whole mess with Jeremy, but you can't stop dreaming or wishing for good things for yourself, especially at Christmas."

"Believe me, I have enough Christmas wishes to deal with as it is." I cast a fleeting glance at the charm bracelet, still anchored to my wrist. I've pretty much given up on trying to remove it at this point.

Maya's words aren't lost on me, though. Now—more than ever, perhaps—I'm fully aware of the power of Christmas wishes. I still don't fully understand what's happening to me or what the charm bracelet is supposed to teach me, but I know better than to wish for something without considering the full implications of the wish coming true.

As much as I'm drawn to Aidan, we can't just pick up where we left off. Nothing has changed since he proposed to me all those years ago. His life is here in Owl Lake and mine is back in Manhattan. I don't know why I have to keep reminding myself of this highly significant and extremely obvious detail.

"You have enough Christmas wishes to deal with?" Maya sighs. "What does that even mean?"

Where to start? "Right now, it means that I seriously need to find a way to get back to the city. *Today.*"

My boss called while I was at the Christmas tree lighting last night, and I didn't get her voice mail until late in the evening when I got home from The Owl's Nest. Her terse message put a prompt end to the walking-on-air feeling I'd had after Aidan's invitation to the classic movie night. The bottom line: if I'm interested in the promotion, I need to come apply in person and tell her exactly why I think I'd make a good manager.

I'm fully aware the demand is a test of my loyalty and determination, and I can't fail. I've worked too long and too hard in the charms department to give up on this chance of advancement now. Still, Manhattan is starting to feel farther and farther away the longer I'm in Owl Lake.

"Are the trains running yet?" Maya asks.

"Not until tomorrow, but I have a backup plan." I throw the covers off and climb out of bed.

"I thought the rental car was your backup plan."

"It was—it still is, actually. Aidan dropped the car off here yesterday afternoon while I was in town visiting his sister at the jewelry store where she works." At the mention of Enchanting Jewels, a warm glow comes over me. It is really such a charming little place, just the sort of boutique where I want to sell my own designs someday.

Not now, obviously. I'd be a fool not to try and work my way up the ladder at Windsor where I've already put in so much time establishing myself. If I'm ever going to get to Paris for Christmas on my own, it's exactly the sort of job I should have.

"I don't know," Maya says. I can practically see her shaking her head on the other end of the line. "I know you want the promotion, but it's not worth risking your life. According to my weather app, the roads upstate still seem pretty treacherous."

"Which is exactly why I'm heading to the local auto store to get a set of snow chains." I nod definitively, pretty darn proud that I managed to come up with a backup to my backup plan.

"Snow chains? Do you really think they'll make that much of a difference?"

I pull another ubiquitous black turtleneck from my suitcase. "Absolutely. My dad used to have some that worked wonders in snowy weather. Unfortunately, he just got a new set of heavy-duty winter tires, so he gave the snow chains away. But that's okay, my eventual promotion will more than cover the cost of new ones."

It has to, because I'm running out of time to get my application in.

"I should probably get going, though. I'll text you the second I get back to the city," I promise.

"Kiss, kiss." Maya makes cute little smacking sounds into the phone. "And be careful!"

When I emerge from the bedroom, my parents are once again enjoying their adorable coffee and bathrobe morning ritual.

"What's it going to be this time—plane, train or automobile?" Dad eyes me over his steaming, cinnamon-scented coffee. He's sipping it from a ceramic OLFD mug, which immediately makes me think of Aidan and our date. Or non-date? Whatever it is, I go all fluttery every time I think about it. "Or have you finally given up and decided to stay here until after Christmas?"

"I don't have a choice. I have to get back," I say, although spending time with Aidan again has begun to make me more aware than ever that life is full of choices, every single day. Maybe I'm more in charge of my destiny than I think.

Or I *would* be, if I didn't have a magical bracelet stuck on my wrist.

"Honey, are you sure you want to work for a place that won't consider you for a promotion unless you interrupt your Christmas holiday and drive through a blizzard to go and beg for it in person?" my dad says softly.

"It's not begging," I say, focusing intently on the tray of muffins on the kitchen island, because I'm not altogether sure he's wrong.

Does my boss realize how much trouble I'm going through to get to Manhattan? Does she even care?

I bite into a muffin, but even gooey chunks of cranberry and white chocolate can't quell my sense of unease. And yet, I can't give up on the idea of at least trying for that promotion. I've spent four years at Windsor. It can't have all been for nothing.

"I hate to break it to you, sweetheart, but the train station still isn't up and running." My mom sighs. "You know, if you decide to say put, you could always volunteer to help with the Firefighters' Toy Parade."

Dad nods. They're tag-teaming me, apparently, and when Fruitcake leaves my side to go stand between them, I get the definite feeling that I'm outnumbered. "The station could sure use the help, and who better than a former Parade Sweetheart?"

I can't help but laugh. "That was over two decades ago. I doubt anyone remembers my reign as Firefighters' Sweetheart."

Every year on Christmas Eve morning, the fire department holds its annual Firefighters' Toy Parade. The event is a celebration of the holidays, but mainly a charity drive to provide toys for children in need. In the days leading up to the parade, the fire department collects and wraps hundreds of gifts for underprivileged kids throughout the state. Then, on parade day, the fire trucks all roll through town with firemen waving from the windows, followed by elaborate floats decorated by local businesses. The last vehicle in the parade is always the ladder truck, of course, with Santa and the Parade Sweetheart riding on top. Tradition dictates that the Firefighters' Parade Sweetheart is always a young child related to one of OLFD's bravest. I had the honor of reigning over the parade with Santa when I was six years old.

"Think about it," my mom says. "It's for a good cause, and I think you'd have a lot of fun!"

"I'll think about it. I promise." I'm sure she's right. It would be great fun, and I'd love to do some volunteer work during the holidays. But with the promotion hanging in the balance, I'm not sure I should commit. From what I remember of the toy parade, it takes loads of effort.

I don't want to make a promise I can't keep and end up letting anyone down. I feel like I've been doing enough of that already.

"In the meantime, I'm off to Pete's Auto Store for snow chains." I fasten the buttons on my coat and grab the keys to the rental car. "Wish me luck?"

My mom nods as she refills her coffee cup and adds a generous splash of Christmas cookie–flavored creamer. "Good luck, honey. Give us a call when you get to the city so we know you're safe."

Dad is less optimistic. "Good luck, but something tells me Aidan will be bringing you home in about an hour or so."

I give my head a firm shake. "Definitely not happening this time."

"Of course not," my mom says, but she's clearly biting back a smile.

I arch a brow at Fruitcake for some sort of validation. He lets out a woof and wags his tail with enthusiasm, so I bend to press a kiss to the top of his warm, furry head. At least my dog believes in me.

Not your dog, remember?

I straighten, take a deep breath and remind myself that I'm a woman on a mission. Nothing will stop me from getting to Manhattan today. Operation Snow Chains is underway.

"What do you mean you don't have any snow chains?" No, this cannot be happening. It absolutely can't.

"I'm sorry, Ashley, but we're clean out." Pete, of Pete's Auto Store, casts me a sympathetic glance and shakes his head. He's wearing a Santa hat, and the white fluffy ball on its end swings back and forth in comical fashion.

I'd laugh if I didn't feel like crying. "You don't understand. I really need them. Can you check in the back and see if you have one more set lying around somewhere? Please? I'm desperate."

"I can check, but I'm not going to find any. We just sold our last pair to the customer who came in five minutes before you did." Pete tips his head in the direction of a fellow auto shop patron browsing the ice scraper display. My nemesis, apparently.

"Thank you." I force a smile as Pete heads to the stockroom.

I can't believe this. Five minutes? *Five minutes?!* If only I'd gotten out of the house sooner this morning, I'd probably already be safely on my way to the city.

I glare in the direction of the snow chain bandit. His back is to me, and it looks like a perfectly nice back, but I despise it all the same. Still, maybe if he knew how badly I need those snow chains, he'd reconsider and agree to sell them to me. Or, since I won't need them after today, maybe we could share them, because joint custody of auto parts between strangers is totally a thing, right?

Something tells me this is going to be a hard sell, but it's worth a shot.

"Excuse me, sir," I march toward him, ready to throw myself at his feet and beg.

But then he turns around and flashes me a self-satisfied smirk, and I stop dead in my tracks. There's no way I'm getting those snow chains. "Aidan?"

What is he *doing* here? Shouldn't he be refilling fire extinguishers or petting a Dalmatian somewhere?

"Morning, Ashley." He lifts his hand as if to wave, but he can't quite manage it because *his hands are full of snow chains.*

I stare longingly at them and then back at Aidan's stormy blue eyes. They've gone dark, like a blue-gray sky right before a blizzard. "I don't suppose you heard me talking to Pete just now?"

He nods. "Sure did."

"I really need those snow chains."

"So I heard," he says in the same flat tone he's used

every time he's caught me in the act of trying to leave Owl Lake.

Date or not, just because we're going to the movies together clearly doesn't mean he's willing to help me get out of here for a few hours.

I have to at least try, though.

"Can I, um, buy them from you?" I start rummaging through my handbag until I have a fistful of dollars to wave at him.

He rolls his eyes. "Put your money away, Ashley."

My hands go still, and a dollar floats to the floor. Neither one of us moves a muscle. I can't seem to look away from his angry, gorgeous face. Why does it feel so warm in here when it's snowing buckets outside and Pete's steady stream of customers keeps opening and closing the front door of the shop?

I direct my gaze at Aidan's broad chest instead of his face, but it's equally distracting. Somehow, I manage to find my voice. "Does that mean you're going to give them to me?"

"Nope."

Ugh. Why does he have to make this so difficult every single time? I want to throw a snowball right at his stubborn head. "Must we do this again? It seems really unfair, especially considering that every time I see you, you're dressed like a firefighter action hero."

He frowns down at the OLFD T-shirt just visible beneath the lapel of his heavy winter coat. "It's my uniform."

"My point exactly." I swivel on my heel and stomp toward the door.

"Sorry, Ashley. No luck in the back, but come back

after the New Year," Pete calls after me. "I should have plenty of snow chains by then."

Of course he will. "Thanks anyway, Pete. You have a merry Christmas."

When I resume my swift exit, Aidan is hot on my heels, tire chains jangling in his grasp. He sounds like one of the ghosts from A Christmas Carol.

The ghost of my *Christmas past,* I think. But wait, that's not right. Aidan is standing right beside me, part of my life again in the present. And as much as I'm afraid to think about it, that means Christmas future is still up for grabs.

"Ashley, wait!" he says once we're out on the sidewalk.

I spin around so fast that he nearly plows into me. "What?"

He backs up, and his blue irises bore into me, unblinking. I hold the stare, refusing to blink either until tears prick my eyes. "You think I'm like an action figure—plastic and unfeeling?"

"That's not what I meant at all," I counter. "I'm just saying that for a man who seems to either be at work or on call twenty-four hours a day, you have a lot of opinions about the fact that my career is important to me."

He says nothing in return, and I know I should probably drop it, but I can't.

"I get it. I've changed. I'm not the same person I was when I left Owl Lake." The admission makes me sadder than it should. Changing and growing is part of life, and I'm proud of all that I've accomplished since I moved away. But being back in my hometown is making me wonder if leaving everything I knew and loved behind was worth it in the end. Everything...and everyone.

I lift my chin in defiance, because no matter what sort of doubts are swirling through my head, he's not being fair. "But you're not the same person either."

"You're right," he says, and there's an ache in his voice that seems to scrape my insides. "I'm not."

I bite down hard on my bottom lip to stop it from quivering.

"Did you really think you'd come back after eight years and find the same lovesick boy you left behind?" He gives me a half smile, like he's trying to downplay the heartbreak behind what he's just said, but I know better. Those words didn't come easily for Aidan.

For the first time since I've been back in Owl Lake, we're getting dangerously close to discussing our history together. I almost hope we actually do, just to get it over with. But the sidewalk on Main Street doesn't seem like the best place to take a painful trip down memory lane.

We're so close that our breath commingles into a suspended puff of warmth in the frosty air. The angry knot in Aidan's jaw is back again, and there's a fire in his eyes that makes me weak in my knees. Then his gaze drops to my mouth, and this huge unspoken thing between us suddenly feels less like history and more like something else—attraction.

My head spins. This feels like the moment in a rom-com when the couple kisses in the middle of a huge argument, and the pounding of my heart is a sure sign that at least part of me hopes that's precisely what's about to happen. Snow flurries dance around us, and the air smells like crushed candy canes and frosted pine—like Christmas. Like *home*.

I'm not sure I've ever wanted to be kissed so badly in my entire life. What is *happening?*

Aidan is the first one to look away. He glances up, and I follow his gaze to see a sprig of mistletoe hanging directly over our heads. It's suspended from the eave of Pete's shop by a red velvet ribbon. Our eyes meet again in a panic, and we spring apart so fast that we both end up slipping on the ice and sliding to the ground.

I'm flat on my back on the sidewalk, looking up at the offending mistletoe when Aidan lets out a muffled groan, followed by a snicker. I laugh and swat at his chest. Big surprise, it feels as solid as a rock.

"Now can I have the snow chains?" I say through a giggle.

He's laughing so hard that he can barely form a response, but his answer is unchanged. It's still a no.

A short while later, Aidan is once again driving me home in a vehicle with flashing lights, but at least this time he's had the decency not to turn them on. I've returned my rental car, because without the snow chains, it's useless to me. Aidan kindly offered to give me a ride home since he's at the end of his shift, and I took him up on it because it's the least he can do after sabotaging my getaway. And maybe, just maybe, I'm the tiniest bit reluctant to see him go after our near-mistletoe moment.

Not that we've come anywhere close to kissing since

then. It's all business as usual, with a mile of distance between us in the front seat of the OLFD utility vehicle.

Its wheels roll to a stop in front of the lake house. I don't even need to glance at the porch to see if Fruitcake is there, because I know he is. My life has turned into Groundhog Day, Christmas edition.

"That's one loyal dog you've got there," Aidan says. "Maybe it's a good thing he doesn't seem to belong to anyone else. I've been asking around for days—I've even checked the other departments in the surrounding counties. No one's heard a thing about a missing golden retriever mix."

The relief flowing through me nearly takes my breath away. After just a few days, I can't imagine parting with Fruitcake.

"So he's really mine?" I ask, throat going thick.

"It certainly looks that way," Aidan says.

I give him a wobbly smile. Loyalty is an admirable quality—one that I probably haven't appreciated as much as I should. "Do you want to come in? Mom and Dad would love to see you."

I regret the question as soon as it's out of my mouth. Again, Aidan isn't my boyfriend. There are probably a million things he'd rather do on a rare afternoon off than hang out with my parents.

But he surprises me by saying yes and minutes later, we're sharing a bucket of my mom's special butter toffee almond drizzle popcorn while we sit side-by-side on the big, overstuffed sofa in the living room. Fruitcake flops at our feet and rests his head on Aidan's foot while my parents flit around in preparation for a "special surprise" they've prepared for me.

I cringe a little when my dad pops a videotape into

our ancient VCR. Surely we're not about to watch the long-lost footage from the year Aidan and I were homecoming king and queen back in eleventh grade. I can't think of anything more mortifying.

But as the old home movie begins to roll, joy warms me from within. It's not footage from high school. On the contrary, it's a full decade older than that.

"Is this the Firefighters' Toy Parade?" Aidan asks, leaning forward with his elbows planted on his knees for a better look.

"It sure is." My mom points at the grainy image of a young, trim firefighter in a Santa hat passing out candy canes to children lining the parade route. "Look, there you are, Ed."

My dad laughs. "That might have been a few Christmas cookies ago."

As if on cue, the camera pans to my mom, working her way through the crowd gathered around the firehouse with a giant platter of her gingerbread firemen and sugar cookie snowflakes. My heart stirs with pride at being part of such a special tradition this year. Mom was right. Who cares if my cookies didn't look—and certainly didn't taste—as perfect as hers did?

Aidan sneaks a sideways glance at me, and when our gazes collide, he gives me a slow smile that builds until my pulse starts to race. I bite my lip and force my attention back to the television.

"This is amazing. I can't believe you found this tape," I say.

"Well, we were talking about the parade this morning, and I knew it was lying around here somewhere," my mom says.

Then she and my dad exchange a meaningful

glance, and just as I'm wondering what their secret communication could possibly be about, the camera zooms in on a six-year-old me.

My hand flies to my throat and I gasp. I shouldn't be surprised, but somehow, I am. This video was taken the year I was the Firefighters' Toy Parade Sweetheart! I'm sitting on top of the ladder truck surrounded by a group of firefighters—including my dad, of course, who beams at me as if I've hung the moon. A glittering snowflake tiara sits atop my head, and I'm wearing a red velvet dress with white faux fur trim that looks like something the Rockettes would rock in their annual Christmas show.

"Look at how cute you were," Aidan says. "The Firefighters' Sweetheart. Who knew? How have I never seen this video before?"

"*I* haven't even seen it," I counter, and then I sit up a little straighter, because he's right.

I was super cute. Whoever was manning the camera at the time—Uncle Hugh, if I had to venture a guess— is asking me questions, and I'm chattering away like a kid who's just done a deep dive into the Christmas candy.

"Wait." My mom shushes us and aims the remote control at the television, turning up the volume a few notches. "This is the best part."

"Ashley, one last question," the camera man says. It's definitely Uncle Hugh. His deep baritone voice is unmistakable. "Describe for us your perfect Christmas—the Christmas of your dreams."

My heart skitters to a stop. Did I just hear that right?

The Christmas of your dreams...

I can't tear my gaze away from the screen, but my fingertips immediately latch onto the charm bracelet, wrapping tightly around the silver charms.

"The Christmas of my dreams would have a dog," my on-screen self says, nodding so enthusiastically that my snowflake tiara bobs on my head. "A big yellow dog, with a huge red bow tied around his neck."

Beside me, Aidan goes completely still as he glances down at Fruitcake. The dog's big pink tongue lolls out of the side of his mouth, and I swear he looks like he's smiling.

"Uncle Hugh was right. He remembered," I say. A sense of wonder spreads through me, and I feel like I'm on the brink of something huge...

Something magical.

"Wait, there's more," Dad says, nodding toward the TV.

Six-year-old me isn't finished with her Christmas wishes. "The Christmas of my dreams would have my mommy's special Christmas cookies, too. And a Christmas tree as tall as the sky with a special gold star on the very top."

My heart is suddenly in my throat. I can't move. I can't even breathe. Young Ashley has just described each and every charm that's somehow come to life on Betty's vintage bracelet. All three of the wishes six-year-old me made that came true.

"Ash? Are you okay?" Aidan says.

I nod without looking at him. I don't trust myself to speak or to even meet anyone's gaze right now. It feels like a flood of tears is gathering behind my eyes, and I'm not even sure why. A shiver courses through me as Aidan slips his hand in mine.

The adorable, innocent parade sweetheart onscreen continues describing her perfect Christmas while she waves a candy cane around as if it's a magic wand. "And there should be cuddly teddy bears, ice skating and a crown shaped like a snowflake!"

My young self gives her tiara a reverent pat as my gaze drops to the bracelet, where a trio of charms rest innocently against my sleeve—a teddy bear, an ice skate and a snowflake crown. I take a deep breath and study the remaining few. The only three left after that are the snowman with the orange enamel nose, the wrapped gift box and the most baffling charm of all: the miniature engagement ring topped with a dainty diamond solitaire.

"Oh! A snowman, too. And dozens of Christmas presents for all the girls and boys," six-year-old Ashley says, jabbing her candy cane in the air for emphasis. "And a happy-ever-after. That's the Christmas of my dreams."

A happy-ever-after, just like a fairy tale. *That explains the diamond ring,* I think. And then my eyes are swimming with tears, and the images on the television blur like a gentle watercolor painting. I'm gripping Aidan's hand so hard that my knuckles turn white.

Young Ashley didn't care about having a glamorous holiday in Paris or a Christmas dripping with rare diamond necklaces. Once upon a time, the Christmas of my dreams was innocent and pure, filled with small miracles and community ties—things I valued most as a little girl, things I'm slowly learning to love again.

Deep down, I don't think I ever really stopped.

As I furiously attempt to blink back my tears, I realize I understand the bracelet now. I still don't know a thing about Betty or where she came from or how any of this is possible, but I know without a doubt that the mysterious charms are somehow magical. There's no more trying to deny it. It doesn't make sense at all, but I know it's true. I know it as surely as I know my own name.

My eyes spill over, and I reach to brush a tear from my cheek, but Aidan releases my hand and beats me to it. His fingertips are warm, and his touch is so tender that I don't think the lump in my throat will ever go away.

I can't believe I ever said no to this man. Perhaps even more poignant is the realization that I've spent my time in Manhattan chasing the wrong things. When I said goodbye to Aidan and Owl Lake, I think I might have said goodbye to myself a little bit too. Or at least, the part of myself that understood what was really important.

The pad of his thumb lingers on my cheek, light as a snowflake. Somewhere in the periphery, I'm aware of my parents tiptoeing out of the room, leaving us alone together. And there's so much I want to say, so very much, but the words won't come. I'm spent, and I wouldn't even know where to start.

How could I possibly explain that I don't know how, and I don't know why, but the Christmas of my childhood dreams is coming true, one charmed encounter at a time?

Chapter Twelve

"So you're really not going back to Manhattan?" Susan grins at me the next morning as she helps me roll a big ball of snow along the ground in front of Enchanting Jewels. "You're staying in Owl Lake?"

"Not permanently—just for Christmas." I pause from our efforts to tuck a stray lock of hair back into my pompom hat. It's been a long time since I've made a snowman, and I've apparently lost my touch. The ball we've just made for the snowman's midsection is distinctly lopsided.

"But you're truly staying, with no day trips away, until after the holidays are over. No more trains or rental cars?" Susan packs another handful of snow onto the snowman's tummy and arches an amused brow. "No more snow chains?"

I jam a twig of an arm into place. "Aidan told you about that?"

"He didn't have to. I heard all about it from Pete

at the auto store—" She lets out a laugh. "—and from Peggy at Mountain Candy, not to mention the ladies who take knitting lessons at the yarn store across the street and pretty much the entire lunch crowd at The Owl's Nest."

"Wow, I guess I've forgotten what living in a small town is like."

"Well, you *were* both lying flat on your backs on the sidewalk beneath a clump of mistletoe." She waggles her eyebrows. "At least, that's way I heard it went down. That's a lot of excitement for Owl Lake."

I'm still not sure what to make of our argument-turned-near-kiss under the mistletoe, so I change the subject back to the matter at hand—the bracelet. "No more snow chains. After seeing that video of myself and realizing that the charms represent my childhood Christmas wishes, I can't leave. I'm supposed to be here and finish the Christmas of my dreams. I just know it."

Staying in Owl Lake until the holidays are over effectively means I can kiss my shot at the promotion at Windsor goodbye, but I feel strangely at peace about it. The second I saw my younger self rattle off the list of wishes, one by one, I knew I couldn't go. Something bigger is happening to me right now than making manager of the charms department, and I'm tired of fighting it. I'm ready to lean all the way in—hence, the snowman.

"Tell me again why we're doing this." Susan sticks the opposite twig arm into place and it promptly falls back down onto the snowy ground. I guess I'm not the only one who's out of practice.

"Because I'm supposed to, obviously. There's a

snowman charm on the bracelet." I offer her my wrist, and she peels back the cuff of my mitten to inspect the charms.

I called Susan first thing morning and asked if I could meet her before her shift started at the jewelry shop. I simply had to talk to someone about the video and Susan was the logical choice since no one else knows about the magic bracelet. I couldn't bring myself to tell Aidan about it last night. He never even asked why seeing the home movie reduced me to tears—he simply wove his fingers through my mine and held my hand until the film ended.

I could have sworn I spotted a glimmer of a tear in the corner of his eye at one point, but I couldn't be sure, and I was afraid to ask. There are still so many things we haven't talked about and I didn't want to ruin the magic spell of the charms.

"What's this?" Susan toys with the engagement ring charm and her grin spreads ear-to-ear. "Maybe you're going to get engaged during the holidays, after all."

It's too bad Maya isn't here. She and Susan have a lot in common, including their enthusiasm for Christmas proposals—and their obsession with seeing prospects for them around every corner.

"That's not what it means." I shake my head. "In the video, I said something about a happy-ever-after. I'm sure the ring is just a symbol for a fairy-tale ending."

My heart pounds hard beneath my holly-berry-red coat. Despite everything—despite the disastrous dinner with Jeremy in the city, despite Aidan's initial frosty reaction upon my return to Owl Lake and our complicated history—I still believe in romance. I still believe in happy-ever-afters, and I still think there's something undeniably magical about a Christmas engagement. I'm just no longer altogether sure who might be best man to slip a ring onto my finger.

"I don't know, Ash. This whole charm bracelet thing has been full of surprises so far. I wouldn't rule anything out." Susan releases my hand, and I tuck the bracelet back beneath the cuff of my mitten.

"I'm not getting engaged." I take a deep inhale of winter air, not quite certain who I'm trying to convince—Susan, or myself.

Because earth to Ashley! I'm out here building a snowman for the sole purpose of making the charms come true so I can usher in my fairy-tale ending, whatever it might be.

I unwind the scarf from around my neck and wrap it around our creation, just below the misshapen ball of snow that serves as his head. The jewelry shop probably opens soon, and I'm sure Susan has actual work to do. But when I glance at the shop door to check the list of operating hours, my gaze snags on a sign situated in the corner window, just beside a gorgeous collection of antique pocket watches. I've always had visions of repurposing old pocket watches into a line of hand-crafted pendants strung on a strand of delicate seed pearls instead of chains. But like most of my other ideas for vintage jewelry design, I've been too busy selling charms at Windsor Fine Jewelry to make it happen.

"Is Enchanting Jewels going out of business?" I frown. That's what the sign says, but it seems like such a shame. The shop is wonderful, and it fits right in on Main Street.

"I'm afraid so," Susan says. "Right after Christmas. The owner is relocating. The family is moving up north, which is why I'm pretty much the only one holding down the fort during the holidays. As it is, we're only open three days a week while Josh is off-duty to watch the girls."

"I had no idea. I'd offer to help out while I'm here, but I already texted Uncle Hugh this morning and volunteered for the Toy Parade committee. He seemed really excited. Apparently, they're short-handed this year."

Susan presses two rocks in place for our snowman's eyes. "Thanks anyway, but the shop's days are numbered and you're only in town for a little while. Something tells me you'll have a great time on the parade committee."

I think back to the video—to the smile on my little-girl face and the hustle and bustle of the parade happening all around me—and warmth fills my chest. "I do, too."

Susan takes a step back and tilts her head, regarding the snowman. "I think we're done here."

"Nope." I shake my head. "Not yet."

I pull a fat carrot from my pocket. Since the silver snowman charm has a shiny orange enamel carrot for a nose, this final detail seems crucial.

"Since you've obviously been carrying that thing around all morning, I'll let you do the honors." With a dramatic flourish, Susan waves her mittened hands at the snowman.

I'm nervous of all a sudden, and I'm not sure why. Three charm wishes have come true so far, so I know precisely what's about to happen. I'll push the carrot into place and the bracelet will make the same jingle noise that it did when all the other charms came to life. I'll be one step closer to the fairy-tale ending of the Christmas of my dreams.

So I take a deep breath and press the carrot into the snow. Our snowman is complete, all the way down to his bright orange nose. Susan and I exchange a glance, and then...

Nothing.

The bracelet doesn't make a sound.

I've obviously done something wrong with the snow-man, but I don't have time to figure out what it could possibly be. Susan needs to open up the shop, and Uncle Hugh is expecting me at the firehouse this morning. So I give Susan a quick hug and make my way to the fire station, a tiny bit relieved to know that Aidan is off duty today.

First of all, I'm a total mess. My ill-fated snow-man adventure has left my face numb and my nose is almost certainly pink from the cold. As for my hair, there's no telling what's going on beneath my pompom hat.

Plus, something changed between Aidan and me last night. I feel like he fully let down his guard in front of me for the very first time since I've been home, and I'm afraid that in the cold light of day, it will go right back up again. Bickering beneath the mistletoe was so ridiculous that it was kind of fun, but I'd much rather see Aidan's vulnerable side again. I have no idea where we stand though, and I definitely don't want to try and figure things out in front of an audience of firefighters. Frankly, I can't imagine anything more awkward.

Tonight is classic movie night at the Palace Theatre, so maybe things will be more clear after our non-date—emphasis on *non.* The mistletoe incident was a huge wake-up call. Ever since my return to Owl Lake, I feel like I've been living inside a snow-covered dream. I'm trapped in a beautiful winter wonderland full of Christmas magic, but it won't last forever. After the holidays, I'll be gone. It wouldn't be fair to start a romance with Aidan when I have every intention of telling him goodbye.

Again.

Not that he's given me any sort of indication that he has any lingering romantic feelings for me. I'm sure he doesn't, and that's perfectly fine. Better than fine, really. It's great.

So, so great.

Still, I get misty-eyed every time I think about the way he held my hand last night...the gentleness in his fingertips as he'd wiped away my tears. Maybe there's a tiny part of me that wishes he did have feelings for me.

My confusion is one hundred percent the bracelet's fault. I wish Betty were here. She'd have a lot of explaining to do. *Loads.* In the meantime, I should probably stop running around Owl Lake with carrots in my pocket, building snowmen in an attempt to get to the engagement ring charm as quickly as possible. It didn't even work, anyway.

No more mistletoe.

No more snowmen.

No more swooning over Aidan.

I repeat these rules to myself while I walk down Main Street's long hill toward the firehouse, in the hopes they might sink in. When I arrive at the station, the ladder truck and the small SUV are all lined up in the apparatus bay, as shiny as if they've just been washed—which they probably have.

As a retired fire chief's daughter, I know perfectly well that the first thing firefighters do in the morning is clean the rigs. A clean, soapy smell hangs in the air, and the feeling of nostalgia that washes over me gives a major tug on my heartstrings. My fingertips reach for a touch of smooth red metal, but I stop short of making contact with the ladder truck's gleaming exterior. I don't want to leave fingerprints. Delivering cookies the other day and seeing the video last night have made me realize just how much the OLFD has impacted my life. This place and these people have left a mark on me—it may be invisible to the naked eye, but I feel it. It's there, and I don't think it will ever go away.

"Ashley!" Uncle Hugh pops his head out of the door and waves me inside. "Come on in. We're just about to get started with the committee meeting."

He wraps me up in a big bear hug once I've crossed the threshold, and as he squeezes me tight, my gaze sweeps over the common area of the firehouse. They've put up their Christmas tree since my mom and I delivered the cookies. It stands in the corner, just past the three rows of plush recliners lined up in front of a giant flatscreen TV. In place of a garland, it's wrapped in yellow tape that says Fire Lane—Do Not Cross. Shiny red ornaments hang from its branches and as always, a firefighter's helmet serves as the tree topper.

But then my attention snags on a flash of something silver-colored beneath the tree's thick branches. When Hugh releases me from his embrace, I peer closer at the Christmas tree skirt.

I feel myself frown. "Snow chains?"

Not just any snow chains—*the* snow chains. Either I'm imagining things, or the very snow chains Aidan and I quibbled over yesterday are sitting beneath the station's tree, topped with a shiny red bow.

"Oh, yeah." Uncle Hugh waves a dismissive hand. "There's a family living in a cabin deep in the forest and the wife's expecting a baby. With all the recent snowfall, we're worried she's going to go into labor and their car won't make it as far as the highway, so Aidan picked up some snow chains for them. I'm delivering them this afternoon. We're going to leave them on the porch, like a Secret Santa sort of thing."

My throat clogs. "Oh, I had no idea."

"You didn't ask," Aidan says as he strolls into the room. He's wearing old, faded jeans and a cozy looking, cream-colored cable-knit sweater instead of his typical firefighter gear. But he's here, even though today is his day off. Does he *live* in his bunk bed in the sleeping quarters?

"Aidan." Swallowing is difficult, because my mouth has gone dry. I'm not prepared to see him, particularly not now, when I've just learned that he had an actual reason for not handing over the snow chains yesterday—a *good* reason.

Major swoon alert. Ugh, I've already failed at the most important item on my list of Christmas don'ts.

"Ashley," Aidan says, and even though he'd be completely in his rights to keep rubbing it in how I'd been so consumed with getting back to Manhattan that I never asked why he wouldn't give me the snow chains, there's an underlying softness to his tone. Whatever magic wrapped itself around us last night while we watched the video hasn't completely gone away. It lingers, like yesterday's snowfall.

Hugh glances back and forth between us. "Ashley's here to volunteer for the parade committee."

"Is that right?" Aidan arches a single skeptical eyebrow. "You know the train station is back up and running, don't you?"

I nod, clearing my throat. "I'd rather be here."

His blue eyes twinkle. "Okay, then. I'm more than happy to put you to work."

Wait. What?

My gaze swivels toward Uncle Hugh. "Aren't you the parade coordinator?"

"Nope." He shakes his head. "Aidan is heading up the parade committee this year."

Of course he is. No wonder my parents pushed me into volunteering. Is *everyone* in town trying to push Aidan and me back together?

"Look at the time." Uncle Hugh pretends to check his watch. He's not fooling me. Like my dad, he's always been #TeamAidan. "I'd better get those snow chains delivered. You two have fun now."

He flashes us a grin, then he grabs the snow chains and heads toward the apparatus bay. I glance around the station in search of other parade committee members, but unless they're waiting to pop out from behind the recliners, surprise party–style, it's just Aidan and me.

Alone.

Again.

"Um, where is everyone?" I ask, glancing warily at the farm table. It's piled high with presents ranging from board games and puzzles to Lego sets and dolls. At least a dozen rolls of wrapping paper are lined up beside the haul.

"Grocery store run," he says.

That explains the engine's absence and the lack of other firemen, but surely I'm not the only civilian on the parade committee. "And the other committee members?"

"We don't meet until tomorrow. Hugh texted me this morning and said we had a new volunteer. He thought if I wasn't busy, I could come in to get you up to speed and get a jump on some of the gift wrapping." His lips twitch as if he's trying his best not to laugh.

"Let me guess—he didn't tell you the new volunteer was me."

Aidan nods. "Interestingly enough, he left that part out."

Our eyes meet, and just like yesterday when we were both lying on the snowy sidewalk outside the auto store, we break into simultaneous laughter. I'm relieved as much as I'm amused. A few days ago, I'm not sure Aidan would have found these silly matchmaking efforts at all humorous. I suppose this is progress.

My face grows warm as our laughter dies down and I realize Aidan is studying my disheveled appearance.

"How did you get here? Did you roll up to the firehouse in a giant snowball?" He gives the pompom on the top of my hat a tug, and my hair spills over my shoulders in a tumble of messy waves.

"Sort of. I've been...playing in the snow." I brush

past him and head toward the table full of gifts, eager to get off the topic of my big fat failure of a snowman.

Plus, Aidan's nearness is making me breathless. I can feel my pulse pounding at the base of my throat, and I need to focus on something other than his soulful blue eyes.

I pick up a boxed jigsaw puzzle. The picture on the box shows a shaggy white dog with a red velvet bow tied around his neck, sitting in a snowy field at the edge of a forest. "This is sweet. It reminds me of Fruitcake."

"We have a lot of that particular puzzle. A card company donated them to our toy drive. Do you think you'll still find it cute after you've wrapped a few dozen of them?"

"Absolutely." I slide out of my coat, ready to get started. If my affection for Christmas dogs hasn't waned in the twenty years since I was the Parade Sweetheart, I don't think it's going away anytime soon.

Aidan sits across from me, and we wrap the pile of the puzzles until each one is covered in glittery paper and smooth satin ribbon. Christmas carols are playing from the fire station's sound system, and we work in silence for a while until Aidan picks up an action figure from the pile of gifts and holds it up to himself.

"Look, it's my twin," he says with a wink.

I roll my eyes. "You're not going to let that little comment go, are you?"

He shakes his head and grabs a fresh roll of wrapping paper. "No, I'm not, mainly because you were right."

"I was?" My hands go still, and I look up from the half-wrapped doll on the table in front of me.

Aidan is focused intently on folding his sparkly red

paper into straight lines—so much so that I have a feeling he's purposefully avoiding my gaze. "I work a lot. It's pretty much all I do these days, so I understand where the action hero comment came from. I'm the last person who should be giving you hard time about being in a hurry to get back to your job."

"What you do is important, though. You're legitimately a hero." I'm very aware of the dangers involved with being a firefighter. Before my dad retired, my mom prayed for him every single time he left for work. As a little girl, my heart would jump to my throat every time I heard a siren.

"There's more to being brave than willingly walking into a burning building," Aidan says quietly.

Michael Bublé's voice swells around us, singing about kissing on a cold December night. A sparkle of gold glitter from an earlier roll of wrapping paper is stuck to Aidan's forehead, and a lump forms in my throat because this is the first real heart-to-heart we've had in nearly a decade. I've missed talking to Aidan like this.

I've missed *us*.

When Aidan finally looks up, his smile is bittersweet. "In a way, I guess it's easier to put my life on the line than my heart."

Okay...wow. That's quite an admission, and it feels like an arrow straight to the center of my chest.

Aidan shakes his head. "Don't. I know what you're thinking, but I didn't mean it as any kind of slam against you. It took me a while to admit it, but you were right to say no all those years ago. We were too young to build a life together back then. We both had a lot of growing up to do, and in the end, it wasn't just you that let our relationship die. That's on both of us.

I could have fought for you, for what we had—I could have waited, convinced you we could take things at your pace. But I didn't. I let us drift further and further apart."

It's the absolution I've been waiting for, but somehow, I always thought it would make me feel better than I do when he says it. Honestly, the only thing I feel right now is sad.

Sad for me, sad for Aidan and sad for what could have been.

"It's always been hard for me—you know that," Aidan says. "After my dad died, I wanted to be the man of the family. Strong. Stoic. I've never had an easy time opening up to people. You were always the only one."

I nod gingerly, because I do know. When I first met Aidan, he was closed like a book. Getting to know him, seeing him open up and share his thoughts and feelings with me, took time. While I've been away, I just assumed he'd found someone else he trusted with his heart. I never asked my parents if he was involved with someone else, because I was afraid of the answer—even while I was dating Jeremy.

Aidan is a good man. He's kind in ways that make my heart twist. It's taken me a while to realize that that sort of man is a rarity. They certainly don't stay single forever.

He shrugs and gives me a boyish smile. "I suppose it's something I need to work on."

"Has there been anyone else?" I ask in a voice just shy of a whisper. "I mean, since me? Since us?"

"Not anyone serious." Aidan averts his gaze. "You?"

"Yes. His name was Jeremy." I swallow hard. Susan knows all about my big breakup, and I'm fairly certain she's told Aidan at least a little about it, but he deserves to hear it from me. "It was quite serious, but we broke up right before I came home for Christmas. I was actually supposed to be in Paris with him and his family right now."

"Paris? Wow." Aidan glances at our surroundings. The Owl Lake Fire Department is about as far as a person could possibly get from the Champs-Élysées. "Is it okay for me to admit that I'm glad you're here instead?"

"I'm glad, too," I say.

And this time when I smile at him, I feel lit from within, like a thousand glittering Christmas lights. Because right here, right now, there's no place I'd rather be.

"All done," I say, placing a shiny green bow on the final wrapped package. The pile of gifts takes up the entire surface of the farm table even though it seems like we just got started.

Jingle, jingle.

Aidan's saying something about the firemen delivering the gifts to the nearby children's shelter, but I'm flipping through the charms on the bracelet. I pause when I reach the tiny silver Christmas gift, topped with a green enamel bow. My words from the video float back to me.

Dozens of Christmas presents for all the girls and boys.

"Everything okay?" Aidan asks, studying me because I've gone suddenly quiet.

Happiness sparkles inside me. "Everything is perfect."

Chapter Thirteen

"You sound different," Maya says an hour after Aidan and I've finished wrapping the gifts for the toy drive and loading them up into the OLFD utility vehicle.

I'm taking Fruitcake for a walk and trying to resist the urge to build another snowman while I explain to my friend that I won't be making it back to the city, after all. Honestly, it's weird how much she can discern simply by the tone of my voice.

"How so?" I ask, although I have to admit, I *feel* different than I did when I first arrived in Owl Lake. The bracelet is making me look at my life in a new light. I'm not quite sure how to explain it, but I definitely feel a little less lost than I did a few days ago.

"For starters, you haven't mentioned Jeremy in a while."

Right. Jeremy—the man I thought I wanted to marry. "The more I think about it, the more I realize how different Jeremy and I are. I can't believe I didn't see it sooner."

"Maybe this trip home has been a good thing," Maya says, but then she sighs. "Although, I have to ask—you're really giving up on the promotion?"

Fruitcake romps gleefully at the end of his leash, tossing snow into the air with his nose. I should probably tell my roommate that I've got a dog now. She's going to think I'm losing my mind. Maybe I am. "I'm sure. It's hard to explain...things have gotten sort of complicated."

"You keep saying that and then just leaving it there, like I won't understand, but I'm your best friend, remember? I can't send gingerbread ice cream through the phone for us to share, but I'm right here and I'm listening. What's going on?"

"Do you believe in magic?" I blurt.

There's a loaded silence on the other end of the line before Maya responds. "What sort of magic?"

"Christmas magic." I swallow. She's going to think I hit my head or something and now I believe I'm a character in a Christmas movie. "Let me explain."

"I'm all ears," Maya says, and her voice is etched with concern.

I tell her everything, starting with the eventful train ride home and ending with the jingle sound that the bracelet made this morning after Aidan and I had finished wrapping the Christmas gifts for the toy drive. I don't leave out a single detail, and even though Maya doesn't say a word while I get it all out, it feels good to finally tell her what's been going on.

When I'm finally finished, I slow to a stop and look around. Fruitcake pants, and his breath comes out in little puffs in the cold air. We've made it almost all the way around the walking trail surrounding Owl Lake.

There's a group of children having an ice-skating lesson on this side of the lake, and they look adorable as they wobble across the frozen surface of the water.

I hold my breath as I wait for Maya to say something.

"So what you're saying is that a mystery woman who looked like Mrs. Claus left you a magical charm bracelet, and now all the wishes you made twenty years ago that are represented by the charms are coming true?" She enunciates each word with extreme care.

"That's about it, yes."

"I told you that you'd have the Christmas of your dreams," she says with a definite note of triumph in her tone.

I can't help but laugh. "You did, didn't you?"

"So that's the entire story? There isn't anything else I should know, is there?"

Fruitcake goes into a play bow and wags his tail while he watches the young skaters. Everywhere the dog goes, he seems enthralled by what's going on around him. He lives completely in the moment, awestruck by the magic of everyday life. Thanks to him— and thanks to the bracelet—I'm beginning to do the same.

"One more thing." I rest my mittened hand on Fruitcake's smooth head and he gazes up at me with his melting brown eyes. "I'm keeping the dog."

After talking to Maya, I have just enough time to get home and change for classic movie night at the Palace.

I'm glad it turned out this way because too much time on my hands would have given me time to debate the "date or non-date" quality of this evening's plans.

The whole thing was Josh's idea, so I'm certain it falls into the non-date category. But the more time I spend with Aidan, the more confused I am about my feelings for him. Because I'm *definitely* feeling something, and anything more than simple friendship is far too worrisome to consider. Once the holidays are over, I'll be right back in Manhattan, at Windsor Fine Jewelry, selling silver charms. As nice as this holiday is, it's just that—a holiday. Thanks to the magic of the bracelet, it barely even feels like real life anymore. Somewhere deep down, I'm not so sure it is. Maybe once all the wishes come true, I'll wake up back on the train beside Betty and find out it was all a dream.

The thought makes my stomach churn, so I push it out of my mind and give Fruitcake a goodbye kiss on the head. It leaves a faint lipstick mark behind, just between his ears, and I leave it instead of trying to wipe it away. He looks ridiculously cute, like Cupid in canine form.

No Cupid necessary, I remind myself. *This is simply a friendly movie outing.*

But when I make my way to the living room, I find Aidan already there, chatting with my mom and dad as casually as if the past eight years never happened. And when he turns his gaze on me, his attention snags immediately on the vintage heart brooch pinned to the lapel of my coat.

"Pretty." He reaches to give the Victorian charm hanging from the center of the pin a little tap. The heart swivels, catching the light from my mom and dad's Christmas tree, and something swells deep in the center in my chest.

"It's one of mine," I say, and when he looks confused, I elaborate. "I designed it."

"Wow, that's incredible." He angles his head to get a closer look. "It's beautiful."

All my emotions seem to bottle up inside my chest. I'm not sure why it means so much to me that he's noticed and admired the brooch, but it does. "Thank you. The original piece was vintage. I like taking old things and making them new."

"Ashley does lovely work." My mom gestures to the necklace she's wearing. It's a rose gold locket I made for her last year for Mother's Day. "I hope the executives in charge of Windsor realize what a great jewelry designer they have in the charms department."

I shake my head. "It's not like that, Mom. I help customers choose which charms to put on their bracelets and other pieces. I don't do any real jewelry design."

"That's a shame." My mom looks disappointed, even though I'm certain we've had this conversation before.

"It's only a hobby," I remind her.

"If you say so, dear. But something tells me it's a little bit more than that." Mom gives her locket a reverent pat.

"Shall we go?" I say to Aidan. I'm ready to leave before this conversation turns into a deep dive into my career.

Windsor Fine Jewelry oozes prestige. If I want to work with jewelry, it's the place to be. Of course, I just willingly walked away from a chance at a promotion, but that's okay. So what if I'm not a manager? I still have a job at one of the most legendary jewelry stores in the world. The necklace I made for my mom is just a little trinket.

Still, a warm glow of pride wraps itself around me as Aidan and I head toward the Palace. I like that he's noticed my charm pin, and I love how much my mother's locket means to her. I can't help it. If I think really hard about it, I can't remember the last time my actual paying job gave me the same feeling of creative satisfaction. As much as I love helping customers choose their charms, it's just not the same as designing something myself.

Windsor is the last thing on my mind when we get to the movie theatre and load up on popcorn, Junior Mints and whipped eggnogs topped with a generous sprinkling of nutmeg. The showing is a double feature of classic Christmas movies—*White Christmas* and *Holiday Inn.* From the moment I nestle into my plush red velvet seat, I feel like time is moving backward. The fashion onscreen is absolutely dreamy, all full swishy skirts with nipped-in waists and glamorous, feminine silhouettes. Just the sort of retro elegance I love.

And the jewelry! There are brooches, delicate watches and intricately designed hair ornaments. I'm in heaven. I turn a smile toward Aidan, but when I do, I find him watching me instead of paying attention to the screen.

My breath catches in my throat. "What is it?"

"I'm just glad we're doing this, that's all," he says, and the wistfulness in his tone makes my stomach flip.

"It's been a long time," I whisper.

"Too long." His expression turns serious while a song and dance number begins on the big, flickering screen in front of us. In the periphery of my vision, Bing Crosby and Danny Kaye are singing about falling in love at Christmastime, but Aidan's gaze holds me in a way that makes it impossible to look away.

And then, in a voice that's scarcely more than a tremulous whisper, he says, "I should have fought for you, Ash."

I swallow hard. "Aiden..."

But he's not finished, and I'm not sure I want to hear the rest. I'm not sure I can stand it. Dancing around our past is much easier than facing it head-on, because the more time I spend with Aidan, the more I'm beginning to wonder if I made a mistake all those years ago.

"I could have asked you to stay...or I could have waited, but I didn't do either of those things," he says, and his smile is suddenly so sad that I'm furiously blinking away tears.

I shake my head. *Don't say any more. Please don't.* "It wasn't your fault. It was mine."

"That's not true, no matter what I tried to tell myself after you left." He reaches to cup my face in the dark theatre. "It was easier to just close myself off. So easy that I didn't quite realize that was the choice I'd made until you came back. Being here with you again makes me wish I'd done things differently."

I can barely breathe. My pulse is pounding a staccato rhythm that seems to beat in time to a simple, three-word phrase.

Definitely a date.

"Sometimes I wish the same thing," I murmur, and I'm shocked to realize I mean it.

Why am I saying this? *You're living the dream, remember? And that dream is in Manhattan, not here.* But when my hands grip the soft velvet of the armrest between us, and when Aidan leans the slightest bit closer to me and his gaze flits toward my lips, I'm consumed with the thought that maybe there's more to life than dreaming. More to life than fancy trips around the world and posh parties and priceless necklaces.

"Ashley." Aidan's minty breath is warm on my face, while onscreen, Bing Crosby is serenading Rosemary Clooney, singing about counting his blessings.

And I realize, now more than ever, how much of a blessing Aidan has been to me—not just yesterday, but today, too. A shiver runs up and down my spine when he leans closer, and I suddenly can't fathom a tomorrow without him. Manhattan seems a million miles away, even farther than Paris.

My breath catches as Aidan's gaze drops slowly to my mouth, and my heart swells. It feels as if I've been waiting for this kiss for the better part of the past eight years...maybe even longer. Maybe even a lifetime. But just as my eyelashes begin to flutter closed, my attention snags on a glimpse of red over Aidan's shoulder.

I don't want to look. I *desperately* don't. I want to stay right where I am, a breath away from the aching tenderness of Aidan's lips landing gently on mine. I want to fall into this moment, to sink into it like a soft feather bed. But for some odd reason, I can't. A chill runs up and down my spine, and I freeze, shell-shocked, as the flash of red comes into sharp focus... the familiar twirl of a cape, the snowy white bun.

My eyes go wide.

Betty!

"Wait," I say, and Aidan's eyes pop open, searching my face.

"I'm so sorry. I thought..." He shakes his head and pulls away, no doubt under the mistaken impression that I didn't want to kiss him, when in reality I want nothing more.

But I can't let Betty get away. I don't know what she's doing here or how she ended up in the Palace Theatre in Owl Lake, but I *need* to talk to her. She's the only one who can tell me more about the bracelet, and I still have so many questions—especially about the tiny engagement ring charm.

"Don't apologize. Please." I rest my hand on Aidan's broad chest. His cable-knit sweater is impossibly soft against my palm, and his heart pounds wildly in the dark. "I just..."

I shake my head, at a complete and total loss for words.

I just think I spotted Mrs. Claus headed toward the lobby for a refill on her bucket of popcorn.

Could this situation get any more absurd?

"I just need to slip away for a quick second. I'll be right back." I scramble out of my seat and tell myself I'm only imagining the glimmer of hurt in Aidan's blue eyes, but it's no use. It's there, because I'm quite literally running away at the very moment we were about to kiss.

I'll make things right with Aidan, I tell myself. I'm not sure how, since we've barely begun to move beyond our sensitive past, but I will. I can't bear the thought of hurting him again, but I also can't pass up my best opportunity to get to the bottom of the magic bracelet.

The theatre is pitch black, and I dart down the aisle until I push my way out the door and stumble into the lobby, blinking against the sudden brightness. Two teenaged boys are working the concession stand, and other than a life-size cardboard cutout of Emily Blunt as Mary Poppins, they're the only people in sight. No Mrs. Claus. No *Mr.* Claus. Not even a lowly elf.

I make a mad dash for the ladies' room but find it empty, even after banging on each of the stall doors and calling Betty's name. There's a hollow feeling burrowing behind my breastbone. This can't be happening. She couldn't have just disappeared into thin air, like...like...

Like magic?

I stare at my reflection in the bathroom mirror. My cheeks are flushed, and my eyes are wild. I can't remember the last time I've looked or felt so alive, and for a dizzying moment, I'm not sure if it's the Betty sighting or the almost-kiss with Aidan that has my heart fluttering like angel's wings. Possibly both, even though kissing my high school sweetheart is *not* part of the plan. And I can't even blame the latest near-miss on mistletoe.

I take a deep breath and head back toward to the lobby to interrogate the teen boys. They don't remember seeing an older woman in a red cape and can't stop smirking as I describe Betty's appearance. It's hopeless. Either I've imagined the entire incident or she's vanished, like Santa up a chimney.

Shoulders slumped, I turn back toward the theater and nearly plow straight into Aidan in the process.

"Oh." I swallow and take a backward step. "Hi."

"Hi." He tilts his head, regarding me with cautious curiosity. "You left in such a hurry, I wanted to make sure you were okay."

"Fine," I nod with far too much enthusiasm. "I'm

great. I, um, thought I saw someone I knew, but it seems I was mistaken."

"Ah." His gaze darts around the empty lobby. I can tell he doesn't believe me simply by the way he tucks his hands into his pockets and can't seem to look me in the eye. "Who?"

"Just a lady I met on the train," I can't lie to him, but at the same time, I know my answer isn't helping him understand why I pulled away so abruptly. Why would I chase down a random stranger from the train when we were about to kiss?

Aidan shifts his weight from one foot to the other, and I have the terrible feeling he's about to make an excuse to leave before the double feature is over. I don't want the night to be over already. I want to go back inside the theater and pick up where we left off, but if history has taught me anything, it's that the most precious opportunities only come around once.

Still, I'm not ready to go home yet. Not even close.

I grin up at him, determined to salvage what's left of our date. "Let's build a snowman."

The suggestion is a flagrant violation of the rules I've set for myself, but desperate times call for desperate measures. Besides, the charm on my bracelet clearly represents a *special* snowman. It has to be this. I'm suddenly sure of it. And, shameful confession: there's indeed a carrot in my pocket.

The corner of Aidan's mouth lifts. It's not a full-on smile, but I'll take what I can get. "You want to build a snowman? Now?"

"Yes." I grin up at him. "Right now."

I hook my arm through his and drag him outside. The sky is as dark as velvet and snow is falling in delicate flurries, soft like feathers. Aidan looks up at the stars blazing bright, and I'm struck by how many times I've seen him standing in this very place, backlit by the theater's marquee. More times than I can count, probably. But this time feels different. It feels like both the first time and the last time it will ever happen, all at once.

"Ready?" he asks, hunching his shoulders against the cold.

I want to freeze this moment in time. I've been so distracted by the charm bracelet that the days since I've been home are passing in a blur.

I nod anyway. "Ready."

"I know just the place." He playfully waggles his eyebrows then heads up Main Street, but his hands remain in his pockets. Earlier, he might have held my hand, but the moment has passed.

Aidan's idea of "just the place" turns out to be the yard in front of the OLFD firehouse. I have to admit, with its pristine expanse of untouched snow, the spot is indeed perfect. The light from the station's windows bathe the yard in a golden glow as we pack snow into the form of three large snowballs, just like the charm on my bracelet. I keep waiting for Aidan to wonder why I suddenly want to build a snowman. I'm not sure how I'll even try to explain it, but luckily, he never asks.

"You're really good at this," I say as he presses a line of pebbles into place along the snowman's body. Five perfect buttons.

He shrugs. "Lots of practice. The twins love playing in the snow, and my sister loves watching us from the warmth and comfort of her living room window. Uncles are in charge of snowmen, apparently."

"They're sweet girls."

"They are." He grins, and then he does a double take when I pull a carrot from my coat pocket.

"I come prepared," I say by way of explanation.

"I see that." He's studying me in that probing way of his again, and my cheeks warm as I remember what he said to me in the theater.

Being with you here again makes me wish I'd done things differently.

I wonder if those words still apply after my quick getaway to go after Betty, just like I wonder if she was really there at all. Was my imagination working over-time to give me an excuse to flee because I was afraid of what kissing Aidan might mean?

Surely not. I know what I saw. She was right there, and I *wanted* to kiss him. I still do—I want it so much that when the tips of my mittens brush against Aidan's gloved fingertips, I go all fluttery inside. I wait, hoping against hope that Aidan will look at me again like he did when Bing Crosby crooned about counting his blessings. But in the end, I can't bear the wait, because the truth is that I know I'm not afraid of what might happen if he kisses me—I'm afraid of how disappointed I'll be if he doesn't.

So this time, I end the tender moment before it begins. I form a frosty snowball with mittened hands and throw it straight at Aidan's heart, where it lands with a muffled thud. Within seconds, we're engaged in an all-out snowball fight, chasing one another around our snowman, who stands quietly in the center of the chaos with his bright orange nose and wobbly grin.

He looks just like the charm on my bracelet, and even though the kiss was a near miss that might never come around again, something about tonight was special all the same. Aidan and I have moved on from the past. I'm certain I'm going to hear the distinctive jingle the bracelet makes every time one of the charms comes to life. I just *know* I will.

But I never do.

The frost-covered yard glitters in the moonlight, and the snowfall is as soft and quiet as a whisper. Aidan is my friend again, which is more than I've ever dared hope for before. The snowman charm remains a mystery. That's okay, though.

For once, I don't give the bracelet a second thought, because the echo of Aidan's laughter commingling with mine in the snow-kissed air is its own kind of magic.

Chapter Fourteen

TWO DAYS LATER, I'M BACK at the firehouse—this time, for the actual toy parade committee meeting.

I've spent the past forty-eight hours or so helping my mom and dad with their jigsaw puzzles, taking Fruitcake for long, rambling walks and running the occasional Christmas errand. I've almost gotten used to the slower pace of small-town life. In fact, I've actually begun to enjoy it. Other than having too much time on my hands to think about the fact that I haven't heard from Aidan since our movie date, it's been really nice.

But he's here now, of course, sitting across me at the fire station's big farm table in his OLFD gear with a clipboard in his hands. We're surrounded by other committee members, mostly other firefighters, plus a few of their family members, most notably Susan. She breezes into the station with Sophie and Olivia in tow, and the girls immediately collapse onto the floor to play with Fruitcake, who soaks up the attention with the long-suffering grace that golden retrievers are so famous for. Basically, the patience of a saint.

"That dog is perfect," Susan says as she slides into the seat beside me. "He's like a canine Mary Poppins."

"He's pretty amazing." I give her a quick squeeze. "It's great to see you. How are things at the jewelry shop?"

"Good. The owner stopped by a few days ago on her way out of town for the holidays, and we started packing some things up. The day after Christmas is going to be our last hurrah. Too bad she couldn't find a buyer. I thought she might because she lowered the sell price to rock bottom." She pulls a plastic bag from her oversized purse and offers it to me. "These are all old pieces we've had on hand for years. Junk, essentially, but I thought you might be able to use some of them for your recycled jewelry designs?"

The bag is full of old silver pins with broken clasps, bracelets with missing links and rings darkened by tarnish, but beyond the obvious wear and tear, the items are quite lovely. At first glance, I spot a gorgeous vintage Art Deco-style women's wristwatch. With just a little cleaning and repair work, I could probably convert it into a lapel pin for my mom for Christmas. "Are you kidding? There are treasures in here."

Susan laughs. "I can promise you that you're the only one who thinks so. Take it. It's yours."

"I don't know what to say." I clutch the bag to my heart. "Thank you, and thank your boss, too."

She gives me a warm smile, then turns her attention to her brother, who's staring down at his clipboard with a tiny furrow in his brow. He hasn't met my eye since I arrived.

I try not to read too much into it. Aidan is tech-nically on duty, after all. He's probably just in action hero mode. I hope that's the explanation for his con-templative mood, anyway, and that he's not reacting to anything bad that's happened. My dad saw some awful things back when he was a firefighter. Aidan isn't re-ally an action figure. He's not indestructible, and he definitely has feelings. A heart. Being a real-life hero takes its toll.

He looks up from the clipboard to nod hello to his sister and casts a quick glance in my direction. The crease in his forehead disappears, the look in his eyes is warm. His words from a few nights ago ring in my head like a refrain from a Christmas carol.

There's more to being brave than willingly walking into a burning building.

Maybe I shouldn't be surprised at the radio silence since movie night.

"There's a snowman out front," Uncle Hugh says as he strolls into the station, coffee cup in hand.

"Yeah, it's been there for a few days. Where did it come from?" Josh asks, then presses a kiss to the top of Susan's head before scooping the twins into his lap and dropping into one of the recliners. Sophie and Ol-ivia collapse into giggles as they burrow into his arms.

A paramedic sitting beside Aidan shrugs. "No clue. It just appeared overnight during my last shift."

Aidan's gaze flits toward mine again, and we share a secret smile.

Uncle Hugh shrugs. "They're popping up all over town. It's like Owl Lake has its own secret snowman bandit."

It's a struggle not to raise my hand. *Snowman bandit, present and accounted for.*

"Should we get the meeting started?" I ask brightly. Surely there's something more important on Aidan's clipboard that we should be discussing rather than my numerous failed attempts at bringing the snowman charm to life.

I can't help it. I want to get to the ring charm. I know it's silly, given my recent near miss with an engagement ring, but I'm only human. I've also possibly spent too much time working at a jewelry store where half of Manhattan's brides-to-be get engaged. When I get back to the city, I'll have to let the Windsor marketing team know that their ad campaign was a little too effective at getting me used to thinking of "Christmas time" right along with "engagement ring."

"What's on the agenda today, fearless leader?" Susan flashes Aidan an exaggerated wink.

"Funny you should ask," he says, glancing down at his notes again. He picks up a pencil and strikes through the bullet point at the top of the page. "I'm officially stepping down as sole chairperson of the committee."

Around the table, mouths drop. Hugh practically chokes on his coffee. Susan laughs as if what her brother has just said is a huge joke. I'm the only person in the room who doesn't seem surprised.

Scratch that—I'm a little surprised, but mostly, I'm happy. And proud. Aidan is trying to change and get more balance in his life. It's a baby step, but it's still a step forward.

My heart skitters as our eyes meet for a brief second. I wonder what all of this means beyond the parade committee. Now that he's moving toward living his life again, is Aidan ready to risk his heart?

Am I?

"So we don't have a committee chair anymore? I don't blame you for wanting to take it a little easier, man. You're always the first to volunteer for anything and everything." Josh says. "But the timing's not great—the parade is just two days away."

Aidan shakes his head. "I'll still chair the committee, but I'd like to have someone step up as co-chair and share some of the responsibility going forward. Next year, that person could move into the role of head committee chair. The remainder of this year could be a training exercise of sorts."

"I see." Uncle Hugh nods. "I have to say, I think this is a wise decision. The bulk of the workload should be shared, and you've headed the committee every single year since you joined the department."

"I agree." Susan gives the table a gentle pound. "One hundred percent."

Everyone nods, effectively confirming Aidan's reputation as OLFD's perpetual action figure. His coworkers are good people, though. The fire department is a family, just like it always has been. And like all good families, they want what's truly best for their own.

"Perfect. We're all in agreement." Uncle Hugh takes a gulp of his coffee.

"Thank you." Aidan nods, and the furrow in his forehead makes another brief appearance. He's clearly uncomfortable showing any sort of vulnerability, even here at the firehouse, his safest haven. "Is there anyone eager to take on the co-chair position?"

Susan raises her hand. *Good for her,* I think, but then she says, "I nominate Ashley."

I blink at her. Did she really just say what I think she said? "Um..."

I can't. I mean, I sort of want to. Actually, I *really* want to. Wrapping gifts a few nights ago with Aidan was nothing like working the wrap desk at Windsor. It felt good to do something with a greater purpose.

But co-chair? It's meant to be a training opportunity. Aidan wants someone who's willing to head up the entire parade next year and I won't even be here next Christmas.

A weight settles on my heart at this realization, even though it shouldn't come as a surprise. My life— my *real* life—is in Manhattan now, not Owl Lake. It seems that my hometown's bottomless hot cocoa, a magic bracelet, countless snowmen, and Aidan's blue eyes have almost made me forget this important detail.

"I second that nomination," someone says. I'm too shell-shocked to register who it is.

"I third it," Josh chimes in.

Aidan's pencil is tapping out an anxious beat on his clipboard. I can't tell if he wishes I would accept or decline. Where's a heaping dose of magic when you really need one? Granted, my magic hasn't been very good about telling me where to go, but it has a solid track record of telling me where not to go, if my failed attempts to reach Manhattan are any indication.

"I don't know," I say. "I'm not sure I meet the qualifications."

This is code for reminding everyone that I no longer live in Owl Lake. Even Sophie and Olivia should be capable of deciphering it.

Uncle Hugh shrugs one shoulder as if my actual residence has no bearing on the matter. "It makes perfect sense. Who better to serve as co-chair than an actual Firefighters' Sweetheart?"

Firefighters' *sweetheart*. The words make me feel all sparkly inside for completely nonsensical reasons.

"That was a long time ago," I protest, but no one seems to care.

"Seems like yesterday." Uncle Hugh grins at me over the rim of his coffee cup.

As I meet his gaze, my attention snags on Aidan and the sudden flash of dimples in his manly face. That tiny hint of pleasure in his expression is all it takes for my resistance to crumble. I'll figure out how to deal with next Christmas later. Video conferencing and email *do* exist. Even Santa plans Christmas from miles away.

Aren't you forgetting something? Santa isn't real.

I run my fingertips over the delicate charms dangling from my wrist. They're cool against my skin, like a kiss of winter air.

"I'm in."

"What's all this?" my dad asks me hours later as I'm poring over three fat binders full of toy parade paperwork at the kitchen table.

Mom glances up from the peppermint tea she's preparing at the butcher-block island. It's part of her nightly ritual and watching her repeatedly dunk her fragrant teabag into her mug as darkness falls and the owls begin gliding over the lake is oddly soothing.

"You haven't heard?" She arches a brow. "Ashley is the new co-chair of the Firefighters' Toy Parade."

Dad shoves his hands into his pocket and rocks back and forth on his heels. "Co-chair, huh?"

"Yep," I say, pausing from my reading to run a hand over the top of Fruitcake's head. He's been sitting patiently beside me since I returned from an early dinner with Susan, Josh and the twins, waiting for his nightly walk. I might as well take him out. My head is spinning with facts and figures. Trying to absorb any more information tonight isn't going to happen.

But volunteering to be co-chair has made me acutely aware that my time here in Owl Lake is limited. The parade is on Christmas Eve, just four days from now. I'm due back at Windsor the day after Christmas. What was I thinking when I signed on for this?

"That's a pretty big commitment." Dad frowns.

I have to be honest, this isn't at all the reaction I'd expected from him. The toy parade is near and dear to his heart. I thought he'd be thrilled to find out that I've taken on a bigger role in the event.

"It is." I nod, burying my fingertips deeper into Fruitcake's warm fur. "But Aidan needed the help, and I've been enjoying working on the committee so far. It was Uncle Hugh's idea, actually. He thought I'd be a good choice since I was a parade sweetheart once upon a time."

My dad nods but says nothing as his gaze sweeps over my pile of binders.

"Ed," my mom says quietly. Something unspoken passes between them.

"What?" My head swivels back and forth between my parents. "Dad, I thought you'd be glad to hear I stepped up to help more. Mom thinks it's a good idea."

"I am glad," he says, followed by a sigh that doesn't sound glad at all. "But do the other committee members realize you're not here to stay?"

"I'm sure they do." I swallow. Then a lead ball settles in the pit of my stomach when I realize I'm not exactly sure of this fact at all. "It didn't specifically come up in the meeting, but everyone in town knows I'm only here for a visit."

"They also know that there was a possible promotion waiting for you back in Manhattan, but that you gave that option up to stay here for the holidays."

"Exactly. *For the holidays*," I repeat.

But even as I'm saying it, I get my dad's point. It's possible that my behavior in the past few days has been sending mixed messages. I've accepted the well-meaning nominations of people I care about for a volunteer position that by its very nature extends into next year. I've adopted a dog knowing full well that my apartment back in the city has a no-pet policy. I haven't bothered checking in with my boss at Windsor to let her know I'm not coming in for an interview. I've been too busy peppering the town with snowmen.

I've also nearly kissed Aidan. *Twice.*

But he knows I'm not staying permanently. I've made that very clear. I'm sure I have.

"I'm always proud of you, sweetheart. Your mom and I are both thrilled at how much you're enjoying your time here at home, and I am so glad to see that you want to spend some of that time helping others." My father smiles, but it doesn't quite reach his eyes.

It seems I'm not the only one who's newly aware of the ticking clock.

Everything has been happening so fast. Have I really been back in my hometown for a week already?

"It's okay, Dad. I'll make sure my intentions are clear. The last thing I want to do is disappoint anyone." I push back from the table and wrap my arms around him, hugging him tight while Fruitcake prances in a circle around us, tail wagging against our legs.

I pull away when I hear the shutter of a cell phone camera. "Mom, what are you doing?"

She holds up her iPhone. "Look at the three of you—it was such a sweet moment. I had to capture it."

The photo puts a lump in my throat, and I think that maybe the reason I haven't reminded everyone I'm leaving so soon after Christmas is because I'm not ready to go, a thought that's only just occurring to me now. And I'm pretty sure a handful of days isn't going to make a difference.

"Can you text it to me?" I give my mom a wobbly grin. "I want to make it the wallpaper on my phone."

"Sure, honey." She taps the screen of her cell and seconds later, my phone chimes with her incoming message.

"And now I'm off to bed," Mom says, slipping her phone into the pocket of her bathrobe before gathering her teacup and heading toward the bedroom.

"Me, too." Dad yawns. "Good night, sweetheart."

"Night-night," I say, and the sight of them walking past our glittering Christmas tree and down the hall together makes me feel unexpectedly wistful.

The holidays are passing in a blur, and soon

Christmas will be over. No more snowmen, maybe even no more charms.

Fruitcake lets out a tiny whine and nudges his head beneath my hand the way he always does when he thinks I need extra-special attention. How have I gone so long without a dog in my life? I bend down to hug his thick neck. Warm, golden fur tickles my cheek.

"I'm not ready," I whisper.

He swivels his soft brown eyes in my direction. There are questions shining in his gaze—questions I have no idea how to answer. I fumble with the silver charm bracelet and marvel at how much has changed in only a matter of days.

I might never be ready to leave this all behind.

Chapter Fifteen

THE FOLLOWING DAY, I START checking off items on my to-do list of things that need to get done before the parade kicks off the day after tomorrow. All the town permits have already been obtained, and I've organized them behind a special tab in my binder. The parade route is set, and the firefighters on duty tomorrow night have already agreed to set up signs so all the participants are clear on where they're supposed to go. Best of all, we've already surpassed our goal for the amount of toys we've collected for children in need. Check, check and check.

I flip through the planning binder again and again, ticking off more boxes on my list as I go. Before long, when I look out the window of the coffee shop where I've set up camp for the day, I see that the sky is growing dark. I've been sitting here far longer than I'd realized. The lights on the big Christmas tree at the top of the hill shimmer in the twilight. The streets of Owl

Lake turn lavender and then brilliant purple as early evening shadows sweep across the snow.

I glance across the street toward Enchanted Jewels, and squint at the sign still propped in the corner window. *Going out of business.* At the meeting the other day, Susan mentioned the shop was for sale, though. Until that moment, I hadn't realized the buyer might be open to selling the business.

Fruitcake lets out a snuffle, dragging my attention back to the task at hand. I don't know why I'm thinking about Enchanted Jewels, anyway. I've got enough on my plate to deal with between now and the parade, not to mention Christmas the following day. Plus I've already got a train ticket back to the city—to my life and my job in Manhattan.

And my apartment that doesn't allow pets, I think, reaching down to scratch Fruitcake behind his ears.

"I know, buddy. You've been so patient today. We should pack up and go for a little walk, hmm?"

He scrambles to his feet, and the patron at the table next to us smiles. Dogs are welcome pretty much everywhere in Owl Lake, and Fruitcake's fan club seems to be growing by the day. I suppose if I had to, it would be really easy to find him a new home. But just the thought of telling him goodbye makes me feel sick to my stomach.

Maya and I will just have to find a new place to live after the holidays. Someplace pet friendly and available immediately—in the most expensive city in the United States. That's possible, isn't it?

Only a person with a magic charm bracelet could believe in that sort of Christmas miracle.

I sigh, gather my binder in my arms and take my

empty coffee cup to the front counter as Fruitcake trots beside me at the end of his leash. We bid goodbye to the barista and then make our way outside. A frosty wind sends ripples through Fruitcake's golden fur, but the cold air on my face feels good. I lift my gaze to the sky, where stars twinkle against the deepening darkness. Yet another thing I've forgotten since I've been away—the breathtaking beauty of a starlit sky.

My gaze flits toward Enchanting Jewels again, and Fruitcake cocks his head at me, tail wagging like a pendulum.

"Don't even think it. There's not a single charm on my bracelet shaped like a jewelry store," I mutter, and then my phone rings, so I turn my back on the quaint jewelry shop and answer it.

"Hey, Ash." Aidan's voice come through the line, and I feel like I'm in high school again. We used to spend hours on the phone back then. We actually talked instead of texting.

"Hi." My smile creeps into my tone, and I tell myself to calm down. Aidan isn't about to ask me to prom. This call is sure to be parade-related.

"I just got off duty and I'm about to deliver a load of donated toys to a church up in North Pole. Pastor Mike, the head clergyman up there, is a friend of mine. We've got several boxes of things for the community served by his chapel. I'm pretty sure your dad once told me you always loved North Pole when you were a kid." He lets out a low laugh that sends shivers coursing through me. *It's just the cold air,* I try to tell myself. *Sure it is.* "I figured it's been a while since you've been there, so I thought you might want to tag along."

He's not talking about *the* North Pole, obviously.

North Pole, New York, is a tiny hamlet only fifteen miles or so from Owl Lake, best known for its Santa's Workshop theme park. The park has been around since the 1940s, so it's not sleek or modern by today's standards. I haven't quite thought of it like this before, but I suppose it could be considered vintage.

"I'd love to," I say. I haven't been to North Pole since I was probably ten years old, and I'm sure what Aidan is suggesting is more of a glorified errand than a date, but I'm tingling with anticipation, all the same.

The feeling goes away when reality sets in and I remember my dad's concerns from last night. I still need to remind Aidan that I'm going back to the city right after Christmas.

"I'll come get you at the lake house in ten minutes?" Aidan says.

"Actually, I was just leaving the coffee shop if you want to pick me up here." I glance down at Fruitcake, who's regarding me with his melting puppy dog eyes. "Fruitcake is with me, though."

"Fruitcake is more than welcome to tag along," Aidan says.

We hang up, and I'm struck by how happy he sounded. Even though he's moving straight from his shift to more work in a volunteer capacity, I can sense a change in him. He's letting down his guard and letting life in. I can feel it. I just wish I didn't have to remind him that I'm leaving so soon. The timing is admittedly terrible. But maybe I'm overthinking things. I've never told Aidan I was staying in Owl Lake for good. He knows I'm committed to my job—so committed that I ran myself ragged trying to get into Manhattan for days on end. He can't possibly be surprised to hear I'm going back once Christmas is over.

Minutes later, I'm once again sitting in the passenger seat of an OLFD vehicle. We're in the small SUV again, and the back of it is piled high with cardboard boxes containing Christmas gifts collected by the firefighters and the toy parade. The community church we're visiting in North Pole will be distributing them to families on Christmas morning.

I've never thought much about the way the toy parade works and the mostly anonymous role the fire department plays in getting so many presents into the hands of children who might otherwise never have a gift to open on Christmas morning. There's very little public attention given to the organizers—and that's deliberate. The firefighters truly want to keep the focus on the children. I think it's one of the things that makes the toy parade's charity mission so special.

I take a sideways glance at Aidan as he maneuvers the SUV onto the state highway that leads to North Pole. He's relaxed, with his elbow propped on the armrest, casually holding onto the steering wheel with just two fingers.

I smile to myself and burrow further into the soft leather seat. "Thanks for asking me to come along. You're right. I haven't been out this way in a long time."

Fruitcake's head pops between us from the back seat, panting softly, and he almost looks like he's grinning. Aidan gives his chest a sweet pat, and before I know it, the dog's chin is resting contentedly on Aidan's shoulder. They look so cute together that I have trouble forcing my next words out.

"Aidan, you know I'm still going back to New York after Christmas, right?" I focus intently on the dashboard in front of me because I'm not sure I can take it if Aidan slips back into character as the cranky action hero who first found me at the Owl Lake train station.

A quiet moment passes between us. The only sounds I hear are the crunch of the snow beneath the tires as Aidan pulls into the church's parking lot and Fruitcake's happy sighs.

The vehicle rolls to a halt in front of a small country chapel with a tall white steeple rising into the velvety night sky. Beyond the church, in the distance, I can see the carousel at the amusement park spinning round and round. The poles are painted red and white like candy canes, and instead of carousel horses, the children are sitting on pretty painted reindeer. They move gracefully up and down as the carousel spins, and it almost seems like they're flying.

"Beautiful, isn't it?" Aidan says, and there's an unexpected tenderness to his tone that squeezes my heart so hard that I press the heel of my hand against my breastbone to try and ease it.

He knows I'm leaving. He couldn't possibly forget, but it's okay. I can tell that any hard feelings that lingered between us are gone, which should come as an immense relief. Somehow, though, the fact that my departure is a given hurts even more.

I'm a mess, basically. Why does being back home seem to get harder every day when it should be getting easier?

"Absolutely," I say, swallowing hard.

We climb out of the SUV and I follow Aidan around

to the trunk. It's not until he opens it and removes the first box that I realize what, exactly, we're delivering.

Teddy bears.

There must be dozens of them—boxes and boxes full of plush brown bears. I inhale a ragged breath, and my own six-year-old voice echoes in my consciousness.

And there should be cuddly teddy bears...

"Hey, is everything all right?" Aidan says, eyeing me with concern, with his arms full of bears. "Where'd you go just now?"

Jingle, jingle.

The bracelet chimes its familiar tune, but this time it doesn't feel magical at all. What have I been doing? Why have I been making snowmen left and right, trying to force my way to the happy ending charm when getting to the end of the bracelet will mean an end to the Christmas of my dreams? There are only a few charms left, and I think I'm just beginning to realize the implications of what will happen when they eventually run out.

Everything comes to an end eventually. My days in Owl Lake are numbered, and each chime of the bracelet is like a countdown, reminding me this is all little more than a dream. Real life awaits.

"Everything is fine," I say. "I'm right here."

For now.

The inside of the church smells like a combination of incense, flowers and lemony furniture polish. I take a deep inhale, letting the comforting scents soothe my fragile emotional state. It's so serene here, so quiet. Nothing at all like the massive St. Patrick's Cathedral on 5th Avenue in Manhattan. I like to drop by there on my lunch hour sometimes to say a prayer or light a candle. It makes me feel closer to God, but not like this. The cathedral may be grand and beautiful, but it's harder to sense God's presence in a massive cathedral packed with tourists than in a quiet country chapel with only a dozen or so rows of pews.

Or maybe that's just me. Maybe I'm more aware of a presence larger than myself here in the Adirondacks, nestled among snow-swept mountains and forests so thick they seem to go on forever.

I glance up at the stained glass windows, where snowflakes pitter-patter against the colorful glass, casting kaleidoscope shadows on the chapel walls in watercolor shades of blues, pinks and violets. Aidan shifts the box of teddy bears in his arms, and when I glance over at him, I'm struck once again by the startling blue of his eyes, as breathtakingly beautiful as stained glass, hidden deep within the evergreens.

"Aidan, good to see you," someone says from the back of the chapel, and when I turn around, I can't help but laugh.

The man who has just entered from the side door off the main chapel—Pastor Mike, I presume—is dressed in an odd combination of Christmas attire. He's got a clerical collar around the neck of his simple black shirt, but on top of his regular clergy uniform, he's wearing an oversized felt Santa suit. Plus, there's a pair of black leather ice skates slung over his shoulder, dangling by the laces. It's as if he took every item of clothing in a Victorian Christmas village and piled them all on at once. I do a double take and then let out a giggle. I can't quite help it.

"I know," he says, gesturing toward his outfit. "It's a lot of look, isn't it?"

"That it is, my friend," Aidan says.

He deposits his box of bears onto a nearby pew and shakes Pastor Mike's hand in greeting, but Mike pulls him into a man-hug that Aidan doesn't seem quite prepared for. Still, there's clearly a warmth between them. I'm happy that Aidan has friends and people in his life who care about him, but it's also strange to think about everything he's experienced since I left. Especially now that the feelings swirling between us are starting to feel all too familiar.

"Mike, this is Ashley." Aidan takes the box from my arms and piles it on top of his while Pastor Mike and I exchange pleasantries.

"Ah, Ashley." Mike's gaze flits between Aidan and me, and the corner of his mouth twitches into a half grin. "I've heard a lot about you."

This comment pleases me far more than it should. Doubly so when I glance at Aidan and notice that the tips of his ears are almost as red as Pastor Mike's Santa suit.

"What's with the skates?" Aidan asks, arching a brow as he takes in the entirety of Mike's outfit. "Not to mention the rest of it. I've never seen you in a felt beard before."

"It suits me, don't you think?" Mike says, stroking a hand down the ridiculous oval of felt strapped to his chin with clearly visible elastic. It's the worst fake beard I've ever set eyes on. By far.

"Absolutely," Aidan deadpans. "You should wear it to your next Sunday sermon."

"I will, so long as you wear yours the next time you save a kitten in a tree." Pastor Mike waggles his eyebrows. A challenge.

Aidan's eyes narrow. "Mine?"

"Yes, yours. You and Ashley are here just in time for North Pole's first annual Santa Skate. I've got a pair of Santa suits set aside for you two, if you're up for it," Mike says.

I glance at Aidan, but he seems just as clueless as I am.

He cocks his head. "Dare I ask what a Santa Skate is, exactly?"

"One frozen pond and dozens of townspeople dressed as Santa, all skating in circles to Christmas music under a perfect, starlit sky for a few magical hours." Mike shrugs. "Sounds like fun, right?"

He had me at magical.

"Yes!" I blurt without waiting for input from Aidan. "We're in."

Aidan glances over at me. "We are?"

"Totally." I grin up at him, despite the nervous flutter in my belly.

There are only four charmed wishes left on my bracelet that haven't come true yet, and one of them is an ice skate. If I'm trying to slow things down and make my magical Christmas last as long as I possibly can, I should be running for the hills.

But so far, most of what Aidan and I have done together has been Aidan's doing. He's the one who invited me to classic movie night, albeit with a little prompting from Josh. The whole reason we're here in North Pole right now is because Aidan called and asked me to come with him. He's also the one who brought up our past and opened the door for us to finally talk about our breakup, whereas I'm the one who keeps running away every time things get serious.

I want to finally show Aidan how much I love spending time with him, even though that time is running out faster than I can stand. Besides, I've pretty much turned into a professional snowman architect and the snowman charm has still refused to chime. I'm beginning to think the bracelet has plans of its own. Maybe we can put on Santa suits, take a spin around the North Pole pond and nothing will happen at all. It's possible, right?

"Let's do it." I nod. I haven't been on skates in years, but how hard can it be? It's probably just like riding a bicycle.

Deep down inside, a nagging voice interrupts my shining optimism. You were never that great at cycling either, remember?

I ignore the warning, because the thought of seeing Aidan on skates, donning a felt beard like the one Pastor Mike is currently wearing, is too good to resist.

"All right, then," Aidan says, and the way his face lights up makes me forget all about the conversation we had in the car just moments ago.

My days in Owl Lake might be numbered, but I'm determined to live every one of them to the fullest.

Chapter Sixteen

M Y SANTA SUIT IS AT least three sizes too big, but by some Christmas miracle, the rental stand at the North Pole skating pond has one last pair of white skates in my size. I do my best not to notice that they look exactly like the silver skate charm dangling from the bracelet on my wrist, but there's no mistaking the ache in the back of my throat. The resemblance is unmistakable.

It doesn't mean anything, I tell myself. All skates look alike.

Except Aidan's skates don't resemble mine in the slightest. When he meets me at our designated picnic table at the edge of the pond, the pair of skates in his hands are made of black leather instead of white, and the blades are long and sleek, like runners on a sleigh.

"All they had left in my size was hockey skates," he says as he drops down beside me on the worn wooden bench.

Fruitcake greets Aidan as if a year has passed since

he's last seen him, even though it's been all of five minutes. Everyone at the skating pond is dressed in matching Santa suits, but there's no fooling Fruitcake. He knows Aidan immediately.

"Hey, boy." Aidan grins and ruffles the scruff of golden fur on the dog's chest. Watching the two of them together never fails to tug on my heartstrings.

"Can you make it around the ice in those things?" I narrow my gaze at Aidan's skates. "They look dangerous."

Maybe this wasn't such a great idea after all. The sight of countless Santas gliding in slow-moving circles around the ice is undeniably charming. An old Johnny Mathis song drifts from the loudspeakers with dreamy lyrics that promise a marshmallow world in the winter—a whipped-cream day—and the commingled scents of hot cocoa and fresh snow hang heavy and delicious in the air. But now that I'm up close and personal to a real pair of skates, I'm beginning to doubt my ability to complete a lap around the pond in an upright position. I'm certain I can't skate and sip hot chocolate at the same time.

"No problem. I played in a peewee hockey league when I was little." Aidan shoots me a wink as he gets his skates on faster than I can make sense of the laces on my own pair.

I can't believe I didn't know Aidan played hockey as a little boy, but it makes perfect sense. Hockey is huge here in upstate New York. And I have to admit that I kind of love that we're still discovering things about each other, even after all this time. Aidan never fails to surprise me, and the charm bracelet has made me realize that not all surprises are bad. In fact, I'm beginning to like them. A lot.

"Here, let me help you get laced up." Aidan kneels in the fresh snow and reaches for my foot.

His hand around my ankle is warm and sure. A shiver flutters through me that has nothing to do with snowy weather. I bury one of my hands in Fruitcake's soft fur, hoping to steady my galloping heartbeat. My dog rests his chin on my lap, and I feel like three of us could be a cozy scene on a glittery Christmas card.

The fluffy ball dangling from Aidan's Santa hat falls in front of his eyes, and he bats it away. I laugh, and he pulls a face. Then our eyes meet, and my stomach does a little tumble. How does he manage to make a tacky Santa suit look so good?

"You look cute in that silly thing," he says, mouth curving into a teasing grin as he nods at my own Santa outfit.

"It's swallowing me whole," I counter. Seriously, how am I supposed to skate like this? "I'm going to end up tripping over it and sliding all over that ice like Bambi. It's not going to be pretty."

Aidan laughs, and the low, masculine sound of it seems to tickle the insides of my ribs.

I bite my bottom lip. "Whose idea was this, anyway?"

Mine. I know it was. It sounded so whimsical and romantic at the time—like a whipped-cream evening, as Johnny Mathis might say. I should probably stop getting enchanted by the idea of a perfect holiday date and concentrate on living in the real world. The last time I thought I was going to have the ultimate Christmas date, I ended up breaking up with my boyfriend of three years. I'm still haunted by the thought of mozzarella cheese.

But the breakup was truly for the best, and my time in Owl Lake has felt far more like a dream than actual reality, thanks to the bracelet.

"This was your idea, darling," Aidan says, and the endearment make me feel warm all over. I'm practically baking inside my Santa suit. "And it was a good one. Don't you know by now that I'd never let you fall?"

Well, then.

Perhaps this experience won't be such a disaster, after all. My gaze swivels toward the pond, and there are skating Santas as far as my eyes can see. This is madness—sweet, hilarious madness. Pastor Mike was right. The Santa Skate is pure Christmas magic.

The clergyman wizzes past us with outstretched airplane arms and a look of mild terror on his face. Aidan calls out to him, and he waves wildly at us until his balance starts to falter. He lurches forward a few steps, then seems to regain his footing. I am so not ready for this.

Aidan ties my laces into triple-knots, then stands and pulls me to my feet. I let out a squeal.

"Ready?" He waggles his eyebrows. Fruitcake woofs as if he thinks watching us out on the frozen pond is going to be every bit as entertaining as the Ice Capades.

I push my Santa hat further back on my head and nod. "As ready as I'll ever be."

Aidan wraps his big hand around mine, and we head toward the pond. I'm a little wobbly on my skates, and we haven't even hit the ice yet. But then I step tentatively onto the frozen surface of the pond and within seconds, we're gliding, hand-in-hand.

It feels like we're floating. Our skates slide against the ice in perfect unison, and it's like Aidan and I are dancing, only better. It's so serene, and everyone around us is smiling and laughing—a merry, moving blur of holiday cheer. This is even better than I pictured it. A whipped-cream date, indeed.

We're surrounded by Santas. There are Santa couples, skating hand-in-hand like Aidan and me, tiny tot Santas and entire families, linked arm-in-arm. I've never seen anything like it before. I wonder briefly why the skating rink at Rockefeller Center hasn't hosted something like this, but I dismiss the thought as quickly as it comes. The Santa Skate belongs in North Pole. It's the perfect place for this.

I take a deep breath as we head into the first turn, and cold air prickles my lungs, like I've just taken a big bite out of a snow cone. My ankles wobble like crazy, but Aidan grips my hand tighter and we make it safely around. In the center of the pond, one of the Santas leaps into the air and then lands on the ice with one foot, executing a graceful pirouette. The crowd erupts into a huge cheer.

Aidan gives my hand a squeeze and when I glance over at him, the wind against my face makes my eyes water. At least that's what I choose to believe, because if I'm so happy that I'm crying, I won't be able to leave this marshmallow world when Christmas is over, no matter what kind of promises I've made or how many times I've reminded everyone that I don't really live in Owl Lake anymore.

Aidan blinks against the wind. His eyes look just as

shiny and wet as mine feel as he lifts my hand to his lips and presses a gentle kiss to my mitten. His earlier promise spins round and round in my head, like a skater twirling on ice.

Don't you know by now that I'd never let you fall?

It's too late, though. I'm already falling...I've been falling for Aidan Flynn all over again since the moment I saw him outside of the toy store back in the city.

I blink hard, then the blade on my right skate hits a groove in the ice. The lovely, floating feeling in my chest winds itself into a tight ball of panic. My feet seem to slide in completely opposite directions.

I'm going down. I just know it.

I let go of Aidan's hand and windmill my arms, trying to regain control, but it feels like the pond is turning sideways. Somewhere above the Christmas carols and the scrape of skates against the ice, I hear Fruitcake barking in alarm. I look toward the picnic tables where he's waiting for us, as loyal and obedient as ever. It's okay, I try to tell him with my eyes. Don't worry about me, I'm fine.

But then my feet slide out from under me and I go airborne.

It all happens too fast for me to scream. All I can do is close my eyes and wait to slam into the ice. But the moment of impact never comes. Instead, I feel a pair of warm, solid arms catch me on my way down.

I gasp, and when my eyes flutter open, I'm clutching the front of Aidan's Santa suit for dear life as he cradles me against his chest. He's still gliding along with the rest of the Santas, carrying me in his arms and smiling down at me.

"I told you I'd catch you," he says.

I'm sparkling inside. "You sure did."

Jingle, jingle.

A tiny piece of my heart breaks at the special ring of another charm come to life, but it's hard to be sad, even though it means there are only three charms left. I'm scared to fall. I've done it before, and it ended in disaster. But there's a candy-cane breeze in my hair, my cheek is nestled against Aidan's shoulder and we're surrounded by Christmas magic on ice.

Maybe it's okay to let myself go, just this once.

Later that night, I sit on my bed and pull out the bag of broken jewelry that Susan gave me from Enchanted Jewels. I can't sleep. Dozens of Santas are skating through my head, and I can't stop thinking about Aidan gathering me into his arms so I wouldn't fall on my face. I have to find a way to occupy my restless mind and emotions, so I do what I always do whenever I'm troubled—lose myself in a collection of abandoned treasures. Running a polishing cloth over the neglected pieces is soothing. Rubbing away the tarnish feels like ridding the vintage treasures of the ravages of time.

Hours into the chore, I find a pocket watch near the bottom of the bag. It's sterling silver, with swirls etched onto the back of its clock face and a serpentine chain. I turn it over in my hands, examining it. It's missing its cover—a casualty of years gone by—but when I wind it up, it clicks a steady beat, ticking out the minutes one by one. My heart does a little leap. I can't believe it still works.

I shine it until it's perfect, my hands moving swiftly over the silver. Times passes in a pleasant, hazy blur as I gently remove layer upon layer of neglect, and when I glance at my phone and see how late it is, my fingertips go still. I sit back to rest against the pillows and take inventory of all the work I've done. It's a lot, but as usual when I'm tinkering with my vintage jewelry finds, it didn't feel like work.

Time never passes this quickly when you're at Windsor.

I start to pick everything up, wrapping the newly shined pieces carefully in a terrycloth bath towel instead of tossing them back into the bag. When I get to the pocket watch, I pause, wondering what I might have on hand that I could fashion into a substitute cover. If I can find something just right, it might make a nice Christmas present for Aidan.

I'm not sure what I could use, though. And Christmas Eve is the day after tomorrow, so making the watch into something special for Aidan by that time seems unlikely. But as I climb beneath the covers, I vow to give it some thought.

My time would probably better be spent working on parade logistics, but hours spent creating never feel wasted. I wonder why that is?

Maybe because my mom is right, and deep down, I *do* wish I was doing something other than working in the charms department. I always meant to start an Etsy shop for my designs, like I'd mentioned to Betty on the train. Somehow that never happened, though. There just didn't seem to be enough hours in the day, while working a full-time job and spending time with Jeremy.

Betty hadn't seemed all that impressed with the Etsy idea, though. She told me to dream bigger, which seemed ridiculous at the time. I do dream big, don't I? Isn't dreaming big what got me to Manhattan and to Paris...almost? What dreams could be bigger or better than that?

I thought that was how I felt, but the longer I'm home, the more content I become and the more I question whether my dreams have been pointing me in the right direction or not. It's been days since I've wondered what I might be missing in the city or what fabulous thing Jeremy is probably doing in France.

I cradle the pocket watch in my hands. It fits perfectly in the center of my palm, and the sensation is almost familiar. Then I pull open the drawer of my nightstand and spot a glimpse of something almost the same size and shape as the pocket watch among my childhood trinkets. And I understand right away—I know just what to do with Aidan's gift. A warm glow blossoms deep inside of me, along with a most inconvenient truth.

The reason I've stopped wondering what I'm missing in New York is because I'm not missing anything at all. When I'm in Manhattan, I rarely have uninterrupted hours like this to create. I always feel like I'm stealing extra minutes here and there. What I've really missed is this—making my own designs and the feeling I get when I make a new memory out of an old one.

I'm just not sure what to do about it.

I look at the charms on my bracelet, searching for answers. The silver teddy bear glints in the light from my bedside lamp. Susan wondered if the charms on my bracelet were supposed to teach me something, and deep down inside, I know that if there's a lesson to the teddy bear charm, it's this—that time keeps moving forward, one minute at time.

Just like a pocket watch with a wind-up spring.

I scarcely have to time to breathe for the next thirty-six hours, much less ponder the intricacies of time. The toy parade consumes almost every waking minute. My favorite duty of all is delivering two glittering snowflake tiaras to Susan's house for Sophie and Olivia, who have been unanimously chosen by the parade committee to be the Firefighters' Sweethearts this year. For the first time ever, we'll have two instead of one.

The girls are positively thrilled—so thrilled that they insist on making matching snowmen and topping both their frosty heads with the tiaras, just to try them out "to see if they work." I take an absurd amount of pictures, intent on capturing as many memories as possible to take with me back to the city. It's such a precious moment that I'm caught off guard when my charm bracelet chimes twice in rapid succession.

Jingle, jingle.

Jingle, jingle.

Sophie and Olivia's laughter is the only thing that keeps my panic at bay.

I know it's silly. Last week, I tried everything I could to remove the bracelet from my wrist—to free myself from the Christmas magic that did nothing but confuse and unsettle me. For a minute there, I might have even been ready to take a hammer to my own arm. Thank goodness I came to my senses.

And then, once I saw the home movie and realized my girlhood Christmas dreams were coming true, one by one, all I could think about was little me's wish for a fairy-tale ending. A happy-ever-after.

The engagement ring charm was right there, and all I could think about was what it might mean. But as I arrive at the fire station on the afternoon of the Fire-fighters' Toy Parade, my very first thought is that now the engagement ring charm is the only one left.

I wish that there were more. This has been the best Christmas I've ever had, and I don't want it to end, happy-ever-after notwithstanding. But things are completely out of my control. That's how it works with magic, isn't it? Wishing for more charms would be like using a magic wish to wish for more wishes. As little as I actually know about Betty, I'm one hundred positive she would agree.

The fire engines are all decked out in Christmas lights and loaded down with bags of candy canes to toss into the crowds. Homemade floats representing the local businesses from Main Street are lined up, ready to go. The old Ford pickup that belongs to the owner of Mountain Candy pulls a trailer decorated with thousands upon thousands of silk flowers bunched together in the shape of various candies. Tall lollipops wobble to and fro in the winter wind. Pete from Pete's Auto Shop is dressed as Buddy the Elf, sitting atop a refurbished Cadillac.

Everywhere I look, I see small-town charm—pure and simple love of a community that comes together every Christmas to celebrate the most magical time of the year. It's definitely not the Macy's Thanksgiving Day Parade.

It's better.

Only one thing is missing—Aidan. I can't seem to find him anywhere, and I was hoping to give him his Christmas gift before the parade starts. Uncle Hugh has taken command of the bullhorn, and he's running this show like clockwork. But Aidan and I are supposed to be giving the final go-ahead. He's got to be around here somewhere.

With just minutes to go before the ladder truck starts things off, I find him. He's stretching an old fire-hose along the start of the parade route, using it as a makeshift barrier to keep the crowd safe. Always the hero.

"Aidan, can I talk to you for a quick second?" My heart is in my throat all of a sudden. Is now really the right time to do this?

Yes, I think, imagining the ticking of the pocket watch I'm about to give him. Time is slipping by. Who knows when the last charm will jingle? It could be at any second. I may not get another chance.

"Ashley, hey." His whole face lights up at the sight of me. Heat radiates through my chest in spite of the snowflakes drifting through the air. "I think we're about ready, don't you?"

"Yes, but I have something for you first." I'm holding a small wrapped package behind my back, and when I present it to him, he tips his head to the side and regards me thoughtfully. My breath catches in my throat, and I feel bashful all of a sudden. Vulnerable, like Fruitcake would probably feel if he accidentally broke free from his leash.

"Merry Christmas," I say, and it comes out far more breathy than I intended. Why is this so difficult? It's only a Christmas gift.

Probably because it's more than just a simple gift. It means something. My hands start to tremble, so once he takes the wrapped package, I shove them into my coat pockets, out of view. Aidan means something.

"Thank you." His eyes fill with warmth. "You want me to open it now?"

I nod, because I don't quite trust myself to speak.

He removes the shiny giftwrap with care, and when he lifts the lid from the box, the pocket watch rests face-down on a bed of tissue paper. He glances up at me, and I smile. Our gazes stay locked for a quiet, breathless moment, and the tender look in his gaze seems to wrap itself around me like a blanket. He knows this gift isn't something I've bought from a store. It's a tiny piece of my heart, wrapped up in red paper. Just for him.

The parade is set to wind its way through Owl Lake any minute, but it feels like time has somehow come to a standstill. We're caught in a tremulous moment, a sublime season that's no longer part of our past, but isn't quite the future either. It's just us, Aidan and me, in the here and now. And I realize if I had one more Christmas wish, it would be to stay here where things are simple and uncomplicated for as long as we possibly can. But I don't even know what a wish or a charm like that would look like. I only know how it feels—like a gift from a Secret Santa, like snowfall on Christmas morning, like midnight on New Year's Eve.

Like every sort of holiday magic all rolled into one.

Aidan smiles into my eyes, and my head spins like it did when he turned me in circles on the ice at the Santa Skate. Then he slowly turns his attention back to his gift. When he turns the pocket watch over, his gaze goes painfully wistful at what he sees.

"It's my dad's old firefighter badge," I say, although that's obvious. It's light gold, with the seal of the OLFD etched onto its center in deep red enamel. An axe, a ladder, a helmet and a fire hydrant are positioned in each corner, and my dad's badge number—seventy-one—is engraved at the top. "From when he was a rookie. He used to let me play with it when I was a kid. The pocket watch was missing its cover and I wanted to find something special to replace it with. Something just for you."

The air around us is filled with lacy snowflakes and crackling anticipation. Now, more than ever, I wish I could tell what Aidan was thinking.

He shakes his head, and his Adam's apple bobs in his throat. "Ashley, I don't know what to say."

But I do. I've been practicing the words for hours in my head.

"You know how much my dad loves you. He wants you to have it. I talked to him about it and he adored the idea—especially when I told him how important it was to me. The past few days have meant a lot to me, Aidan. More than I can put into words, really." I feel more self-conscious right now than if I were standing on Main Street dressed as one of Santa's elves. "I wanted to give you something special. I hope that's okay."

Aidan's eyes sparkle, and I feel warm all over.

"Of course it's okay." He presses the watch to his heart, and the gesture is so poignant that I can't bear it. "Thank you."

"Merry Christmas," I say, and my voice goes all wobbly. I've never been great at hiding my emotions, but being back in Owl Lake has reduced me to a raw nerve of feelings and hope, want and expectation, too rich and sharp to keep under wraps. Or maybe it's not Owl Lake. Maybe it's just me, remembering what it feels like to want to kiss someone so badly that I can barely think straight.

"Merry Christmas," he says, and as he takes a step closer, his gaze drops to my lips.

He feels it too, then—this heady, glittering pull between us. It's not just me. It's us–Ashley and Aidan. Years are slipping away, one by one, and this time, neither one of us is doing a thing to stop it.

This is it. This is the moment when we're finally going to kiss, and it's perfect. It's the exact right time. Just like the watch, we're making something new out of something lost and forgotten.

My pulse is racing, and I'm so happy I could cry. Visions of mistletoe dance in my head as I lean toward him, welcoming his warmth, his evergreen scent and the years of shared memories that dance in his eyes. This is where I belong...right here. Always and forever.

But just as Aidan lowers his head to mine, someone in the periphery calls my name.

"Ashley!"

Then my perfect Christmas kiss ends before it even begins as I realize who's walking toward me.

Jeremy.

Chapter Seventeen

I MUST BE IN SHOCK—*REAL* SHOCK, like during a medical emergency—because I can't seem to feel my limbs. I know everyone around me must be talking because I can see their mouths moving and I can see the children along the parade route clapping and cheering. But I don't hear any of it. My head is filled with a terrible roar, like the rumble of snow tumbling down a mountain during an avalanche.

I shake my head and do my best to will things back to normalcy. Jeremy can't be here. He's in Paris, on the other side of the world. There's got to be some mistake.

"Ashley, are you okay?" Jeremy laughs, as if his nonsensical appearance in Owl Lake is some sort of hilarious joke. He reaches to cup my elbow, and I'm so stunned that I let him. "I'm sorry to catch you off guard like this, but I wanted to surprise you."

Surprise me? I let out a shaky exhale. "Mission accomplished. I'm surprised."

And not in a good way. I'm more confused than

anything else, honestly. I sort of feel like one of the firefighters milling about should wrap me up in one of those silver space blankets they give people who've experienced a sudden loss of body heat.

The parade is seconds from starting, and I just gave Aidan his Christmas gift. There's still so much for us to talk about, so much to say. He was about to *kiss me*, for real this time, and now he's standing awkwardly between Jeremy and me, clearly feeling like a third wheel. My special moment with Aidan has been ruined, and now that Jeremy is here, I'm not sure we can get it back.

I glance in Aidan's direction, and when our eyes meet, I see him tuck the pocket watch I've just given him into his coat pocket. Out of sight.

His gaze flits toward Jeremy, and he extends his hand for a shake. "Hello, I'm Aidan Flynn. Welcome to Owl Lake."

"Jeremy Davis." Jeremy takes Aidan's hand and pumps it up and down without bothering to remove his fine leather gloves. He clearly has no clue who Aidan is or what he once meant to me. I know for a fact that we've talked about it, but like so much else about me, he seems to have neglected to pay any attention to the details.

How could I have possibly wanted to marry this man?

My eye flit once again toward Aidan, even though looking at him right now hurts. Any and all traces of Aidan's charming dimples vanish as he searches my gaze. He recognizes Jeremy's name, and he obviously wants to know why my ex-boyfriend is here in Owl

Lake when I told him Jeremy was spending Christmas in Paris.

Join the club. I shrug but Aidan turns to check on the fire truck getting into position at the parade's starting line before he can see it.

I've got to get control of this situation right now. Aidan and I have a job to do. Together. I gave him my word.

"Jeremy, the parade is just about to start, and we..." I gesture at the empty space between Aidan and me, which feels cavernous all of a sudden. "...we're in charge, and..."

My words are tumbling over one another, and the seconds are passing too quickly. Jeremy doesn't even seem to be listening. He's too busy grinning from ear to ear, reaching for my hands and squeezing them tight.

"Ashley! Aidan! There you are. Hugh is looking—" My dad's voice trails off as he walks up to our awkward trio. He does a double take at the sight of Jeremy, and his smile freezes in place. "Jeremy. This is, ah, certainly a surprise."

My mom bustles up beside him, with Fruitcake's candy cane–striped leash wrapped around her crocheted mittens. When she spots Jeremy, her mouth forms a perfect O of surprise.

"Look, honey." My dad's spine goes rigid and he draws in a long breath. "It's Jeremy."

"I can see that," Mom says, and then she reaches to give Jeremy a polite hug. "Merry Christmas, Jeremy. We thought you were in Paris!"

"I was." Jeremy nods. "And Paris is beautiful this time of year, as always. But it just wasn't right without Ashley."

He flashes me an apologetic smile, and it's the most contrite expression I've seen on his face in the entirety of our relationship.

"Oh." I shake my head. "You don't need to apologize."

He didn't actually apologize, though, I think. There's a difference between implying something and saying it out loud—a huge difference that I'm more aware of now than ever. If I'd had time to actually tell Aidan how I feel before Jeremy popped up, I wouldn't be feeling so terribly uncomfortable at the moment.

All I did was give him the watch and tell him the past few days have been special. I stopped short of saying the words that mattered most.

I still love you.

"That's okay. You'll see Paris next year." Jeremy winks at me, oblivious to the thoughts swirling through my head.

What is going on?

"It seems like you two have a lot to talk about. Why don't you stay here, Ashley? I've got the parade under control," Aidan says.

Wait.

I shake my head. That's not what I want at all. I know Aidan is only trying to be nice, but I don't want to stay here on the sidelines. I want to be right in the center of things, helping to run the parade, just like I promised. Just like I chose, when I made the decision to volunteer. I haven't seen a Firefighters' Toy Parade in what feels like an eternity, and I don't want to be a visitor in my hometown anymore. I want to be a part of it—this year and for many more years to come.

All of them, I realize as my throat goes tight. All of the years, the entirety of my Christmas future.

I've been running away from Owl Lake for as long as I can remember, searching for something I couldn't quite name. Adventure? Glamour? Excitement? I'm not even sure anymore. I just know that the closer I got to that ever-elusive something, the emptier I felt. I don't belong in Paris. I don't even belong in New York anymore. I belong right here, in the town I've loved with my whole heart for as long as I can remember.

"Um..." I remove my hands from Jeremy's. Has he been holding them this entire time?

But I don't have a chance to finish what I was going to say. Aidan doesn't even get the chance to turn and make his exit, because the moment I let go, Jeremy reaches into the pocket of his elegant black overcoat and pulls out a small, square Windsor-blue box.

My mom gasps and all my breath seems to leave my body in a sudden whoosh. Wordlessly, Jeremy drops down on one knee right there on the snowy sidewalk.

This is it—the scene playing out before me is the exact scenario I'd pictured in my head when Maya hinted that Jeremy was about to propose. Only instead of taking place in New York or Paris, it's happening in my hometown. In front of my parents and my dog and the greater population of Owl Lake.

In front of Aidan.

"Ashley, I should have never let you walk out of my life," Jeremy says.

Fruitcake, excited to find one of the humans kneeling down to his level, wags his entire back end, wiggles toward Jeremy and licks the side of his cheek. For some reason, I expect Jeremy to react with mild disgust, but he doesn't. He laughs it off.

A crowd is forming around us, intrigued by the sight of an unfamiliar, well-dressed man kneeling in the snow in front of one of their own. Women press hands to their chests and sigh with delight when they catch sight of the little blue box in Jeremy's hand. My parents, Aidan, Jeremy and I are immediately swept up in a chorus of oohs and ahhhs. Curious onlookers are pressing in on all sides, effectively blocking Aidan's exit. He's going to be forced to stick around and witness the rest of Jeremy's proposal.

And it's all so *wrong*. Everything about it feels wrong, from the way it's so quickly turning into a public spectacle to the fact that the man is kneeling down in front of me with a tiny velvet box in his hand is the wrong man.

Be careful what you wish for.

So much has changed since the day my train rolled into Owl Lake. Everything, really. Back then, I was secretly waiting for Jeremy to show up, tell me it was all a big mistake, and beg me to agree to be his wife. This proposal is everything I thought I wanted—so perhaps it's what I deserve.

"Ashley James, *veux-tu m'épouser, mon amour?*" Jeremy says, and then opens the ring box with a flourish.

A cushion-cut diamond solitaire in a pristine platinum setting glitters against a black velvet pillow. Somewhere behind me, a man says, "Whoa, look at that rock."

Someone in the vicinity groans. I'm pretty sure it's my dad. My mom elbows him sharply in the ribs.

I stare at the diamond in confusion, and it's only then that I realize that all the times I've imagined my proposal, the engagement ring in the box was never a fancy modern sparkler like this one. It was vintage rose gold. An antique, with a modest emerald-cut center stone, surrounded by a decorative halo of tiny diamond chips. A ring steeped in history, just like Aidan and me.

He's the man I've been waiting for, all this time.

I feel him stiffen beside me, and it takes every bit of courage I can muster to look at him. This isn't how Christmas Eve was supposed to go. We should be enjoying the parade together right now, and instead, Aidan has just watched another man ask me to marry him.

At least I think that's what Jeremy just asked me. I can't be one hundred percent certain, because I never quite got past the first French lesson on the language app on my phone. Maybe someplace deep down, I didn't want to go to Paris as badly as I thought I did.

"Ashley, sweetheart," my mom says. She gives me a tight smile, her subtle way of reminding me that Jeremy is still kneeling at my feet, waiting for an answer, while I'm desperately wishing I could turn back the clock to a time before he popped up in Owl Lake—maybe even farther back than that. Maybe I'd go all the way back to the night eight years ago when Aidan proposed.

My bottom lip starts to tremble, and I feel like I might cry. The time I've spent in my hometown this Christmas is too precious to me to wish it away. I've learned things about myself I never knew, and in many ways, I feel like Aidan and I are closer than we ever were before.

I've changed. He's changed. *We've* changed. We've grown into the people we were always meant to be— people we might never have become if we'd taken different paths in our lives.

As painful and embarrassing as this moment is, I know Aidan isn't going to stand by and let me walk away again. He said so himself.

I should have fought for you, Ash.

"I'm sure she's still just surprised," Jeremy says to my mom as he rises back to his feet. He's brimming with confidence at the thought of my unspoken yes. Or *oui*, as the case may be.

"Of course she is," Mom says in return, though she sounds a lot less certain.

Dad just shifts uncomfortably from one foot to the other. Fruitcake's tail has stopped wagging altogether.

But I'm barely paying attention, because my eyes have finally found Aidan's and what I see there causes my chest to constrict in a terrible, terrible way. The man who sat beside me in the Palace Theatre a few nights ago and whispered about all the ways he wished he'd done things differently has vanished. Action-hero Aidan stands in his place, more distant and closed off than I've ever seen him. His arms are crossed, and his eyes are cold and vacant. The angry knot of muscle in his jaw hasn't made an appearance since the day we collapsed beneath the mistletoe on the sidewalk outside of Pete's Auto Shop, but it's back in full force right now. There's not a trace of the vulnerability he's shown me in the past week.

He takes a backward step, and I can *feel* him slipping away.

I know better than to wish he'd tell me right here and now not to marry Jeremy. Aidan is a good man, and he'd never want to publicly humiliate someone like that, nor would he interfere with anyone else's relationship. I just need a tiny hint of reassurance, but he refuses to even meet my gaze.

Do something. Say something. Please. A bone-deep coldness sweeps over me, and even though I'm surrounded by so many people I know and love, I've never felt quite so alone.

The lights on the fire engine at the start line flash yellow and red. Caution! Emergency! But today is Christmas Eve, a time to celebrate. The people around us turn their attention toward the parade, now kicking into full swing. Uncle Hugh must have given up on Aidan and me.

He's not the only one. Aidan's last words before he disappears into the crowd are for Jeremy.

"Merry Christmas," he says quietly. "And congratulations."

I'm not marrying Jeremy, obviously.

Aidan might think I am, and in this incredibly awkward moment in time, Jeremy definitely thinks I am. I can't quite get a read on whether or not my parents think my answer will be yes, but frankly, I have far more important things to worry about right now—

starting with correcting Jeremy's misguided assumption that we will ever be man and wife.

Thankfully, the crowd of observers hovering around us has dispersed, with everyone's attention refocused on the parade. Mom and Dad have moved to the frontlines to see if Hugh needs any help with anything since he's taken over for Aidan and me. Main Street is lined with people on both sides, all the way from the firehouse to the inn at the top of the hill, where the parade will come to an end in the spot where the town Christmas tree stands.

Has it really only been a handful of days since I watched Aidan place the star atop that tree? It feels much longer, even though my time in Owl Lake seems to have passed in the blink of an eye.

"Your parents' dog is really friendly," Jeremy says, doing a quick sidestep out of Fruitcake's reach.

We're standing off to the side, away from the crowd and beneath the pretty white gingerbread trim of Mountain Candy. Over Jeremy's shoulder, I can see Enchanted Jewels, where the snowman that Susan and I made a few days ago still stands. He's crooked and uneven, much like the cookies I made on my first day back in town. I wouldn't have it any other way.

Fruitcake is attempting his famous nudge maneuver, prodding Jeremy's hand with his nose in hopes of being petted. For once, it's not working. Fruitcake's furry brow wrinkles in confusion as he peers up at me.

It's not you, it's him, I want to say. But first I need to clear the air with Jeremy. And as far as he and I are concerned, it's not him, it's me. I want a different sort of life than I thought I did a few weeks ago. I want a life with dog hair stuck to my jeans. I want cobblestone streets and old stone churches instead of skyscrapers and fancy Windsor-blue carpet. I want to design and make my own jewelry all day long instead of squeezing in time in spare minutes here and there after spending eight hours a day behind the charms counter. I want more nights steeped in the scent of my mom's peppermint tea, more evenings skating in a Santa suit by the light of the moon and quiet mornings by the lake listening to the ethereal birdsong of the owls.

My eyes fill with tears.

I want Aidan.

I blink my tears away and rest my hand on Fruitcake's broad, golden back. "Fruitcake doesn't belong to my parents. He's mine."

Jeremy frowns. "Who said anything about fruitcake?"

"You did." I ruffle Fruitcake's head. "Fruitcake is the dog's name, and he belongs to me."

"Um, I don't understand." Jeremy's gaze narrows. "You can't have a dog."

"Yes, I can..." I take a deep breath. *Here it goes.* "... if I stay here instead of going back to Manhattan."

Jeremy's forehead creases. "But we can't stay here. Our jobs are in Manhattan. Our *lives* are there."

I nod, because he's just captured the essence of our dating relationship so perfectly. Our *lives*—his and mine. Never *our life, never truly something unified and equal.* Jeremy and I never shared the kind of closeness Aidan and I once did. I used to tell myself it was because young love was different and that I loved Jeremy differently but not less than I'd loved Aidan. Now I know the truth—I never really loved Jeremy at all. It's hard to give your heart away when it already belongs to someone else.

How could I have gotten things so wrong?

"Jeremy, let's sit down. We need to talk." I nod toward one of the pretty park benches situated by the walking trail surrounding the lake.

"Okay," Jeremy says, and he follows me until we're sitting on opposite ends of the bench with Fruitcake planted between us at our feet. The dog insisted. I'm pretty sure he knows what's coming. Call it canine intuition or just another spark of Christmas magic.

"I can't marry you," I say quietly, looking Jeremy straight in the eyes.

He blinks back at me as if I've just said something nonsensical. "I don't understand. The whole reason we broke up before I left for Paris was because you wanted to get married and I didn't. But I've given it some thought and decided I'll do it, since that's what you want. It's the whole reason I'm here."

"Right." I force myself to smile. "I know you ended your trip early and came all this way, but we're just not right for each other. Do you remember what you said to me that night at dinner before you left for Paris?"

His brow crinkles.

So I fill in the blanks. "You said 'marriage isn't for people like us,' and you were right."

"I was?"

"Well, mostly right. Marriage isn't for people like you—at least not now. You're not ready to get married, Jeremy, and that's okay. You said yourself that you're living your dream, and I don't want to take that away from you. You deserve someone who wants the same sort of life that you do, because the thing is..." I give him a tender smile. "I'm living a different dream."

He looks around, taking in the sight of the town I love so much—the snowcapped mountains and clusters of blue spruce trees, glistening with icicles, the quaint downtown area with its mom-and-pop shops and old fashioned theater—and the heart of it all, the frozen lake that sits at its center, silvery smooth like a mirror.

"This is really what you want?" he asks.

"Yes," I say without hesitation.

"Is this about the promotion? Because I could probably pull some strings and make sure you get equal consideration for it, even though you weren't able to apply for it in person."

I didn't realize he knew about the promotion, but it makes sense that he's been in touch with work while he's been away. He'd never completely step away from Windsor, even during the Christmas holidays. "Thank you. That's a very kind offer, but no. This doesn't have anything to do with the promotion."

"Well." He lets out a breath, and I get the feeling he's not too disappointed that I've turned him down. In fact, he seems a little relieved. "Maybe this is for the best."

Fruitcake swivels his head back and forth as if trying to keep up with the conversation.

Jeremy arches a brow. "I'm allergic to dogs."

Once we've agreed that we're better off as friends than life partners, Jeremy is anxious to get back to Manhattan. I half expect him to tell me that he's allergic to the Adirondacks as well as dogs, but if that's the case, he keeps the matter to himself. Lucky for him, there's one last train back to the city tonight.

In truth, I'm ready for him to go. I'm sure I've missed the parade by now, but it's still Christmas Eve. I want to meet my family and friends down at The Owl's Nest like we'd planned.

Of course, it won't be exactly like we planned. Aidan won't be there—I'm sure of it. And his absence will cut me to the quick. Where's Maya and her pint of her gingerbread ice cream when I really need her? I might have thought I was heartbroken after I broke up with Jeremy, but this time...

This time, I'm certain of it.

"Come on," I say, wrapping my arms around my midsection in an effort to hold myself together until Jeremy gets on a train and I can properly fall apart. Aidan and I are over, and this time, it feels permanent. If we can't find our way back to each other after a magical Christmas like this one, I'm not sure we ever will. "Fruitcake and I will walk you to the train station."

We follow the walking trail halfway around the lake until the station comes into view. It's all lit up for Christmas, with twinkle lights wrapped around the oversized grandfather clock out front and a cluster of evergreen trees, branches laden with snow, on the platform. I didn't even notice all these details when I first arrived in Owl Lake ten days ago, but I was a different person then.

"Pretty," Jeremy says, pausing in front of the train to gaze up at the lights and smile. "I can see why you love it here."

Fruitcake woofs his agreement, and I can't help but laugh. "I'm glad."

"I should get going, though." He glances down at the sleek silver watch strapped to his wrist. From Windsor, no doubt. "This is the last train, and it leaves in two minutes."

Wow, it's gotten late. I had no idea it was almost ten o'clock. The parade is definitely over. I've missed the entire thing, and suddenly, that realization makes me unfathomably sad.

"Go," I say, waving Jeremy toward the train.

He looks at me for long, quiet moment until his smile turns bittersweet. "Merry Christmas, Ashley."

And with a quick hug, Jeremy is gone. Just as he runs up the steps of the train, the horn blares, long and loud. I tuck my hands into my pockets and watch while it pulls away from the platform. I remember the last time I sat on that very train. I felt so lost, so adrift. Little did I know that the place I was traveling to would feel even more like home that it ever had before.

And to think it all started with a magic bracelet tucked into a handknit Christmas stocking that's hanging from the mantle back at home.

Fruitcake leans his solid weight against my legs. He's still here, the first of the charmed wishes to come true. Each of them taught me something new, and it's not until now, alone at the train station on Christmas Eve, that I finally admit to myself how much I'd hoped the last charm would have something to do with Aidan. I wanted that ring charm to represent our happy-ever-after together. I wanted it so much that it seems almost unbelievable that I was wrong.

"Wear this and have the Christmas of your dreams," I whisper into the cold, dark night.

And then I pull back the cuff of my coat to look at

the bracelet and run my fingertips over the charms that brought me back home...but it's not there. At first, I think it must have slipped further up my sleeve, so I search and search. I flail out of my coat. My stomach lurches and I feel like I might be sick. It can't be gone.

How can this be happening? Over and over again, I tried to open that clasp and it wouldn't budge. The bracelet can't be lost. It just can't.

Please, no. Please.

But it is, and there's no telling where I could have lost it. I've been all over town today. It could be anywhere, buried forever in the holiday snow.

Sorrow closes up my throat. My magical Christmas—the Christmas of my dreams—is officially over.

Chapter Eighteen

’M NOT SURE HOW LONG I sit there on the cold, hard ground of the train platform, weeping into scruff of Fruitcake's neck. It feels like hours, but when my phone buzzes with an incoming text from Susan, the time reads 10:21.

Just got seated at a table by the window at the Owl's Nest. Where are you?

A tear drips onto the screen of my phone as I type out my answer.

At the train station, but I'm on my way. See you in a few minutes.

I sniff and shove my phone back into the pocket of my coat. No doubt Susan thinks I'm engaged to Jeremy, just like everyone else in town. After all, news travels fast in Owl Lake. It's a wonder she still wants to spend Christmas Eve with me.

"Come on, Fruitcake, let's go. Enough wallowing." I give my dog one last squeeze and scramble to my feet.

I've lost the charm bracelet, and I've somehow lost

Aidan, all in the scope of a few hours. This isn't the way I expected my magical Christmas to end, but there you have it. If I ever run into Betty again, we're going to have a *serious* chat.

Still, I know there's a lot to be grateful for. I have my family, I have my dog and I have the memory of very nearly the most perfect holiday a girl could wish for, even if the ending wasn't what I'd hoped so desperately for it to be.

But my wrist feels unsettlingly light without the comforting weight of the silver charms. I feel untethered, like I could float away. So I tighten my grip on Fruitcake's leash as we make our way from the platform to the front of the train station, where the old grandfather clock towers over Owl Lake, just as it always has.

The station is eerily silent. With the departure of the last train, there's no reason for anyone to be here. The parade is over, and the crowd of people that lined the streets earlier have all gone their separate ways to celebrate the holiday with their own special Christmas traditions. Merry Christmas, to one and all.

Snowflakes swirl down from above, and the night is so quiet, I can hear them land all around me in soft little wisps. Flutter, flutter, flutter. I take a step, but then I pause, because another sound breaks the silence—it's faint at first, barely audible. But it builds and builds, just like the sudden pounding of my heart. I peer into the darkness, and my breath catches in my throat as the lights of a fire engine sweep into view.

It's the ladder truck, and it's heading this way.

Fruitcake goes completely still, on high alert with his ears pricked forward and his big, bushy tail held high. The closer the fire truck gets, the more animated he becomes, until he's prancing gleefully at the end of his leash as it rumbles into the parking lot of the train station and comes to a stop at the curb just a few feet away. Fruitcake pulls away from my hold, running up to wait by the driver's side door. The truck is still decorated with twinkle lights for the parade, and a row of light-up candy canes line the top of the cab.

I shield my eyes with my hand and squint at the windshield, but I'm almost afraid to look. Please tell me that's Aidan behind the wheel of the big red truck, and please tell me there's not a burning building behind me that I'm woefully unaware of. The very thought that he might be here...for *me*...seems too good to be true, the ultimate Christmas wish. There aren't enough charms in the world to represent how badly I want it to be the case.

But when the fire truck door swings open and my gaze settles on the hands that belong to the uniformed man gripping its edge, my knees buckle. I know those strong, capable hands. They're the hands of a man who can steer a car using only two fingers. Cradle a sleepy puppy in a single palm. Loosen a necktie with one swift tug.

Gather packages outside of FAO Schwartz on a crowded, fated morning in December.

Aidan.

If I say his name, I know I'll break down. Still, the fact that he's here has to be a good sign, right?

When he reaches the bottom step of the fire truck, he pauses to look at me. One glance is all it takes for me to see that he's come here with his heart on his sleeve. His eyes are full and alive, brimming with equal parts hope and vulnerability. The joy that swells in my heart is almost crippling. I press my fingertips to my lips to stop myself from crying out loud. I don't think I've ever been this happy in my life—not just for me, or for us, but for him.

Aidan is here, and at long last, he's ready to put his heart on the line.

He jumps down and rushes toward me with Fruitcake hot on his heels. Longing whispers through me, and then he's just an arm's length away, close enough for me breathe in his evergreen and campfire scent. Close enough to throw my arms around him and kiss him silly, which I nearly do. But there are things we need to say first—things I've been waiting to say for eight long years, even if it took me all this time to realize it.

"Ashley." Aidan inhales a gulp of air. He's out of breath, as if he's sprinted all the way here from the end of the parade route—which he basically has, albeit with the help of an emergency vehicle.

And it dawns on me what the text from Susan was all about. She wasn't simply wondering where I was. Aidan must have asked her to help him find me. No one else in Owl Lake has any idea I'm at the train station.

"Please don't go," Aidan says. "Please."

When his voice breaks on his final word, something inside me breaks along with it. Not my heart this time, but any last lingering bit of my resistance. We belong together, Aidan and me, no matter what Betty's magic bracelet seemed to think.

I shake my head. "I'm not going anywhere. I was only here to say goodbye to Jeremy."

"Goodbye?" Aidan says, and the unspoken question mark floating between us nearly makes me cry.

"I'm not marrying him, Aidan. I can't, not when I—"

"Don't say it." He cups my cheek, presses his forehead to mine and a shiver courses through me at his touch. "Please don't. I need to be the one to say it first."

I nod, and my lips begin to quiver in earnest.

Aidan reaches to still them with a brush of his thumb. "I'm in love with you, Ashley. I don't want to spend the next eight years wishing I'd had the courage to tell you how I feel. I've *always* loved you, and I want to build a life with you. Whether that life is here or in Manhattan or Paris doesn't matter. I lost you once, and I don't want to lose you again."

At this, my mouth curves into a blissful smile. Fruitcake lets out a contented sigh. Aidan is offering to give up his entire life here in Owl Lake, just so we can stay together. But he doesn't belong in the city. Aidan belongs right here, and I can't imagine him living anyplace else. He's as much a part of our hometown as the firefighter's crest stitched onto his coat, right above his heart.

"I love you, too, and I'm not going back to Manhattan. Owl Lake is my home." I tip my face toward his until our lips are just a whisper apart. "And I'm home to stay."

With a smile that lights up his entire face brighter than any Christmas tree, he lowers his mouth to mine. The kiss is electric, filling me with warmth and a joy so sublime that my heart feels as if it might burst. We don't need mistletoe, and we don't need Christmas magic. Aidan and I finally have the only thing we need—each other, with hearts wide open to everything fate has in store for us this Christmas, and each and every Christmas to come.

I press my hands to his chest when he pulls away, and his heart beats a furiously against my palm, steady and true.

I peer up into his beautiful blue eyes. "Can I ask you something?"

"Anything," he says, tucking a wayward lock of hair behind one of my ears.

"What made you change your mind?" I swallow hard, because we both know that back at the parade, he was almost ready to let me walk away for good. "What made you come find me?"

His expression turns serious. Thoughtful. "I wanted to right away. The second I left you there with Jeremy, I regretted it. But I thought I'd missed my chance. I thought it might too late to tell you how I really felt. And then..."

I tilt my head. "And then?"

"And then I saw a flash of something silver in the snow, right beside my foot. When I bent to take a closer look, I found this." He reaches into his coat pocket, pulls out a delicate silver chain and holds it up between us. Charms swivel and dance in the glow of the twinkle lights that surround us. "It seemed like a sign."

"My bracelet!" With a trembling hand, I wrap my fingers around the charm bracelet and clutch it as if I'm taking hold of every dream I've ever had.

The choice is mine now. Without the bracelet stuck on my arm, I can do whatever I choose. And I choose this—the here and now, and a happy-ever-after I've wanted since that day I rode atop a fire engine with a glittering tiara on my head, waving a candy cane as if it was a magic wand. The Christmas of my dreams doesn't have to be over. It's mine for as long as I choose to live it.

I hold out my arm, and when Aidan fastens it to my wrist for me, the clasp works just fine. While I'm marveling at it, I barely notice Aidan reaching into his pocket for something else.

He clears his throat and I look up to meet his gaze.

"There's one more thing," he says, opening his palm to reveal a small wrapped package topped with a shiny silver bow. "I couldn't let you leave before I gave you your Christmas present."

It's small and square, and when I take it from him, my breathing slows as a memory from long ago takes over. Aidan grows quiet, and his expression is suddenly so reminiscent of the Aidan I first fell in love with, the young Aidan I used to know, that I half expect the arms on the big grandfather clock beside us to start spinning backward.

I tear off the paper. The box is new, but the ring inside it isn't. It's vintage rose gold with delicate filigree and an emerald cut center stone—the same ring he offered me when he first proposed.

"Oh, Aidan," I say.

Jingle, jingle.

A gasp escapes me before I can stop it.

The bracelet! It never made its magic chime when Jeremy proposed. I'd been so disappointed in the strange turn of events that I failed to even notice.

Aidan gives my chin a gentle tap and guides my gaze back to his.

"Before you left for college, you gave that ring back

to me and told me to ask you again someday. So I'm asking." When he smiles, there are lines by the corners of his eyes that weren't there the last time he proposed. A few silver bristles are visible in the scruff on his jaw.

We've been apart now for as long as we were together, but I wouldn't have it any other way. We're ready now in a way we weren't then. Ready to make our own magic. We're taking something old and making it new again, just like the jewelry I love best. Perfect. Vintage. Timeless.

He caresses my cheek with a touch as gentle as a snow-kissed Christmas. "Marry me?"

I can't get my answer out fast enough. "Yes!"

Then I wrap my arms around his neck and kiss him, soft and slow. Aidan is charm and warmth and all the Christmas magic I need. He's my home, my Christmas dream.

And I'm a firefighter's sweetheart once again.

Epilogue

"ARE YOU ABSOLUTELY SURE ABOUT this?" Susan takes the check I've just handed her and slides it back toward me across the glass counter of the main jewelry case at Enchanted Jewels. "Because I don't want you to rush into anything on the day after Christmas. I could probably get my boss to give you a few more days to make up your mind if you need more time."

"She's sure," Maya says and slides the check back toward Susan with a perfectly manicured fingertip.

That's right, Maya's here in Owl Lake.

After Aidan and I shared the news of our engagement with our family and friends at The Owl's Nest on Christmas Eve, the scene at the bistro turned into a full-on holiday engagement party. Dad stood up to say some very kind words about Aidan and me, then bought a round of cinnamon hot toddies for everyone who was there—with the exception of Sophie and Olivia, obviously, who sipped peppermint white chocolate cocoa topped with whipped cream and sprinkles while their tiaras wobbled on top of their heads.

The only thing that could have made the night better was if Maya had been there, so I decided to video call her from the party and give her the big news. When I told her Aidan and I were getting married, she let out a such a loud squeal that I thought my phone case might crack. Thanks to modern technology, she got to "meet" Aidan and Fruitcake and join in on the celebration.

But being someplace digitally isn't quite the same as actually being there, is it? So after spending Christmas morning with her mom and brother in the city, Maya took the train to Owl Lake and showed up on the doorstep of my parents' house just as we were about to start playing a board game with Aidan, Susan, Josh and the girls.

Aidan found it especially funny that Maya brought a pint of gingerbread ice cream with her in her purse. It was more like gingerbread soup by the time she got to Owl Lake, but that didn't bother Sophie and Olivia. They shared a bowl at the table while we all played a rousing game of Candy Land. Fruitcake made himself comfy at our feet while he chomped on a giant soup bone—a gift from Aidan. It was the best Christmas Day I've ever had.

But after Aidan and his family went home and Maya got settled in the guest room, I went to have a heart-to-heart with my mom and dad in the kitchen. I told them I wanted to buy Enchanted Jewels, and that I'd already completed an online loan application at the credit union that services the OLFD. I still had one last

Christmas wish I wanted to make come true before the clock struck midnight.

Before Betty gave me her charm bracelet, she told me I needed to dream bigger, and I'm taking her at her word. My mom and dad generously offered to co-sign my loan, so I was approved first thing this morning. And now here I am with my closest friend from the city, handing over a check for the modest purchase amount to my soon-to-be sister-in-law.

"She's *definitely* sure," Maya says, waving a hand around the charming shop. Most of the cases are only half-full since today was supposed to be closing day, and I can't wait to fill them up with my own repurposed designs. "Ashley is going to start her own jewelry empire. It's going to be the shining star of Main Street."

Susan and I exchange an amused glance.

"I'm not sure I'd call it an empire," I say with a laugh. "It's going to be nothing at all like Windsor."

"No, but it will be *yours*." Susan grins. "My boss is thrilled. She emailed the purchase contract over this morning, because the roads are getting bad again and she's not sure if she'll make it back to Owl Lake today. She and her husband do a lot of traveling during the holidays."

"That's too bad. I was looking forward to meeting her," I say.

"Maybe if she gets stuck in snowbank somewhere, Aidan can go rescue her in his shiny red fire truck." Maya waggles her eyebrows and the three of us collapse into giggles.

But our laughter is quickly interrupted by a bright, cheery voice. "A rescue won't be necessary, dears."

Susan, Maya and I nearly jump out of our skins.

How odd, I think. I could have sworn we were the only three people in the shop.

"Sorry, ma'am. You startled us," Maya says.

"She does that a lot," Susan says. "I swear, Mrs. C, sometimes it's like you appear out of thin air."

I press my hand to my chest. My heart is beating is a mile a minute, and when I look up, it nearly stops altogether. "*Betty?*"

She smiles and her eyes go all crinkly behind her red glasses with the holly leaves and berries in the corner of the frames. "Why, hello there, dear. Ashley, was it?"

"Wait." Susan glances back and forth between us. "You two know each other?"

I blink, not entirely sure how to answer the question. "Um…"

Susan and Maya are wide-eyed as they wait for me to elaborate, but then Betty subtly presses a finger to her lips while they're busy looking at me. *Shhh.*

Seriously? I can't tell my two best friends that Susan's boss, the woman who owns Enchanted Jewels, is my stranger from the train? She's the source of the charm bracelet that tinkles on my wrist every time I move, and I'm supposed to keep it a secret?

"We, um, met once on the train," I say, waving a dismissive hand.

Right. No big deal, but I think the woman who owns this place might be married to Santa.

"Yes, and what a journey it turned out to be," Betty says.

Understatement of the century.

"Indeed." I laugh, because I just can't help it.

Maya's brow furrows. She knows me well enough to recognize when I'm being evasive.

If Susan suspects anything, she hides it well. She offers her boss a gentle smile and flips through the simple purchase agreement until landing on the signature page. "It's great that you're here. You two can sign the paperwork together."

"Marvelous." Betty claps her hands.

I can't stop staring at her. I can't believe she's here, after all this time. Questions are spinning through my mind, and I can't ask any of them if I'm not supposed to tell Susan and Maya that the first time I saw my charm bracelet, it was dangling from Betty's wrist.

I wrack my brain, trying my best to remember anything and everything Susan told me about her boss and why she might be selling the store. The details were scarce, but they take on a whole new meaning now that I know Betty is the living, breathing person behind the entity known as Enchanted Jewels, LLC on the paperwork.

The owner is relocating. The family is moving up north...

No. It's not possible, is it? Up north, as in the North Pole? And I don't mean the small town with the amusement park, just twenty minutes away. I mean the kind I thought only existed in storybooks and Christmas carols.

"I must hurry, dears. I have a train to catch." Betty opens her handbag to reach for a pen. As she sifts through the bag's contents, I spy a pair of knitting needles. They look like the same ones she used to knit the Christmas stocking that still hangs from the mantle in my mom and dad's lake house.

"Another train?" I arch a brow.

She finally finds a pen and plucks it from the purse. The ink is red, because of course it is. Is it even legal to sign a contract with a red pen? "Oh, yes. It's my favorite way to travel. So convenient, and you meet the most interesting people."

I practically have to bite my tongue to stop myself from making a comment about the larger choice of destinations that come with a sleigh and eight flying reindeer. Susan and Maya would probably think I've lost my senses. Who knows? Maybe I have, but I don't think so. It feels more like I've found them. For the first time in a very long time, I'm following my heart and I quite like where it's leading me so far.

Betty's hand is poised above the signature page when Susan asks us both a question. "I know you each had some time this morning to go over the terms of the agreement via email, but is there anything else you'd like to know before you sign?"

I glance at Betty, and there's a sparkle in her gaze when her eyes meet mine. I have a feeling I'll never get the answers to the questions I want so desperately to ask, and that's okay. Some things are better left unexplained. She's given me so, so much already. It wouldn't be right to ask for more.

"Just one question," Betty says as she angles her head toward me and smiles. "How was your Christmas, dear?"

I answer without hesitation. "It was magical."

The End

Spiced Walnut Crust Cookie with Chocolate Ganache and Sea Salt

A Hallmark Original Recipe

In *Christmas Charms*, the James family bakes and delivers Christmas cookies to the firefighters every year. As a thank-you gift to her old flame Aidan for rescuing her, Ashley joins in on this tradition and tries to replicate one of her mother's recipes...with mixed results.

Maybe she should've made her mom's chocolate and walnut cookies instead! These Spiced Walnut Crust Cookies with Chocolate Ganache and Sea Salt are easy to make, and so good you'll want to start your own holiday tradition of sharing them with your friends, family, and loved ones.

Prep Time: 30 mins.
Cook Time: 20 mins.
Serves: N/A

Ingredients

- 7 tablespoons unsalted butter, softened
- 1/3 cup powdered sugar
- 3/4 cup walnuts, finely ground, divided
- 3/4 cup all-purpose flour
- 1 teaspoon cinnamon, ground
- 1/2 teaspoon cloves, ground
- 1/4 teaspoon sea salt
- 1 cup dark chocolate chips, melted

Preparation

1. Preheat oven to 350°F.
2. In a medium bowl, combine butter and powdered sugar.
3. Mix with a wooden spoon until smooth or use an electric mixer with a paddle.
4. Add in 1/2 cup ground nuts.
5. Sift together flour, cinnamon, ginger, cloves and salt in a bowl.
6. Add to the dough. Mix until well blended.
7. Place dough on parchment paper and roll up.
8. Refrigerate for at least 15 minutes.
9. Unwrap and roll into quarter sized balls, place on prepared baking sheet and bake 15 to 20 minutes.
10. Remove from oven and let cool.

11. Melt chocolate chips in microwave in 30 second intervals.
12. Top cooled cookies with chocolate, sea salt and remaining walnuts.

Thanks so much for reading
Christmas Charms. We hope you enjoyed it!

You might like these other books
from Hallmark Publishing:

An Unforgettable Christmas
Wrapped Up in Christmas
Christmas in Evergreen
A Royal Christmas Wish
A Timeless Christmas

For information about our new releases and
exclusive offers, sign up for our free newsletter at
hallmarkchannel.com/hallmark-publishing-newsletter

You can also connect with us here:

Facebook.com/HallmarkPublishing

Twitter.com/HallmarkPublish

About the Author

Teri Wilson is the Publishers Weekly bestselling author/creator of the Hallmark Channel Original Movies *Unleashing Mr. Darcy, Marrying Mr. Darcy, The Art of Us*, and *Northern Lights of Christmas,* based on her book *Sleigh Bell Sweethearts.* She is also a recipient of the prestigious RITA Award for excellence in romantic fiction. Teri has a major weakness for cute animals, pretty dresses and Audrey Hepburn films, and she loves following the British royal family. Visit her at www.teriwilson.net or on Twitter @TeriWilsonauthr.

You might also enjoy

CHRISTMAS in BAYBERRY

A small-town Christmas romance from Hallmark Publishing

❄

Jennifer Faye

Chapter One

Last week of November
New York, New York

BIG LAZY SNOWFLAKES DRIFTED TOWARD the ground. Standing in front of the large glass windows of the Manhattan skyscraper, Wesley Adams had an excellent view of the late-November sky, making it seem like the city was inside a great big snow globe that someone had given a shake. Or maybe that's just how life felt right now—shaken and turned on its head.

He started walking, refusing to let the entire day go sideways on him. If he kept moving, he could meet all of his deadlines. He glanced at the black leather wristwatch with the gold face that his mother had given him when he'd graduated from college. It had been all she could afford—probably more than she could afford—and he loved both her and the watch dearly.

For a senior business advisor, there was so much work when the end of the year rolled around. Worst of all, everything needed to be done at once. For Wes, when it came to holidays or a deadline, the deadline always won out. There were always risk analyses and restructuring deals that needed to be completed ASAP. Business didn't take holidays. It was the mantra of Watson & Summers.

Wes rushed down the hallway toward his office. Even though the holiday season was upon them, the office was devoid of decorations. Not one tiny Christmas tree or so much as an ornament was to be found anywhere on the floor. There wasn't even holiday music playing over the speaker system. Mr. Summers, as he insisted on being called, thought bringing Christmas into the office would encourage employees to act as if they were on holiday instead of proceeding with business as usual. Wes didn't agree, but it wasn't his place to argue the point.

As usual, Wes was prepared to work through the entire Thanksgiving weekend. He was certain it would be the same for Christmas. Too much work and not enough time. He told himself that being in the office was the way he liked it—a chance to get ahead.

After all, he was in line for a promotion to assistant vice president. If he could land the prestigious position, it would mean more money—money he could use to rent a place for his mother here in the city, near him. As his father had passed on a few years back, Wes worried about her living all alone in Florida. It was so far away. And she didn't like to fly.

Of course, she insisted she had all of her friends, should she ever need anything, but sometimes he wondered if she was truly as happy as she let on. Or was she saying what she thought he wanted to hear?

He wouldn't put it past her. All she'd ever wanted was for him to be happy.

Right now, he had fifteen minutes to verify the projected five-year growth report and print out an income statement for his next meeting with an important client. He'd meant to get it done this morning, but one impromptu consultation had led to another. No wonder the work on his desk piled up.

"Hey, Wes," the president of the firm called out to him.

Wes stopped in front of the office door. He peered in at the older man, who had just a few gray hairs left on his head and permanent frown lines marring his face. "Hello, Mr. Summers. What do you need?"

His boss's bushy brows drew together. "Do you have the report on the Wallace account?"

"I do. It's in my office. I'll get it for you."

"No rush. As long as you have it to me by eleven."

Wes nodded. He checked his watch again. Fourteen minutes till eleven. So much for not worrying about getting the report to Mr. Summers right away. His mother had always said, *If you want something done, give it to a busy person.* Had that been some sort of prediction about his life?

After the promotion, things would slow down. He'd have staff under him to help balance out his workload. It would all get better. He just had to hang in there until the first of the year. That should be easy. Not a problem at all.

He couldn't help but smile at the world's biggest lie.

Wes stepped into the hallway, noticing Mr. Summers' assistant at her desk. "Good morning, Jan."

"Good morning, Wes." The older woman's ivory face

lit up as color bloomed in her cheeks. She peered at him over her black-rimmed reading glasses. "Thank you for the Boston cream donut. I was going to save half for lunch, but one bite led to another. It was so good."

At least once a week, he made a point of stopping at the bakery on his way into the office. It was a small way to thank the people who helped him throughout the week.

"Glad you enjoyed it. How's your mother doing?"

"Better, now that her cold has passed," Jan said with a smile. "She's promising cookies and pie for Christmas. And she's making a nut roll just for you."

"You're both too good to me." He'd gotten to know Jan's mother a few years ago, when he'd volunteered to help move Jan's mother into a senior's high rise.

Jan whispered, "I've got my fingers crossed for you. It won't be long now."

He knew she was talking about the promotion. He grinned. "Thanks. I've got to run."

"Let me know if you need anything."

He greeted other co-workers but kept moving, because time was money and there was never enough of either. Still, he liked to acknowledge the friendly people he worked with every day.

"Morning Joe," he said to the mailroom guy, who was pushing a full mail cart down the hallway.

"Morning." A few years younger than Wes, Joe attended night school. He liked to say that he was working his way up through the company—starting on the ground floor. "I left those files you put a rush on in your office."

"Thank you. You're a lifesaver."

Joe smiled and continued pushing the loaded mail cart in the opposite direction.

Buzz. Buzz.

Wes stepped into his office and fished his phone out of his pocket. It was his mother. He really didn't have time to speak to her. He had the pages to print, the report to get to Mr. Summers, and he had to get back to the conference room in—he checked his watch—ten minutes.

It wasn't like his mother called all that often. She could need something important. He pressed a button and held the phone to his ear. "Hey Mom, is everything okay?"

"Of course, it is. Is that any way to greet your mother?"

He moved to his desk and perched on the edge of his chair. His hands moved rapidly over the keyboard as he entered his password. "Sorry. It's just that you don't normally call during business hours."

"I did this morning, because I need to discuss some business with you."

His finger struck the wrong key and the printer started spitting out five copies of the necessary file. He tried to stop it, but the computer froze. With a frustrated wave of his hand, he let the printer finish producing all five copies. Fortunately, the report was only three pages long.

"What business?" he asked.

"Do you remember Bayberry?"

"Bayberry the candle? Or the town in Vermont?"

"The small town."

He checked the time. He was down to nine minutes.

"Of course, I remember. We lived there briefly when I was, ah, fifteen."

He envisioned his mother smiling and nodding her head. "That's right. You have a good memory. Well, I was just talking to my friend there. Do you remember Penney Taylor?"

He remembered a girl in school with the same last name. She'd been in his class, and he'd had the biggest crush on her. They'd lived in Bayberry less than a year, however, when his father had announced that they had to move because he'd landed a new job. Wes hadn't taken it well. He'd intended to ask the girl to the Candlelight Dance on Christmas Eve. He hadn't thought of her in years.

"Sorry Mom, but I don't know your friend."

"No worries, dear. You'll like her. She's the sweetest."

Why was he going to like her? He didn't have any plans to meet his mother's friend. "Mom, I don't understand, and I really have to go. Can we talk about this later?"

"My friend, Penney, owns The Bayberry Candle Company."

She said it as though it was supposed to mean something to him. "I'm not following."

He grabbed the file for Mr. Summers. Wes's gaze moved to the time on the lower right corner of his computer monitor. Five minutes and counting. He moved quickly. His elbow struck a stack of reports for his meeting. He reached out. They fell into his hands.

"My friend, she needs you to come to Bayberry and advise her on her business."

He was touched that his mother was talking him

up, but he couldn't drop everything. "Mom, I can't just leave the office." He straightened the papers. "It doesn't work like that. Right now, I have to get to an important meeting. Can we talk more later?"

"Sure. But there's something else you should know—"

"Mom, I really have to go. I promise to call you back. You can tell me all about your friend's situation this evening."

"Okay, dear. Love you."

"Love you too." He disconnected the call, grabbed the file for Mr. Summers and rushed out the door. If he hurried, he'd make it to the meeting in the nick of time.

He hoped Mr. Summers was out of his office or tied up on the phone so he could drop the file folder off and keep going.

Mr. Summers looked up and smiled. "Wes. Just the man I need to see."

Wes glanced in the office, finding Chad lounged back in one of the leather armchairs. Chad with his white-blond hair and too-bright teeth, was another senior analyst—also very eager for the assistant vice president position.

"That will be all, Chad," Mr. Summers said.

"Yes sir. You can count on me. If you need anything else—anything at all—you know where to find me." On Chad's way out the door, he paused and grinned at Wes. "Don't worry. I'll make sure all of your accounts are handled." And then he tucked his thumbs in his gray suspenders and sauntered down the hall in his designer suit and shiny shoes.

My accounts? What?

Chad must be confused. That was the only reasonable explanation. Although when Mr. Summers gestured for him to enter the office, Wes got a sinking feeling in the pit of his stomach.

He entered the very spacious corner office. The two outside walls were glass, giving a jaw-dropping view of the city. Right now, though, Mr. Summers had his full attention. Why did Chad think he was taking over Wes's accounts?

Wes stepped up to his boss's very large oak desk. "Here's the file you requested. Everything should be in there."

"Thank you." Mr. Summers took the folder, then gestured to the two charcoal gray chairs in front of his desk. "Take a seat."

Wes was torn between doing what the president of the company wanted or speaking up about his pending meeting. After all, Mr. Summers had the final say on who got the promotion. Wes had to stay on the man's good side, but he also had to get his work done.

Wes's mouth grew dry. He swallowed hard. "Sir, I'm expected in the conference room on the twelfth floor right now."

Mr. Summers leaned forward, resting his elbows on the large oak desk. "They can wait." His gray brows drew together in a formidable line. "This is important."

Wes had no idea why Mr. Summers was so worked up, but he couldn't help but wonder if this had something to do with the promotion. Was Chad being promoted over him?

He took a seat, perching on the edge. Then realizing he needed to appear wholeheartedly interested in what

Mr. Summers said, and not ready to rush out the door at his first opportunity, Wes slid back in the chair.

Mr. Summers got to his feet. "Can I get you something to drink?"

"No, thank you."

"Well, I think I'll get something."

The man was certainly not in any rush to get this conversation over with. Maybe the promotion had been decided upon early. And if it was bad news, he didn't think Mr. Summers would waste time with pleasantries—in fact, he was quite certain of it. He wasn't one to draw out bad news.

"Sir, I want to tell you how happy I've been here at Watson & Summers for the past nine years."

"Has it been that long?"

"Yes, sir. I've learned a lot."

"That's good to hear." Mr. Summers turned with a glass of sparkling water in his hand. "I know you're up for the promotion."

"Yes, sir." He sat up straighter and smiled. "It's an amazing opportunity."

"You do know there's only one spot open and a number of strong candidates."

Wes could feel the promotion slowly slipping from his grasp. After being uprooted numerous times as a kid, moving from town to town, crisscrossing the States, he liked the thought of staying in one spot for the rest of his life. There was something to be said for putting down roots.

But if he didn't land this promotion, he was going to have to rethink his plans. Manhattan wasn't the cheapest place to live—far from it. As of right now, he didn't have a Plan B.

Mr. Summers took a drink of water. He set the glass aside. "I have a way for you to gain an edge over the competition."

Wes couldn't help but be suspicious. Mr. Summers had never showed any favoritism toward him before, so why now? Still, he shouldn't look a gift horse in the mouth.

"Thank you, sir. I appreciate this—"

Mr. Summers held up a hand to stop him. "You haven't heard the plan just yet."

Wes had a feeling there would be no chance of turning down Mr. Summers—not unless he also wanted to say goodbye to his bright future at the company. And that was not something he intended to do.

"I need you to go to Vermont."

"Vermont, sir?"

"Yes. Bayberry, Vermont, to be specific."

"Bayberry?" Wes tried to process this turn of events. First his mother, now his boss. "Have you been speaking with my mother?"

"Your mother?" Mr. Summers' forehead creased. "Why would I speak to her?"

Wes cleared his throat. "What do you have in mind, sir?"

Read the rest!
Christmas in Bayberry is available now!